Monster

Other books by Jowita Bydlowska

*Drunk Mom*

*GUY*

*Possessed*

# M( )NSTER

Jowita Bydlowska

A Novel

Anvil Press // Vancouver

Library and Archives Canada Cataloguing in Publication

Title: M( )nster : a novel / Jowita Bydlowska.
Other titles: Monster
Names: Bydlowska, Jowita, author.
Identifiers: Canadiana 20240376226 | ISBN 9781772142242 (softcover)
Subjects: LCGFT: Domestic fiction. | LCGFT: Novels.
Classification: LCC PS8603.Y395 M66 2024 | DDC C813/.6,Äîdc23

Cover by Rayola.com
Cover image by K.J. McCusker
Interior layout: Michał Kozłowski
Represented in Canada by Publishers Group Canada
Distributed by Raincoast Books

The publisher gratefully acknowledges the financial assistance of the Canada Council for the Arts, and the Province of British Columbia through the B.C. Arts Council and the Book Publishing Tax Credit.

Anvil Press Publishers Inc.
P.O. Box 3008, Station Terminal
Vancouver, B.C. V6B 3X5
www.anvilpress.com

Printed and bound in Canada.

*For Samantha*

# ONE

IT'S LATE IN May, the orange 7 p.m. sun descending slowly behind the buildings just visible from the tall windows of the bookstore. The air smells metallic, of city and dried blood, silver-grey fumes from cars, lights and noise but also spring, a moist animal muzzle rooting, the creature part of me picking up on it, stirring in its sleep.

You stand out in the lineup—especially here, amongst the neurotic-thin men who like books—with your wide athlete's body, a tight T-shirt, your inky beard, a black square bag hitting your hip as you step out to talk to the person in front of you, some nerdish girl (nerdish girls are probably exotic to you, you can corrupt them easier). This place is full of them; later I'll try to recall the girls you talked to, once I noticed you. There was a girl with glasses in a pale pink dress, who fretted and flirted, and one with wispy hair who was soft and pretty, pretty like a sheep, her big animal eyes never leaving your face.

The store's ceilings are high, European-city high, wall-to-wall shelves with books with their colourful spines, some pulled out and displayed half-open, a few with their full faces vying for everyone's attention. I don't know if they've done any studies of how much time it takes for a book to command attention. I look at my own debutante, its purple cover and the letters in the title font arranged from fat to skinny, the wrong approach considering what the book is *not* about. Today is her birthday so everyone is picking her up, carrying her, caressing her anticipation-shivering vertebrae but after tonight, who knows if they'll bother with her?

There's a big table with a plate of sweaty cheese cubes and grapes and cheap champagne, and plastic glasses. On my smaller table I have a flute with not so cheap champagne. Voytek's hoots and laughter come from all sides of the large room as he runs around entertaining our four-year-old. He is the one who brought the not-cheap champagne and opened it in the bathroom in the back of the bookstore—Psst hey, hey, he said and pulled me with him. His alligator eyes.

Inside the bathroom, Voytek barked not to look at him so I didn't, I supported myself against the sink and looked at the word *PROUST!* printed on the cover of a book stack and listened to the sounds behind me, the clink of the buckle of his pants, squeak of shoes, the jarringly fussy whisper of my crinoline underskirt being lifted. (I'm wearing a See By Chloé silver A-line dress, the colour of the cars outside, a cascade of skirts like waves, with a cinched waist and corset-like top. I have never read Proust.)

I giggled and my husband asked in an offended tone if I did not enjoy myself.

Of course I do, I said and kissed his mouth, tasting grapes and cheese, and a crypt.

Fine, he said, grunted repeatedly, came, pulled up his pants, and produced the champagne as if that was my reward for lying to him.

I didn't *not* enjoy myself. But I was distracted, our daughter was in the storage-slash-employee room, sitting with one of the young women who worked at the store. As we straightened ourselves out, I thought about how the young woman recognized my husband, judging by how she stared at him when we first walked in and how quickly she volunteered with Ruby when Voytek said something about having to talk to me in private; she knew what he was hinting at, I was irritated with her for conspiring.

But Ruby was behaving, so I couldn't be too mad. The young woman must've told her to be quiet, must've distracted her with a book with pictures of corpses, or surgeries, so she could eavesdrop on my husband grunting like a stag as I stared at *PROUST!* while getting railed.

Afterwards, Voytek thrust the bottle at the girl and said, Can you hide this somewhere?

She nodded, her eyes reptilian like his, flashing above her face mask. She was wearing a bowtie and a man's suit. It was a look. Rejecting femininity. Opposite of me in my giant skirts, my thighs still wet with the stag's sperm. I felt my face get hot, I was blushing and no one was even looking at me. Ruby wrapped herself around my legs, sniffing me, her face in my skirts.

Actually, you should have a splash, where are my manners? Voytek said and the girl laughed and said she was working and my husband said, It's just one glass, it's a special occasion. Right?

And I said, Please. Have a glass.

What's the occasion? said the girl as if she didn't know about the book launch, in the store where she worked and where she had volunteered to watch the child of the author who was having this book launch, the author married to Voytek Tak—the Voytek Tak whose books the girl's father had probably read in their original form, before translation, and felt angry about, having been his unpublished contemporary. I saw the girl as a child, sneaking into her parents' bedroom to read *all* the forbidden books—corpses, surgeries, but especially the one that launched Voytek into a bad-boy-lit orbit, made him a phenom in his time. Many years ago. There was a lot of sex in the book and people wrote about that, about how it was too explicit and unnecessarily vulgar. But also fresh, edgy.

Voytek still has sway. A look passed between him and the girl—*that* kind of a look. Maybe it was more pronounced because the bottom of her face was covered. Either way, if they could, of course, they *would*, if only because of the girl's father's imaginary rivalry, or they would because she heard him grunting, maybe pictured it all, his exertions in the bathroom, and she'd want to make him grunt like that herself, or they would because he poured her a glass of champagne, as if she were an adult, on par, or they would fuck because people fuck. I watched her watching him while they clinked their glasses; it was as if I wasn't even there. Then again, I've been told I have a tendency to be paranoid and imagine things.

I'll take care of her, Voytek said, meaning Ruby.

I love kids, said the girl and Voytek laughed, I don't. Go, go, he pecked me on the cheek and smacked my bum.

What is everybody doing in there? said my best friend, Lisa, who surprised me right outside the storage door, black nails like talons wrapping around my upper arm, her face all overdrawn eyebrows and caterpillar lashes, no mask, her red lips like a scratch. Her hair looked freshly blown out.

What are *you* doing *here*? I said.

Waiting for you! Anyway, this is John! Lisa cooed and pushed a small human male at me, his arm shooting out as if activated by a button. I shook his hand. I thought of a slang one of my husband's students introduced me to: NPC, a non-player character.

John wants to write a book, Lisa said. It's about his grandfather's immigrant journey as a mill worker and then starting a factory. But that's only a disguise because it's really a self-help about becoming a successful businessman. We should have lunch next week to discuss, she stared at me, a hint of a smile luring in the corner of her mouth, and I understood. There would be no lunch next week, there was no book—there was maybe some half-baked idea—but John was *not* an NPC, not tonight; tonight John was the most important player, at least for however many hours he paid Lisa for.

Yes, lunch, of course. Absolutely. I have to go, excuse me, I said and let Lisa kiss me on both cheeks.

And then it was time for me to go and stand at the little podium and nod during the introduction and shake my head in fake annoyance as my editor told cute anecdotes about being forced to work with me and my generous use of the word "fuck" and how he had to take it out but also how he had to "put some fucks back in," which made people laugh quite genuinely, and then I said things about being forced to work with *him* (some chuckles, clearing of throats), and then I made a joke about health magazine covers insisting on all of us women having to "get our body back" as if our body ran away somewhere where in reality all it did was have a child, or had to commute to a boring office job (genuine laughs), and then I thanked everyone, including people like Brett Fraser from marketing, whom I didn't know at all—I memorized names on the way—and I said something about feeling true in my body and the long windy road, but feeling true, yes, that's the word, *true*, true, I had healed, and there was more applause and then one more joke about the cheese not being a diet cheese and then it was time to sit at my smaller table, and then there *you* were in the lineup.

I don't know why I'm telling you all this, but I need to give our story some kind of a beginning. Those are the frames leading up to the moment I meet you, notice you talking to whoever it is you are talking to, that camera bag hitting your hip. In my memory, I can smell you from where I stand, your minty cologne mingling with the outside, the cars and the spring and the setting sun. I stare, hypnotized, as someone says something about being true to her body, many women say that, true-to-their-bodies women say they are *true*, and my husband hoots, and Ruby squeaks, and then our old babysitter with her own daughter appears and says, Show Yoveeta what you got there!

Her daughter opens her palms and there it is, a dying butterfly. The girl sets out to explain about butterflies in a determined, mechanical voice.

I smile, look behind her, lock eyes with your camera lens.

The daughter doesn't budge, she's a big girl, she has to finish her speech, eggs, pupa, chrysalis, caterpillar. Le-pi-dopterist. The females of some gypsy moth have no wings, all they can do to move is crawl, she finishes. Her mask is dangling off her ear, it's stained yellow on the inside.

Her mother apologizes and I say good-naturedly that it's fine, it's no problem. This encourages her, Oh, oh! Tell Yoveeta that you rode a Leviathan!

I rode a Leviathan, the girl sighs.

I picture the girl atop a giant serpent. I say, What?

It's the biggest rollercoaster in Canada. It's very scary, the girl says in the same monotone. Her mother's open face smiles and I smile back into it. North Americans feel proud of the most bewildering achievements—riding roller coasters or being able to eat twenty hot dogs in one setting.

That's amazing, I say.

I look down at the girl's hands. The butterfly is dead.

(You will say later, pillow-to-pillow, how I struck you as elegant, gracious, putting up with that situation at my own book launch.

I never told you that I fired the babysitter a week later. I liked that she made the effort to pronounce my name right but that wasn't enough. She was even more of a pushover than I am, I didn't like seeing her being bossed by her little girl. I worried my own daughter was going to pick up on this kind of behaviour, become a little bitch, halt lineups with her needs, her own butterflies. It was bad enough she had me for a mother.)

I sign both copies of the babysitter's book, write something sweet and personal, possibly even, "With love" but nothing you would get extra money for once I'm up on eBay, dead and marginally more valuable. I'm not witty like my husband who writes about birds and the seasons and each moment's significance and hope and dust and death. He knows lines, poems. He studies things like poems, he has a degree. In Poland, they are talking about setting an official plaque outside of his birth home, and he's not even dead. But he has written about communism, and he is an import Polaks could all be proud of, he has won awards. His signed books are already on eBay.

The babysitter's daughter closes her hands, rubs them together.

I get up and excuse myself. In the bathroom I splash my face with some cold water, pinch my cheeks, stumble over the pile of screaming *PROUST!*s, straighten them, take a few deep breaths, come out, do it all over again, smile and touch hands and try and fail to listen, and say thank you. I am not meant to be out and in public for this long; over the years I've shrunk my world—or rather I've grown inwards, depending on how you look at it. I've become somewhat unsure of reality, not convinced that this isn't all a spectacle put on for me. Right now, I want to go home where I talk to the walls about my hopes, more specifically where I go to dream about freedom. I don't have a clear concept of it, I just want to one day not be hungry for anything or anyone.

My husband appears briefly at my table with a new glass, and he tells me I'm doing great, I'm a star, and then the girl in the pale pink dress, and then you, finally *you*, finally you are here. I have to look up, and neither of us smiles, we know, we already know, and the air feels different, like there's more of something, extra gravity, objects with greater charge create stronger electric fields. I raise the glass and take a little sip, my eyes on you the whole time.

We talk with our eyes for six champagne seconds, the light outside the windows now heavier, more decadent, more golden; a small swath of your hair turns deep-fire red when you tilt your head, my head tilting with yours in a perfect mirroring gesture. You rub your beard self-consciously; it's a new beard, a test beard, and after tonight, I will never see you with a full beard again.

You talk. You are charming, confident, loose, that camera bag banging against your hip, the fire in your hair turning black, deepest dark. You apologize for taking the picture of me (you don't have to, everyone else is doing it, this is what this is for). You say you are new at your job, now that you're here, you claim to not have had the foresight that it would be a dumb idea to try to interview me during this time, during my own launch. You laugh as if we are both in on a joke.

I laugh when you ask if you could, actually—could you? you say, Oh lawd, please, m'am, I'mma get fired, I need this, it's my big break.

You make a face, bat your lashes, fold your hands in a prayer.

(Later you'll write that you don't care about books like that, self-help, memoir, and you don't have a girlfriend anyway to give a book like that to. That's how you let me know you don't have a girlfriend. And that you don't give a shit about the book I wrote.

It's your lack of subtlety I like. Your lack of apology.)

I roll my eyes and say, It'll have to be another time.

Another time? Perfect. That works, I'll email you, I'm sorry and thank you, thank you, you say and you leave, the air relaxes, fills with other smells of other people. I don't relax, but I keep talking, signing more books, more of everything, more of it a blur, blur of Lisa hugging me too long and too tightly to the disapproving looks of Covid-conscious strangers. The light outside goes, is gone, the metallic greys of cars gathers, intensifies, the red light of Stop, Don't Walk. Then it's over, the girl from the storage room rustles by, maskless, she throws a line, a little smile, my husband is a fish, a hook, he sinks. I wonder if they'd exchanged numbers. I am tired, I am talking to someone or maybe I am not talking any more, my body is wet and hot underneath all the waves of See by Chloé.

Voytek and I walk home as Ruby falls asleep in the stroller. We want to enjoy the celebratory mood a little longer, I am buzzed from the champagne and from being famous. All I can think of is your face—you're not a story yet, you're already an altar, my future daily devotional.

I rewind the evening, try to see if there's anything to stamp you out but no. At the launch, all women told me about their bodies, stories of triumph, sacred but wasted (on me); the women said I helped, or that was the gist of what they all said. I was indebted to all of them holding my book close to their chests, their furtive glances and nervous smiles, their spelling out names of sisters, cousins, friends who they were buying their second copies for. There were moments where I felt like getting up and screaming. I wanted to make a scene like people do on reality TV, flip the table upside-down, kick the shelves. A few women held my hands in theirs, too many hands cupping mine—when did people replace handshakes and elbow-bumping with this gesture? Or was it because we were freshly out of another lockdown and were overwhelmed with the permission of intimacy? Seeing so many mouths all at once was shocking. Each time a mask would unhook, there it was, that confessional duckbill, their eyes flitting, and I'd feel my stomach constrict. It wasn't quite my stomach either but the thing that lay dormant in that area where all of my hunger would start. Now that I was here, with my book, I was accountable to the world for not letting *it* out; I told the world I was in charge and not the other way around. But I seemed incapable of paying attention to all of that for too long, my book and my success and my stomach.

I forget most people from that evening, no one else's face is sharp, in focus. I retain no guilt about that, not remembering the women, and myself, and our pain or victory, I remind myself that I'm not indebted to anyone after all—it was Voytek who told me people feel intimate with authors, especially with memoirists; they think they have learned your secrets and now you owe it to them to learn theirs. You don't.

I stay with your ghost for the rest of the evening as I walk with my husband in the warm May night. At one point he asks if we should share some French fries and pulls me toward a shouty, comic-sans food truck with a big clown logo painted on the side. A headache comes on instantly as the smells hit my nostrils, grease and cleaning products. There is a woman in the back of the food truck scrubbing something, she looks at me briefly, the bags under her eyes are deep, bruised.

Just small, I say in a small voice to my husband who knows what he's doing. I hold his eyes and he nods.

The logo clown passes me the fries and wishes me a good night. My hand is shaking as I jam three clammy strips into my mouth, contemplating their warmth and softness, the simple—and therefore perfect—saltiness, the kick of the vinegar. I'm flooded with sensation, the masticated deathly chunks travelling down my throat, my own internal Leviathan.

I have no words for what I know yet but before bed, in the bathroom, my head bent over the toilet, throwing up the fries, my terrible form of prayer, I have a vision. I don't know if I should blame you, my husband or my body. But I do have a vision, in the paradox of slowing down while I speed up I become many things at once, an open shell, a pearl swelling, shuddering rib cage, something more visceral even, a white-deer carcass, steam, a pomegranate geode of pulsing guts. I feel excavated. I have another vision: of your closeness, your physicality, how it will be unbashful, demanding of my yielding. Skin against skin, hard of muscle and warmth. Your cock that I will ask to invade me, that I want to be a rock to climb over, a crystal to impale myself on, the tip of you stirring ribbons of red and pink inside me, the wetness between us in my breath, and the milky bitterness of you on my thighs, our sweaty hair, my smell briny and sweet and warm like blood, you taking, claiming, my desire pooling underneath and all around me in my nakedness, shame and shamelessness sliding against you, to keep you and push you away but keep you again, as I devour everything and for once, I don't want to, or understand how to, purge and I am content, filled, whole.

# TWO

I FELL APART slowly but by the time I realized I was no longer whole, too many pieces of me were missing. Most significantly, in one swoop I lost my home and my language and I found myself in a strange, impersonal place with over-manicured front lawns and highways as wide as fields. The trees seemed too far away. The buildings were grey, stern. The people in my new small town dressed without care, in baseball caps and garments with threads that unravelled easily from pant legs and sleeves. The food was plastic and sold in obnoxious quantities: large tubs of three-coloured "Neapolitan" (nothing to do with Italy) ice cream, sacks of salted peanuts, body bags of synthetic potatoes: chips. The food was easy but its easiness was deceptive, there were chemicals in it that made you addicted to it, the same way there were formulas in TV shows that didn't require one to think, not like books did. In case there was any doubt whether what you watched was funny there was often a laughing track, and sad shows were punctuated by sad pianos or violins. Later I found out even the books were easy, the ones that were popular at least.

Here, it was a frictionless buffet that hooked into your neuroreceptors, releasing unlimited dopamine, the hook invisible and prone to get stuck. It could take years (of therapy, of self-help) to find it and unhook yourself. As a result this new world was full of people who had no idea how to entertain and feed themselves, unaware of not knowing how to until their bodies and minds started to fail them. I am, of course, guilty of that too, having always reached for false nourishment that filled me with Nothing.

The new language was simple but unwieldy, melodic but also like a too-large cube I had to find a way to fit into my mouth. My tongue had to touch foreign places when I said words that didn't exist in my own language but now gave instructions and destinations, *a, the*...I later learned they were called *syncategorematic* words, words that when used alone fail to signify, words that require more words to have logic, meaning. (If I were to describe in a word how it felt to immigrate I would say it was syncategorematic. Or, having lost everything and having gained what I didn't understand, I grieved yet was curious.)

I went to school during the day where no one talked to me because I didn't talk. I was invisible against the metal jaws of lockers, or rustling through dead leaves of autumn mornings and afternoons, to and fro, back to my non-home where my father and mother were either silent or yelling in our native language.

But don't mistake this for a story of loss. I was never a loser, that's not how I saw myself. I knew I was smart and I knew I was beautiful. I spent my free time feeling lonely and restless, running my hands over my developing body, dreaming of someone, a boy, to take me away. I couldn't go back, I understood that I had to want something of this place, something that would make me feel as if this was my place too. The easiest thing for a girl to want is a boy, so I wanted a boy, a boy to put his tongue inside my mouth, to pass me the English cube of his language. I felt I would've been motivated by love, or at least by desire or by being desired. I knew about desire; I learned a lot from my Best Friend's Dad, how to hold things steady: a wheel, a cock, your ground. A boy could ground me. But the boys, and later, men, were disappointing. Their English was often far worse than mine, which I eventually absorbed from books and old movies. This is why I shared my body only. This is why when spiritual reconciliation with this new place refused to happen, I remembered the bad food that used to comfort me, and between sharing my body and feeding my body, I was almost fulfilled. In control. I could easily expel both the boys and the food, and I could keep moving until I found *it*. I suppose that *it* was love because as doormats, aprons and coffee mugs—the tabernacle contents of all households in America—told me, *home is where the heart is.*

I thought I was clever in placing my dislocated heart with Voytek, the only man I'd met who, I thought, understood my particular woes. The only man who was both better and worse than my Best Friend's Dad—the first man to rein me in. Voytek came from the same place as me and he made a home here, easily, like it was his right. Like he was a colonizer. He had not only adapted but he had a voice here; unlike a typical immigrant resigned to his fate—a man like my father—he wrestled with the new language until it obeyed and gave him that voice. And unlike me, his immigration was a choice. I thought of Poland as a dead mother, but he spoke of Poland the way people speak of a person who was problematic and beautiful, a mother for whom men murdered other men, but who drank or stayed in her room with darkened windows, and pills. He visited her and then he was fine. I never went back, it was too painful to see her grave.

Here is a man, I thought, I could feel steady with, grounded. He praised me, he told me I was different from all the other students, different from his wife.

I wrote first because I couldn't speak, still building fluency in the new language, and he got this and told me there was even more to it. He said I had *a thing*. I was *a real talent*, he could tell. He said: I *see* you.

Here is one man, I thought then, who knows I have *a thing*—knew it before I even knew it myself, he could show me how to get a voice, get my thing out, tell the world. Here is someone who sees me, maybe even sees what I fail to see when I stand in my room in front of a mirror trying to decipher what all of this is for, when I write also trying to decipher what all of this is for. Here's a man for whom my body is not a problem the way it is for me, a man who can contain it.

He was obsessed with my body—he photographed it constantly, touched it and licked it and dressed it in ribbons and lace and leather, and stockings, always—but he also said he loved my brain. A man who made pronouncements about world-renowned brains said he loved mine, can you believe that? His public persona was that of a weary Polish intellectual, a writer of mostly historical fiction, an occasional social commentator who charmed both male and female television hosts, intimately leaning into armchair rests as he told anecdotes from the old country in his sculpted, accented English. I watched him on screens the way women watch music idols or actors, in disbelief that this was the same man who kneeled at my stockinged, high-heeled feet and told me to call him a bad dog, a bastard, his one hand running up and down my calf as he frantically, teenagerly rubbed his cock with his other hand. The same man who said he wanted to commune with *me*, show *me* his most private, tender underbelly. And he showed it to me, his writing, unpublished pages that were raw and unedited, clunky sentences tripping over themselves that told the story of his inner life, not the suave wit he was in public but an unsure man at the mercy of other men but more importantly, women, their hair and their thighs and necks and shoulders, and how they looked at him, like he was something they could toy with. I was jealous of all those women, the ones before me, and the ones he lusted after still, but I also saw in his writing how afraid he was of us, all women, and I figured I could show him a different side, I could be gentle and nurturing. And knowing how he worshiped us, I thought he would never leave me, even if I had to resort to all those female machinations he found so mysterious, temper tantrums and pouting and making dramatic entrances and exits that would always keep him on his toes even when he felt that he had landed a good one, a safe one, me. It wasn't premeditated and none of that was coherent; I only understood what I thought later on, but the point is I believed I found the man I had been looking for and I had to keep him. Here is a man who is *home*, I thought. And later, when he got us an actual house—here is a home that is a home. I needed it to exist to be complete.

You will ask me many times why I stayed for so long knowing what I suspected (not *knew* as it was too dangerous to *know* for a long time). This is why I stayed: Because I finally had a place of my own and for a while it seemed as if I'd finally arrived—at that elusive destination all people strive toward, where we finally feel like we can rest, and evolve and thrive. I didn't understand that I didn't need the man anymore to make it a home until the man tried to take it from me.

I'm telling you this because a night will come, and you will ask me, What do you need? What do we need to do? But instead I will go over what led to it all: the house, the long walk, the nostalgia, the sudden idea that was not sudden at all but seemed like a snap. My voice will be high-pitched, foreign to me. Can you help?

You will shake your head. We'll be sitting in your car, lights off. The bottom of the road. My chest will be rising and falling, panting as if we'd just made love, the realization dawning on both of us, my panic—is this the end? But then you will blink slowly, one steady click and lock, like the shutter in your camera, capturing something that only *I* had seen before, unfurling, trembling, shimmering.

And you will place your hand around my wrist and you will say calmly, so quietly your words will be cold and still like the water of that night, No, let's just go. This will be a promise. And with that you will prove to me that I can be grounded again, and that you understand.

The rest of this story is to fill in the blanks, everything that I owe you.

# THREE

I GET AN email from you about fact-checking a few items, and you ask if you might ask more questions, and then ask them anyway: When did you start writing? When did you first publish? Why write about hunger? Is this metaphorical? What's your favourite food? What's on your bed stand? Do you have an eating disorder? Childhood stuff?

You are indiscreet and trying to buy yourself an *in*—I fall for it—and you finish the email with an anecdote of once watching a co-worker eat in secret, a skinny, morose woman with a permanently red, swollen face. She always refused the office birthday cake but once you saw her steal the leftovers from the fridge, place them in her tote. You waited outside the kitchen discreetly so that she wouldn't get spooked and a couple hours later, when you ran into her on the way out, she talked too fast and her eyes were bright, too bright; it was as if someone turned on a light inside her. You have never seen her so happy and you even had half a mind to ask her out for a drink—you had noticed suddenly, for the first time, that she had a long elegant neck, and such full lips—but you could tell she wanted to be alone, to be away. She begged you with her eyes to let her go and you didn't understand; you knew she had a crush on you, her behaviour made no sense. *But it was as if she couldn't wait to get home to be with her new, secret lover,* you write.

My body zaps with a sweet charge, there's a pulse between my ears, a spasm in my fingers, Return, Space, when I read the quick lines and what's in between them, you wanting to talk, to connect, that anecdote that shows me you understood something about bulimics. Hand-written letters, now relics of history, are a lost site of romance, but electronic correspondence can be breathless too. Ours is, from the start.

I answer your questions: *It was when I was eighteen and it was a story about a man who gets killed by a vending machine. It's not a book about dieting. It's not a self-help, it's a self-discovery. I could never eat enough, there was this longing inside me but this isn't about food. Metaphorically but also not. It's important to read it to understand it. Maybe you have a female co-worker who could read it and summarize it for you? Maybe even her, the lady with the cake. It's a book about being true to your body, about finding home in your body. Female bodies are not like male bodies, we are empires that wage wars. But on ourselves–j.*

I reread my corny little media spiel. You should feel duped. I feel duped.

You email right back, *It still sounds like a book about eating to me. Like justifying restrictive eating. Twisted.*

*Sure,* I write, *maybe it's a little twisted. But it isn't about that. Call me.*

You call me. I listen to you explain what you want to do with the article. Something about women lying about healthy eating to cover up body dysmorphia. You were shook up by your co-worker, is it like that for me? Am I okay with you writing, saying that? You know it's controversial, it should be controversial for a man to write an article like that, no?

You asking or saying? Either way I'm okay, I say. I'm not. It doesn't matter. All publicity. You writing the story, it's probably bad, and it's going to make me look like a traitor. Letting a person with a body that's not a woman's body write about a woman's body. I'm wary of you exploiting your co-worker too but maybe, I hope, you can be sensitive, gentle. I have no way of knowing. I'm ready to betray myself, and her, and all the other women just like that—I can't even justify it as some instinct or a gut feeling that I have about you, although it would serve our story to say that I knew right away I had such a feeling. Or: it hasn't even been a day with us and I've already sold out to appease you.

My lower back feels tense, cramped. I'm sitting on a tall Lucite stool, one of four, something my husband insisted on last year and had installed professionally in the kitchen-dining room, like a real grownup. He was so proud of that. The stools are the only piece of furniture I love, but they make no sense, clash spatially, visually with the heavy chairs and leather couches crowding the adjacent living room, which is far too small. I spin on the stool, then I extend one leg and hoist it onto the kitchen island, like it's a ham hock I should prepare for a party later; the ham hock is still covered in a sheen of sweat from my one hour on the stationary bike. The bike stands in the corner of the kitchen, my husband hates it there. To burn even more calories, I bring it upstairs from the basement, forget to bring it downstairs.

You say, How are you true to your body if you're not feeding it when it's hungry? It's disordered eating, I read about it, it's called orthorexia, every portion is measured and weighed on a little scale, certain foods forbidden after certain hours. You need protein to survive. Carbs make you happy but I know that carbs can activate craving for more carbs.

I don't measure things on a little scale. That's not me. I just pay attention to hunger. It takes twenty minutes for the brain to get the message that hunger is satiated. No matter what, the idea is not to stick my—your finger down your throat. Once a week, you can go out, I don't know, to an Italian place and order a real Neapolitan pizza, with the rubbery, thin crust, those large holes in the dough; the type of dough is called cornicione, look it up, it's an airy, raised edge, that's crunchy on the outside and soft on the inside. I can eat that thing once a week, I say.

(I think about it now, cornicione, an assault of its salivating memory with the added auditory pleasure of your phone voice. I notice the slight rasp, how you elongate certain words, the toffee of your "I kno-o-ow." I would like to taste it against the corner of my mouth.)

I don't know what the hell I'm talking about so I change the direction, try to give you better quotes you can use, something about how being true to your body also means acknowledging you are destroying yourself if you're not eating properly, if you're starving yourself on purpose. People like me, we have to be vigilant. We have to attend to our obsessions, know how to curb them. It's an ordeal.

Speaking of food. Can I take you out to dinner?

No. I'm married.

I know. Can I take you out to dinner?

I hang up, gently as if I was stroking your cheek, your head, apologizing.

Five minutes later, you text me a menu from a restaurant in your neighbourhood. I don't know if this is a dare.

But there is no point resisting because I know that sooner or later. Both you and the food.

Of course I want to prove to myself that I am immune, can handle both temptations. I look at a small, slightly zigzagged pile of copies of my new book like it's a guarantee, or, better, a protection, but how can an object made out of paper shield me from Monster? Because that's another revelation about our meeting: if there is one thing I cannot deny about myself, it's that this is the instinct I have, from the get-go, the fist I suddenly felt unclench inside when our eyes first met—a certain, ancient recognition.

# FOUR

ON THE DAY of our follow-up interview (our date), I am delirious with excitement and so turned on that as I sit on one of the fancy stools to do my makeup, I slide side to side and almost cum right there and then. I look across the kitchen to the dining room where Voytek is reading to Ruby in her high chair, her mouth and chin beige with peanut butter. This image snaps me back to propriety. I smear tiger grass cream on my face to make myself paler.

I wear all white to our outing. I feel virginal, and also like my outfit is a warning to myself—and to you—to keep this innocent. I've never cheated on Voytek and although I feel what I feel, I lie to myself that I don't feel what I feel. You are writing your article, this is a professional meeting (this is a double-think).

I spot you sitting to one side, through the glass door, but when I enter the restaurant you are not there. An illusion.

Jowita? you say from the opposite side.

I'm not usually the kind of a person who walks into windows or doors, the kind of a person fooled by reflections; when I sit down and feel like I've lost the game already. You've stood up to greet me, but I pretend not to notice, suddenly too shy to give you a hug. You sit back down, you are friendly and warm, you compliment me on my white top, you say my hair looks great when I wear it down. An intimate comment that suggests you've been looking at pictures of me, most of which show my hair pulled back because that's how Voytek likes it.

Such nice weather, isn't it, it's so warm outside, like a real summer and there's that perfect breeze you don't get in August, August is like a sweaty hooker, One of us blathers on.

Ha ha, One of us laughs.

One of us says, I've missed being—eating out in a restaurant, it's funny what we take for granted.

And then we talk about the restaurant where we're at, how it has a great reputation, all those five-star Yelp reviews. I tell you I'm impressed with your choice.

You pick out a bottle of white, Manousakis Nostos Crete. I like the confidence with which you order, like you're a much older man, a man my husband's age. You tell me you worked in a French restaurant for a year, which is why sometimes you're assigned food pieces. And you like the line drawing of an old man on the label. Indeed when the bottle shows up, there's a picture of a little old man in a dark vest tilting a glass to his lips.

He is exactly what my grandfather looks like, you say and you laugh.

Or my husband, I say and we both laugh.

That's not true, you say and I hate it that you know who he is. I instantly regret my joke.

The wine is fruity, full of sunshine. The pretty brunette waitress compliments your choice, she looks at you with fondness like you're her younger brother she can't believe is all grown up. She tells us the specials and I can't hear a thing, I'm gripping the menu; in my mind, the names of dishes swirling in my own colour-coded caloric zones of GREEN, YELLOW and RED.

(Like every person fucked up over food I have beliefs over what's safe versus what could make me lose control. I wish this was only about the fear of fatness, but it's worse; it's about not being able to escape, getting a taste of something addicting, something I'd never get enough of. If I'm afraid of happiness, I'm more afraid of it ending; I don't understand contentment, satiation, calm, but I hope to achieve it by never testing its parameters.)

After the waitress leaves, I say, You do the honours. But please, nothing too heavy—I point to the two code-RED plates, Calamari and braised lamb, the two dishes I really want but can't have.

You nod and smile. I remember your co-worker with her secret cake, how you said her eyes shone—here was a woman who knew she could escape her hunger because she would feed it and fool it, her head bent over the toilet. Me? I am trapped at this table.

You order the first dish. Over the course of the evening you'll order dish after dish, increasingly challenging in their complexities although deceptively small, as if designed not to scare people like me. I don't know if you know what you're doing but our eyes meet every time a new dish is delivered and I nod slightly, ready for more. The truth is, as much as I want to control this, I already capitulated when I agreed to meet with you.

(Did you know I saved the menu? I'm not one for mementos but this one is not a memento, it's the map I'll need to remember how it all started.)

A dozen oysters. Enough has been written about oysters, their poetry, their innuendos. Both of us eat them no-nonsense: radish, a drop of sauce, slurp, next. This is the only dish we don't lock eyes over, we ignore the erotic connotation.

We share the Tomato Salata: heirloom tomatoes, ricotta, coarse pepper, salt. The purple-red fruit erupts in seeds as I quarter it with a fork, I let its taste linger in my mouth, chasing it with the white softness of the silky cheese. I steal a look at your forearms, no tattoos, no scars, but lots of dark, wiry hair that I love, this evidence of your testosterone, your maleness. You catch me looking and you smile a secret, quick little smile as if you told yourself a joke. You cut me another piece of tomato, top it with the cheese. I place the morsel in my mouth. Your forearms make me think of foreplay, fingers brushing against secondary erogenous zones, the neck, the insides of knees and elbows, the waist.

Nova Scotia scallops, citrus, hollandaise, tarragon—served on wide shells, like costume jewelry, the sweet, soft orange crunch curdling the tarragon in my mouth, the scallop a small, flat tongue. I let out a quiet moan.

That good, eh? You reach for the second shell and slide the whole thing down, down into your mouth, your throat, you smack your lips afterwards.

My father used to say scallops were like biting into a virgin thigh, the whole experience of them, you say and watch me blush. I picture a grey-haired man rolling a tartan skirt over a set of trembling thighs, white cotton panties, the man's wolfish mouth on pale skin, a set of dark, mischievous eyes—like yours—looking up as his teeth pierce through.

Dakos Toast is served on sourdough bread with feta, peas and marinated chanterelle mushroom. This is the first code-YELLOW dish we share.

The restaurant is pleasantly noisy, a Friday night crowd, laughter echoing against the tile-and-wood walls and servers flirting behind the bar, and very quietly some jazz, and, at one point, someone tapping a fork against glass, maybe an engagement, a retirement toast, there's discreet, expensive applause. Maybe none of that is there, maybe this is a scene from all those movies playing in my head at all times. To be honest, I don't really hear or see anyone but you.

What do we talk about? Mostly, we talk about the food we're eating. I'm reminded of my days of sneaking around with Voytek, all the foodie mannerisms I took on, of closing my eyes in feigned ecstasy, my nods, and, yes, moaning, and the superlatives, each bite "spectacular," or "unbelievable," "insane," or simply "sooo good." You do it too, although with less flamboyance than me. You mostly watch me eat with such intense fascination it's as if I were performing a difficult ballet or playing an instrument. I appreciate your restraint, I appreciate that you prefer to watch. And I do perform for you, a woman who eats and who thinks nothing of it.

We eat Tuna Crudo—warm Florina peppers, oregano, capers, ramps, a crispy fried onion garnish—in semi-religious silence. The meaty fish is the colour of bloody bruises. I picture the imaginary virgin's thighs, imagine your father's teeth.

I'm aware of the numbers adding up, rising toward the number I decided once, long before that night, was safe. But like a safe word, the number isn't actually safe; it's a fictional agreement, the number of calories I came up with that I believe will prevent Monster from showing up at a given meal. (It's 800, if you must know.)

The waitress shows up to clear our dishes, asks, How is everything? I consider telling her *everything* is about to take a different turn; I want to say this cryptic thing, say it out loud, to warn you, or to see if perhaps you are cruel. If you know exactly what you are doing to me. If you figured me out, as with your cake-eyed co-worker, to see if you were right all along about me writing a book full of covert diet tips.

Everything is great, you say, looking at me. I say, Everything is great, and the waitress says, Do we want to order anything else? The ribs are out of this world.

I panic. But only for a brief moment. I'm reminded of the time I went to a party and a girl approached me and a boyfriend, and flirted with both of us. She stroked my arm and playfully punched his. She was bossy, hair in a tight braid, tattooed drummer arms, bright lipstick like a wound. Can I kiss you? she said to me while staring at my boyfriend. We kissed, our bodies hot and drunk, her leather vest like a third skin between us.

Sure, let's try the ribs, I say, my voice small. If someone were to hold a stethoscope to my chest I wonder if they'd hear what I hear in this moment, a whooshing second beat—it erupts from within increasing in volume, exploding in my ears temporarily but loudly enough so that I have to shut my eyes in what I hope looks like a foodie's dreamy anticipation.

The fragrant (Mennonite-farmed) lamb meat falls off the bone in hard-butter-like chunks; I scoop a sliver of it, as if trying on a new sexual technique, using the tip of my tongue. I can't help but think of one of my favourite killers, Jeffrey Dahmer, who was so turned on by bones that he opened his victims' chests and torsos to examine how they were "put together." I share this with you, testing you, wanting to punish you a little for the ribs and everything else.

Ah yes. There's a new movie about him, you say, nonplussed, and slide a whole rib into your mouth, sucking off the purplish bits. You think I am talking about pop culture, not about what frequently occupies my mind. I don't shock you, I appear just like every other person, obsessed with Netflix.

And maybe it is wanting to prove to you I am *not* that person that makes me stop the waitress and order (the code-RED) Medouli.

Are you sure? you say. It's the deep end. There's no coming back from that, you lick your lips, like a wolf that runs in your family, but your eyes are soft. And suddenly, I know you understand a lot more than I thought you understood. You can sense that almost none of this is about having a meal at a fancy restaurant. You are not cruel and this isn't a test. You're not waiting for me to break. You can't hear Monster, its sudden whooshing heartbeat, but you have compassion. (Later, when I ask how you knew, you will tell me that you read my book, the easiest of explanations, no magic.)

This is your favourite restaurant, you tell me, Look at the way the light hits and bounces off all that crystal and the mirrors, the atmosphere, it's so feminine... women love this place, you say, and then you look at me and wince and say, Sorry. God, that was a stupid thing to say.

Sorry for what? I laugh with my head slightly thrown back like an unhinged American.

The marrow-rich bone arrives with a side of sourdough and meyer lemon. The plate is sparkling with big chunks of coarse salt. I don't know what I was expecting but not this oily, heavy substance that you show me how to scoop with the bread after sprinkling the salt and squeezing some lemon on it. There is no information whether Dahmer ate bone marrow—he ate hearts, he was partial to them—but now that I can see the inside of this bone I think how sacred and prohibited this is, something no one should have access to, as taboo as when people try to insert body parts into other body parts that should not go together, a tongue and the deep, dark cave of an asshole, for example. Exactly the type of thing that Dahmer would be into. I don't share this with you, how cannibalistic I feel taking this food inside, how depraved. I wonder if this is a prelude to what you and I will do after this meal, maybe not tonight but eventually. This is so categorically RED-coded, the final, greasy chunk of it setting off the alarm inside me, coating my anxiety only temporarily with its heaviness and flavour. It does exactly what every forbidden food does to me: calms me down while simultaneously announcing a loss of control so total that I might as well make peace with losing it. No more safety net, my book, my words means nothing.

The bottle of wine is gone, the food washed down and stuck in my panicked stomach. You order two more glasses, a consolation prize. It's a lot more difficult to care about anything once alcohol is involved and I suppose this is my one salvation, being sufficiently drunk makes me relaxed enough to not bolt out of the restaurant. I do excuse myself to go to the washroom and stick a finger in my throat but it's no use, my throat is not interested in opening, my drunk mind telling me it doesn't matter, this is fine, one big mistake that I can still recover from. When I feel my face turn hot from the effort I have to stop. I am vain and want you to find me beautiful, I don't want to look as if I'd cried, or worse, did what I'd set out to do.

When I come back, we talk some more about the menu. You say you get it now why dogs are so attracted to bones, wasn't that just the most delicious? They can smell their secret.

Whose secret? Dogs?

You laugh and say, Bones. The secret of bones.

My stomach is an animal graveyard, I giggle back.

We are drunk and full and frantic and the bill is suddenly here, you snatching it before I have a chance to. We tell the waitress how wonderful, so delicious, everything was, how amazing; we throw every compliment we can think of and she assures us, You've had one of the best culinary experiences in town.

Outside the restaurant, groups and couples pass us by, so many people masked and still timid but on the brink of screaming from the pressure of having to restrain themselves for so long. Me too, although our first evening is anything but restrained.

Can I kiss you? you say and before I have a chance to say yes or no, you grab my hand and pull me towards you and take my face in your hands and press your juicy, murder-stained mouth against mine. My nipples stiffen and my head spins and I lean into you wanting to feel your hardness. I rub against you and, for the second time that evening, let out an involuntary moan.

# FIVE

IT IS AS it was in the beginning, except I am the wife now. My husband comes home in the bird-screaming hours, sleeps in his office. I hear him bump, hiss, bump, *fuck*, but I can't move because I am stuck in a dream where I'm waking up only to realize I am still asleep. I am in our marital bed.

This is not the first morning like this but it's the first morning when I don't feel like getting up and running at him with my teeth and claws bared.

Later on he comes downstairs all wrinkly suit, under-slept but giddy, he squeezes Ruby's cheeks, he kisses me on the top of my head, he closes the cupboards loudly, chips a glass against the metal sink while getting water, and when I open my mouth, words come out of it that I don't intend to say: Does she have better tits than me?

He looks sheepish then—the way men do in movies about cheating—and he says, No, no, you have way better tits.

I shove another slice of toast in my mouth, force its scratchy edges against my throat to cork up the scream. I am also still full of your kiss; it has sunk and expanded, it's kept me full for two days now.

My husband says quietly, It's nothing, just a student—a former student, he adds. I don't know if in his excitement he has forgotten about the last time it was *just a student*, or if he's referencing me, a *former* student and if that is supposed to appease me.

Our daughter claps her hands and starts whispering gibberish, possibly thinking that this is a game of whispers.

Voytek keeps talking, he says he already posted the grades so he didn't do anything wrong, he didn't sleep with a student, a *former* student yes, but not a *student*-student, he won't stop talking, *not anything inappropriate, no grounds,* and I say, Shut up, shut up, I'm not your boss, I'm not firing you for fucking a student. Nobody's ever gonna fire you for fucking a student.

What's that supposed to mean? he hisses.

Ruby tilts her head. She is in her high chair eating an omelette with her hands. I feel so tired of the fight I should be having but am *not* having. I think of that one afternoon in Voytek's office many years ago when he handed me my folder and praised me for getting an "A" and told me I was a real talent. Said to email him. So I emailed him later that week to ask to meet to talk about where I should pitch the short story I got the "A" on and we met in a bar on College and drank two bottles of cheap wine to celebrate my certificate.

Was this *former* student a real talent too?

Voytek was once married to a poet in New York. An expert on self-immolation, I was patient in the beginning; it was one of my assets. I was discreet, I knew my role. My roles—I was not just his lover, I serviced and worshiped him too. I massaged his bad knee, I wheeled a small suitcase filled with organic meat he needed a special permit for, I told him he was a genius. The actual wife didn't seem real and he never talked about her. When we traveled together he called me his wife in front of hotel staff, waiters, drivers. When he had to call her, I would always walk away, make room for the private drama of his actual marriage.

On the trips, I felt important because I was with an important man that people lined up for at various desks outside of various conference rooms to get their books signed. He charmed old ladies and young women as he sat behind whichever desk, his pen paused as if whatever was being said was so riveting he was forgetting he was in the middle of writing his own name down.

I watched from various corners, a little creep, a black cat. I couldn't go to his signings, at least not officially—some of the people who came to signings would remember the poet in New York, his wife, they asked about her, about her poetry, about their dogs. I became curious and asked about her too. He dismissed me, but I found an essay collection where he and other old men wrote about the women they loved. He had told the world his wife had no body hair, no pubic hair; that she came across fairy-like, ethereal and delicate; he referred to her as "pale fire," and after I read the essay I couldn't speak to him for hours, couldn't explain why I started to cry when he kissed my neck and whispered something about the warmth of my skin, my sweet smell, my *secret, private beauty.* The words, although specific and spontaneous, sounded hollow. I knew he'd said the same words many times before as he kissed other necks. The first transgressions I resented Voytek for were not of Voytek's doing; I resented his past, the fact that he loved before me. I couldn't tell him about any of it because it would make me seem petty and ridiculous so I kept quiet, muzzled with my unjustified indignation. The irony of being a mistress jealous over the wife only added to my distress.

If he caught me crying or sulking with no explanation, he would disengage, leave me to my misery and that in turn would make me even more miserable. The childish charm of a pouty young woman wore off quickly and early on.

But he stuck around, forgave me easily. After the readings and the signings, we would go out. Sometimes we went out to dance—where I danced and he sat and watched, an orange rind in his mouth as he sucked on it and stared, an old-fashioned in his hand, on his leg, a knee brace that made me feel tender towards him—and we always went to the movies. Whatever would be playing in the local theatre, even gun-and-car movies or rom-coms with Julia Roberts. We rarely ate out, but when we did it was always something obnoxious, a steak or a whole fish with a head. He said he liked a girl with an appetite and I never told him that after those dinners, those trips, I would come back to my silent apartment and not eat for days. It was fine, I was not distracted by hunger, I liked how its pain kept me alert, sharp. I didn't desire anything or anyone but him, and school and work and sleep were secondary to my vigil; I measured the passing time in With-Voytek and Waiting-for-Voytek. I stopped partying and socializing, I lived plainly, my apartment was like a white shoji screen. I was a paper cutout of a girl. Actually, it wasn't until I became a mother that I experienced clutter.

I excuse myself from the breakfast table to go to the bathroom upstairs. On my way, I see that Voytek's computer, his email specifically, is open. Maybe it's lack of sleep, his head filled with the stories he plans to tell me, or with her tits. The email is addressed to someone called Margot Ziti, and in this email he calls her *baby*, something he's never called me before, it's not a Voytek word, and he talks about how their one *magical* night together gave him hope, how pathetic he feels for even writing this, how he was in love once with someone but he couldn't fathom leaving his pregnant wife (me), and for two years he went to the woman's house in the ravine and he still thinks of her all the time, sitting in a window of her reading nook; she'd read him poems out loud, and he imagined himself living there with her—my hands shake but I manage to take a picture of the email with my phone, and read the rest in the bathroom as my guts give out and I empty my body from both ends. In the email, Voytek tells Margot Ziti that she is *a real talent* and that she's got *a thing* he can't quite put his finger on. He's so distracted by this woman already he's resorted to tired lines, stock phrases.

He shouts from downstairs that he's taking Ruby to daycare and going out to work. I don't know what he means about work, the semester is over. He's no longer writing any books either, he has told me nothing inspires him anymore. Perhaps he is inspired again, and that possibility hurts me more than anything else.

I find Margot Ziti online. She is dark-haired, with an enormous nose, a prominent jaw and pleading eyes. Not a typical beauty, she reminds me of someone you'd see in *The National Geographic* preparing her younger sister for a wedding to a Sherpa. My husband likes the *jolie-laide* type. I write her a message and attach a picture of me, Voytek and Ruby. I'm playing the wife's part in a film about being betrayed. I don't feel a lot of emotion, maybe even some relief to finally have such blatant proof. You have asked me when I finally knew, for sure, and *this* is when I was forced to stop hiding from what I already knew. It is dramatic but at the same time it is banal, a strange let-down to something that I'd imagined for so long. I'm not sure what I wanted, how I wanted to find out. I suppose if this really was a film about being betrayed, I would've walked in on him buried balls deep into his betrayal.

I take out my phone and stare at your number. I don't even know you, but I already talk to you all the time in my head. I imagine your outrage when I tell you about my discovery. Although I don't know if I should tell you, wouldn't being cheated on mean that I am easily replaceable? When a woman is cheated on, isn't there often that smug, unfiltered thought that suggests there must be something wrong with her, that she couldn't keep her man no matter how beautiful, smart, accomplished, kind?

Margot writes back. Her friendship with my husband is not *pedestrian*, or her feelings aren't. She writes she can *transmute* those feelings into friendship.

I calculate. They would've known each other for the duration of the spring course, so roughly two weeks. What feelings? She uses other big words: *transfixed*, *philia*; she is enamored with a writer, a man that students more advanced than her write long papers about. She writes that she is not a home-wrecker, she's genuinely fallen for my husband. *In this photo*, she writes, *your daughter looks sweet and a little lost, and you look not unkind but he looks melancholic.* I didn't ask her to review the picture but she offers her judgements freely, as if she had a right to him, to my daughter too. I am mortified by the ease with which she offers these judgements, by the fact that she doesn't retreat and apologize but instead stakes a claim. (I remember then another student, this crazy redhead who didn't know how to use Voytek's interest in her to serve her, who let whatever happened between them destroy her instead of taking advantage of it like I did). I have a bad feeling about Margot. I wonder if she, like me, understands that Voytek's weakness is not young women but that he has a blindspot where he can't see he's as much of a prey as they are.

Kill her, the thought pops into my head.

I picture her in some sad student apartment, a kitchen with stained cupboards worn out from constantly cycling through tenants. Margot is on a yoga mat, practicing bending, being serene. Based on my Facebook research, prior to meeting my husband she went to India to become a yoga teacher. She prayed, wore batik vests and parachute pants, and headbands; she stood next to men with legs set into triangles. She looked happy and sweaty, that nose always demanding attention.

In my murder fantasy, it's dark inside because it's too bright outside, a shouty kind of a summer day. Margot's ass is in the air and her face is down, and I walk in and grab the heaviest object—a Buddha, some kind of stone deity—and smash it over her head. She folds into herself, falls right onto her nose, and crashes into the yoga mat. *This is a woman threatening your home, your daughter, your daughter's home,* I think as I bring the statue down again and again. Somehow I am a version of my daughter that is a hybrid of her and me, the teenaged me who came here on a plane and tried, and failed for so long, to find a safe place to stay. It's her I'm really angry about, protective of. It's not the man who is at stake, it is me.

There is pink foam coming out from the corner of Margot's mouth. She whimpers, tries to grab my legs, is too slow. I, on the other hand, have to be quick, I have to raise that Buddha and bring it down again and again. I've run amok, my strength is supernatural, my body full of adrenaline as if our roles were reversed, as if it were me on the ground fighting for my life instead.

Research shows that there are two types of murderers: organized and those who snap. I turn out to be a bit of both—I've come over in rage and with an intent but I snapped when I saw her serene pretzel form.

And because I'm not the first kind, I don't have any ideas about how to clean it up after. Would I have to buy chemicals, lime, a saw, a small ax, industrial-strength garbage bags? And would I be caught on camera with my suspicious cargo? What camera? You never know. So would it make more sense to just leave her there, how would anyone ever guess our connection anyway? In my fantasy, Margot's body is strewn about, flecks of white bone, watermelon and pomegranate and Halloween.

I get off of the toilet. I splash my face with some cold water. I am dizzy, I am sweating. Inside me, there's stirring, my hunger waiting to pounce.

I leave the house and walk slowly to the ugly little mall in our neighbourhood and I buy a mickey of vodka in the liquor store. I sit on a hill overlooking the playground and I drink the vodka straight from the bottle, the liquid scorching the soft tissue of my mouth, my throat. I am becoming lighter. Mentally too: I even laugh out loud. I think about how dumb and evil all of this is, my husband's principle of making sure the grades are turned in before he fucks his students, the murder I've committed in my head. There are a few hours before it's time to get Ruby from her daycare, maybe I will sober up by then, or maybe not. I'm not sure if I am still sitting or if I am lying down, everything swerves and spins. Eventually I am no longer a part of reality as I unspool from my body and rise in the air like a balloon.

# SIX

THE SKIN GETS thinner. It's soft, velvety, it loosens. I am fascinated by the process of ageing as much as I'm also terrified by it, terrified of losing my looks. I've looked up prices for getting my chin, my forehead, my cheekbones, brows, or nostrils altered. There's nothing wrong with me yet, but in a few years I will be middle-aged and still a woman, and therefore offensive to a world full of Kardashian symmetry. Without the scalpel's interference, all the years of love and loss accumulate and concentrate; orgasms and disappointments show up in lines, in the depth of our eye sockets, cheekbones. We become calibrated versions of ourselves, grotesque.

I pinch my face, peer into my own eyes. Did my husband's betrayal carve out some new lines, is there more depth to me, a particular look of being above it all? I stand in front of the mirror and I try to catch, pin this new woman, surprise her with a sudden glimpse but whenever I look it's still just me, slightly blurred.

Since *our* first encounter, there's been a shift, another dimension taking shape on a different timeline, under the skin. I've become aware of this shift, I imagine I can feel twitches of something stretching, uncoiling, waking up from deep slumber. Every time as I look away from myself, there's an imperceptible nod, and we both know that a change is coming, morphing the old me and whatever it is I'm becoming into one. But one what?

I step into the shower and scrub my body, first with a loofah and then with my fingernails when that doesn't seem like enough. I'm not dirty but I feel soiled. I woke up to Voytek parting my ass cheeks, whispering in my neck that I'm getting too bony, a *little birdie* he said, his fingers kneading my hip bones, his cock sliding down, poking like a blind worm till it found my girl hole. His cock felt like old rubber and it hurt at first but I closed my eyes and fantasized about being a young girl losing her virginity and I lubricated and it was fine, nice even, but there was an anger hangover, the virgin's anger and I couldn't recover from it fast enough. I came but the orgasm was no-nonsense, contractions and an obligatory moan, a discharge of built-up responses, and then I wanted him off of me immediately. For once I was grateful for his usual disdain for cuddling and lingering on. We were done, finished, here's the receipt.

I come back from the bathroom and as I pick out clothes for the day, Voytek comes in and says he forgot to tell me, he has great news! He doesn't wait for me to ask what the news is, he tells me he's writing a new book, a memoir about his time at Fool's Paradise, a writer's residency in Scarborough, and a misunderstanding that occurred between him and some of his students. He says he's been feeling *hopeful*, truly *inspired*. I don't ask by what or whom. I know by whom. But it doesn't hurt. It has nothing to do with me and when I try it on for the pain—poking the thought like a loose tooth—there isn't much to it. I'm not trying to show myself up, I genuinely feel fine, yes, I think of you and I feel fine. I feel fine, better and prettier. Voytek kisses me on the top of my head to say goodbye, and without thinking I wrap my arms around his waist, a tender gesture that surprises us both. He stiffens momentarily but relaxes and in a soft voice says he loves me. I say it back. His earlier morning intrusion feels distant, unreal.

After he leaves, I take some selfies, pouting, smiling, trying to catch beauty and fit it onto my face. I check Voytek's location on my phone and it doesn't load. I shrug, as if someone is watching me perform my resignation. And then the universe rewards me for being so strong, and indifferent: a text from you that says, *Hope you're keeping well.*

I feel elastic, pliable with sex appeal. I exaggerate it as I glide against the walls. I play loud techno but it's not quite right so I switch to classical, something that sounds like evening rain, like spring and joy. I slow down my movements, move my hips in a wave, hands above my head, showing off my long neck.

I'm thinking about you, I can't think of anything else. I don't know why I'm not running after my husband, demanding Margot's head on a plate. With you I'm emboldened, carefree, silly and they—they can have each other. You're hoping I'm keeping well and for you I should keep well. You and I could have a future. We could stay up all night to explore my body, press your parts into my parts. I could rub my cheekbones in the sweat on your stomach. I would like to defile this face. I want it to break out in a red rash. I want to be allergic, asphyxiated from you, then mouth-to-mouth from you. I want you to watch me in the morning, notice the new lines, the time passing, my sharpness. I want you to write an ode to my moles, breathe in my breath, pry me open to examine my teeth, slide your fingers in there too, slide in your soft cock. Stuff me. Not with perverted food this time. I want to come to as I gasp for air with you expanding in my mouth.

We could do this all the time.

I try to imagine the intimacy of growing old together; it'll be different from how it's been with Voytek for so many years, his stooping shoulders, his man breasts, nipples with aggressive long hairs, the mouth something small died inside of—I've never had to imagine anything, the ageing kept happening right in front of me. But with you, I have to think up these future changes, they will seem fair both to you and to me as we will both go through them. It excites me that we will age at the same time and I'll get to ease into your worn-out slippers shuffling, your dandruff, your used-up testicles, your preferences, your future constipations, greying beard, magnesium milk. Everything I've been thrown into with him, I could shift that over—all of that could be yours to expose me to and I would love you for it even more, slowly, unlike the way I've rushed accepting the degradations of Voytek's ageing, if only to prove to him, to myself, I could fully love him. It is true that at this point in our story that I am still very much bound to Voytek, but I toy with these sorts of dreams. It surprises and delights me that I let myself do that.

What many men might not know about women is that when we fall for you, what we fall for is your future ugliness, not your beauty. (This is the opposite of how men fall in love.) It was Voytek's knee brace that softened my heart, his fluffy hair, his greying, once-white robe, the way his reading glasses were always a little greasy, the Scotch tape holding his cracked Blackberry screen together.

I knead and touch my face, and for the rest of the morning I don't answer emails, I ignore phone calls. Voytek's mother, Voytek's editor, Voytek's sister. No Voytek. I massage indentations, stimulate collagen, and stretch my neck. I pinch the skin under my eyes. I don't know how I'm going to manage to make it till it's time to go get Ruby, I feel so restless, charged as if I were earth and seeds, Heliamphora trying to violently push through, to eat, eat.

At the daycare it's the usual tumult of small bodies, dirty plastic toys, and smells: cooking, porridge, crayons and a faint whiff of excrement. Children screaming for mothers and fathers and mothers and fathers screaming for children.

I wait for my daughter, who is one of those deliberately careful four-year-olds who already tries to dress herself; she is meticulous about matching and colours and shoes. Today, when I came in, she nodded in my direction, and we smiled at each other politely, acknowledging our roles. Since turning three, she has rarely run towards me and I've learned not to rush her or call her, I respect her struggle with a body that's not accustomed to being fully functional yet. I wonder if she dreams of longer limbs, of speed, of being able to attend to herself the way she wants to attend to herself, not like this, with chubby arms and fingers that don't understand the sequence of shoe lacing. Most of the time, she wears Mary Janes, it's one less humiliation for her, she only has to remember that the indents in the middle mean Left or Right. I wait for her to finish dressing. I notice the colours of Easter dioramas hung on the walls are paler than usual, burnt out by the sun. I think of death before wheeling her outside, nothing specific, no one specific, just all of this ending one day.

Outside, the light is gentle and there's a breeze but I'm chaotic, uneven.

Jowita! A voice breaks through and my brain arranges all the information that is *you* as *you* materialize. I panic, unsure if I should perhaps turn around and pretend you've mistaken me for someone else. I am not prepared. I have nowhere to run, where would I run? A big soundless yawn opens up inside me, a stretch of a spine within the spine, your voice activating the secret stirring. There's a pulse between my legs and I relax.

Is he a fwend, mummy? Ruby says from the stroller as I stop and wait for you to approach us. Your walk is good, like you understand your distances, how objects relate to your presence, and what you look like when you're being looked at. Some of it is put-on I'm sure, but I'm captivated by everything I'm seeing, I'm a woman who's falling in love.

There's a coyote infestation, you say by the way of greeting. A man was attacked in the bluffs and you know, they're not above digging up a corpse. Someone said they saw a few of them outside their backyard. Like even around here. They're big things. They look like wolves. In a playground too, you say and nod at the stroller.

I picture a large animal lunging at Ruby, dragging her out and I hate you in this moment, hate that you brought a new fear to all the other fears I have about my daughter. And what corpse? I remember murdering Margot, if only in my mind, leaving her body to be eaten outside in a yard.

So I shouldn't try to pet it?

Oh, you should try for sure. Mind if I walk with you for a bit? you say and crouch down to say hello to Ruby who says hello back and who shows you her favourite Barbie, with shorn hair, whom my husband and I call "Butch."

I'm just going to the park, I say, feeling guilty for not having more exciting things to do with a stroller and the child in it.

Okay. What are you gonna do in the park?

I say, Look for coyotes? I don't know. Do they really eat people?

They do not. Maybe just the remains. You don't want to be eaten up, you say, your eyes never leaving mine. You make me nervous and you know it, you seem to take pleasure in watching me as I say words, try to arrange them into sentences.

You laugh when I say something about feeling chaotic, which is better, I say, than having spent my whole day looking at myself in the mirror and dancing to techno. I didn't feel prepared for this part of the day, the one where I'm a mother... I am giggling, blathering on. Your laughter makes my blood rush. This is a chance encounter, and now I'm going to expect to be running into you or you into me; we've probably passed each other before and never noticed, but now we are important to each other and the universe is conspiring. Or you're stalking me.

We walk and this is filler, a scene of a casual encounter, a man walking beside a woman with a stroller, a man who's not the creator of the child in the stroller, a man who can charm and walk away and continue living his life wherever he lives it. The memory of your mouth on mine seems uncertain, like a dream I had.

In the restaurant you were somewhat restrained with personal information but now, walking, you tell me about yourself, say you live in one of those micro-condos that are popping up anywhere there's a tiny bit of space left, an old parking lot that suddenly explodes into cranes and rebar, towers of boxes stacked one on top of another, each containing a person or two, a flat screen TV, a bed, a couch, a kitchen island. All those young people, like chickens in cages. All preparing to launch into the world and suburban houses with others like them, but for now fucking and eating takeout in their assigned compartments as they learn the final lessons of time passing too fast.

You don't seem bothered when I make my observation and ask if I always talk like this, like I'm writing aloud, am I writing a new book or something?

Yeah, I am writing a book or something, I tell you, and in that moment decide that our story will be the next story I write—and I think how I should make even more effort to notice things about you that would convince someone other than myself that this could be worth risking everything for, which is one definition of love: risk. Now, I know too that I could leave my husband, and I am already thankful for you giving me the impetus, and on that first walk you have no idea.

We walk and you laugh again, louder this time, at something that Ruby says. At the sound of it, a shiver cuts through. There's a new clenching inside me, a loop of pain and pleasure—already, and this is your laughter only, only the timbre of your voice. I wonder what sort of things you whisper when you fuck in the morning. (I will find out soon that you whisper exactly what my fantasies dictate: you become an older man with a virgin, a teacher, a daddy, a werewolf shapeshifter, or a whole gangbang, or a fat man—you can be anything I want you to be, you will read me before I can even finish the script.)

I insist we walk up to the lights and don't jaywalk, even though there are no cars coming from any direction. A few times I have an urge to grab your hand and hold it. Falling in love might not be a conscious decision but from that first air shift, those six champagne seconds I knew and now I know I was right.

That night I have dreams about you dying. Various tunnels and bottomless wells. That is my other clue—I only ever dream of people dying when I love them. I dreamt of my daughter falling off the birthing bed and landing on her head the same night she was born. With Voytek, it was speeding trains, cars, blood on the windshield. And I always dream of my house on fire or flooding, me trying to carry out soaked walls, failing, the whole thing just sinking to the ground.

# SEVEN

WHEN I WAS pregnant with Ruby, Voytek's friend Kazek opened a bar in a nice area of town, near the large park with ravines, where people from Hollywood shot movies on the cheap, famously a movie about a demon girl who haunted the wooden castle playground. She stood still with her dark eyes glowing at the top of slides or in windows of the castle before disappearing into the sickly bruised dusk, taking whichever child she'd set out to murder, with her. All that was left were hats and mittens and a doll with a broken neck. They eventually connected the disappearances to an orphan adopted by a friendly family and called an exorcist.

Kazek's bar had a framed poster of the demon girl on a wall and despite being named after a flower, everyone referred to the bar as The Demon. And that's how I thought of it on the hollow nights waiting at home for my husband who would text he was going out for a nightcap to Kazek's. He would be jailed for life once the baby arrived, was I that insecure and needy that I wanted to encroach on his last days as a free man? It was my fault that the baby was coming, it was me building it in my treacherous body. I was the one who forgot to take the pill all the time, no? It wasn't the pill's fault. It was fine. No, really, fine. Those were all jokes, of course, but honestly did I mind if he were to just enjoy himself one more night?

There were many one-more times but who was I to give a grown man a curfew? I had trapped him already, he was mine for life now, I had destroyed his marriage, seduced him at that bar where we met to talk about me being a real talent. I told myself such things when I would feel desolate and alone in our first apartment, with an exposed brick wall and his masculine leather furniture. I brought almost nothing material into that apartment—a bookshelf, a lamp, some paintings I'd found in thrift stores. What I did bring the most of were problems, the biggest one in my belly.

When Voytek stays out all night again and texts about nightcaps and crashing at Kazek's, I say nothing. I know how this could go. Besides, I am not alone now. Ruby is asleep, her breath like sweet little clouds smelling of spit and milk when I check up on her and gently kiss her velvet cheeks. And there's you too. We keep texting, and right now nothing is more important and beautiful. When the three dots appear on the screen, I hold my hand between my thighs squeezing them, permanently on the brink. You text you can sense I am alone, yours only. I allow myself to cum after we say goodnight.

In the morning, my husband and I stand in the hallway and we look at each other like we've just taken a pause in a particularly uneventful boxing match. I put Ruby down and he opens his arms. He smells clean like he has just had a shower. He doesn't say sorry. Sorry for what?

He releases me from the hug.

How was The Demon?

Great. But you know. Like everyone else, worried about the pandemic, Voytek says. His eye twitches.

Ruby wraps her little arms around his thighs and he picks her up, buries his face in her neck. She squeals. The bar isn't even open, I checked online. Kazek is honouring the lockdown.

(An image of Margot's dank student kitchen flashes in my head, Margot on the edge of a sink, Voytek's head between her legs.)

I say, I'm sorry to hear that.

I made sure I drank his most expensive Scotch, Voytek laughs. It was the least I could do. I crashed on the couch. He spent two grand on a vintage Olivetti Valentine typewriter. I had no heart to tell him a good keyboard doesn't make one a good writer.

Great details, I think as I make him a tuna salad sandwich and a salad, and heat up a tomato soup for Ruby. We watch a cartoon about an overgrown mouse and a small cat. I notice dust everywhere, in too many places, the TV console, a stack of books, so much of it and too impossible to get it all so might as well leave it.

After Ruby goes down for her nap, I follow Voytek to our bedroom and we go to bed. This is something we do frequently, during the day, with both of us working from home. And today I do it because I need to confirm what I already know. I will be alert for any change, a different thrust or grasp, more inspired aggressiveness or tenderness, anything out of our norm. Or to see if he will turn me down claiming tiredness, or a hangover. Or if he asks for a costume, something we haven't done since before Ruby was born.

No costumes. And he doesn't turn me down. He is exactly as he always is. We arrange ourselves in our spots, press and kiss and lick, every touch so rehearsed, it's as if we're playing a game of shape-sorters with our bodies. Maybe I was wrong then? I cannot detect another woman on him today, I have no proof. And maybe because of that, somewhere in the middle of this, I have a thought about how the past few weeks, the ones with you in them, have been a mistake. Like a fever, or COVID, something I caught and that caught me, changed me but only temporarily.

In the beginning, Voytek's kisses are automatic, perfectly impersonal, like a countdown, one Mississippi two Mississippi; he Vs my labia with cold, dry fingers, hooks one inside to draw out moisture. But when I turn my sigh into panting, it's as if something loosens and he murmurs into my shoulder, something about me being his bad girl, *bad girl birdie.* It occurs to me—and not for the first time—that that's who I am to him, really, a bad girl, and not a wife, but a spoiled brat birdie he's been tasked with taking care of. But there's sentiment in that too, I'm *his* bad girl and that is better than not being his girl at all.

He kisses my labia, inhales me loudly, ostentatiously, he Mmmms like I'm a delicacy, the sweetest thing he's ever tasted. I'm trying to focus, push you out of my thoughts. I should just leave you be. It is my duty to salvage this. For Ruby. With Margot *and* you, that's going to be too many variables. I will make Voytek love me again and I will become a dutiful, fulfilled wife and mother, and we will renovate the rest of the kitchen, then we'll open the attic. We will have parties with seven different types of sandwiches, even a garden party in our tiny backyard and I will hold my husband's arm and lean my head onto his shoulder and call him "honey" and recount interesting anecdotes from all the trips we'll take together, to Paris and to Havana and Berlin and everyone will feel a little envious but also reassured that we've worked it out—some guests will remember that it was a close call for us at one point. Ruby will grow up without having to own *two of each* for each of her homes, she will never know the small pain of not being able to fall asleep because she's left her favourite stuffy at mommy's, or daddy's.

He grunts and speeds up and that's my cue. I whine and groan and rock my hips, scratch his back. *I'm here, I'm here,* I tell his body, embrace him with my legs and with my heart too—I feel that I love him, I feel pity and guilt. And gratitude.

It was a close call, your passionate mouth, your Monster calls, you seducing my phone, keeping me away from the man who has committed to this—this repertoire, of fucking, of parenting, of home. He is here and he hasn't left yet, not really, and I have it in me to forgive him again the way I have so many times before. He's only human, he's only a man.

He shudders and gurgles, he sounds like an angry dying creature as he orgasms. His eyes are shut, his face twists. I force myself to look at him with kindness and then suddenly all I see is a lost boy, neglected, looking for a place between welcoming legs. They must be my legs.

I pull him towards me, hug him, don't let him wriggle out. I say, It's okay, it's okay to let him know that I *know* and that all of that is behind us now. It's funny that I keep thinking of forgiveness yet he has never said he was sorry and he has never asked to be forgiven. But he is the weak one and I am fine to do all the work for both of us, and for our home that we will recreate now.

He stiffens but then lets his body go limp; he falls right into me.

*

We book two nights in a hotel in Niagara Falls where there's a water park and an arcade. We once spent Christmas in that hotel, it was horrifying, American, with televisions in each booth in the restaurant that offered a menu of burgers and iceberg lettuce with croutons. The waterpark was in need of renovation with peeling paint and used-up structures vaguely resembling palm trees, and the fully, unintentionally preserved 1980s arcade—it was all charming in its own way, and a perfect place for screaming children. Ruby squealed with joy and cried from over-stimulation.

You text asking if we could meet again, you have something to tell me. I wonder if you're sensing the pulling-away, if it's making you panic. *I'm sorry* I say in my head and hope that you will get the message.

I send Voytek and Ruby to the pool and claim a headache. I go to the restaurant and order a pizza and I eat it fast, while drinking a whole jug of water. I try not to think about what I'm doing, if I am doomed now.

I make myself sick easily but after I'm done, I'm still stuck with myself. The act of expelling does nothing for me, there's no relief. But for the rest of the evening I don't answer your text.

At night, Voytek touches me again, and I squeal quietly to hide a sigh. He places my hand on his dick. I move it mechanically, my mind wandering despite my best efforts, your text flashing under my eyelids. I clench my vagina, arch my back, repeat. How would he ever know I'm faking? In our many years together, Voytek hasn't looked at me once during sex, so much of our fucking has been about just getting each other off. I'm thinking about you again, our kiss, your unanswered text. What would it be like with you?

Those juvenile feelings are fleeting, I tell myself, and remind myself that Ruby's well-being and the future Voytek and I are planning are more important than being happily in love. Besides, happiness is dangerous for the reasons I've already outlined.

But, wait! I'm happily in love now! I tell myself when Voytek inserts himself into me, inserts his dirt and my forgiveness. *This is love,* I tell myself as he penetrates me, eyes shut, mouth shut until a few minutes later when he lets out a low-pitched cry, and shudders on top of me. He pulls out, rolls over and doesn't make a move to gather me in his arms. Did we use to cuddle when we first started dating? I can't remember. But I remember one rainy afternoon now, when he met me in the coffee shop on campus and took me to his office and undressed me with great care, rolling my tights down my legs and laughing softly at my nervousness, my trembling. I was a graduate student by then and he had handed in my marks a long time ago. It thrilled me to be in the same office I used to visit to discuss which literary magazines I could pitch or why I wasn't getting along with my handling editor (a woman who would cut entire sentences she deemed politically incorrect and unnecessarily offensive).

In the same office, Voytek kissed my goosebumped legs up and down, behind my knees, and bit me gently inside my thighs. He licked and finger-fucked me slowly. He was methodical, luxuriating in our togetherness. For the first time, it was as if we weren't sneaking around and stealing time. Of all of our past fucks, that's the one I remember the best. He turned off the lights and pulled the blinds half-down, rain pitter-pattering against the window, he locked the door. It only rattled a couple of times during that late afternoon, urgently, desperately, and I remember picturing another *real talent* student on the other side of it, a thought that made me cum in Voytek's mouth.

After the sex is over and he's asleep, I reach for my phone and re-read your text again. If I reply, I will jinx this, I will bring back the wrong energy, invite more betrayal and disaster. I am the sort of person who says she doesn't believe in omens but I absolutely do believe in omens and superstitions and what people's birth date says about their personality.

I wake up too early full of anxiety and too jittery from it to fall back asleep. I worry I will collapse if I try to get up so I stay still. A notification on my phone takes me to an interview I gave to an Instagram magazine called *[ ]*. I've talked about my pain like it is a commodity, given interviews about the still-rotting places in me that I publicly claim to have healed. To connect with my readers, I've opened old scars, scalpel in my tongue, pulled out all the veins, lobbed their wet sticky ends at them. I answered women's questions about their own festering lacerations, man-made and self-made—their fat asses, their secret eating and puking, how do they, no, better yet, how did *I* overcome all of that? Self-love. Support. Making meaningful connections, I recited my spiel and they kept pulling on my veins, stretching them, and I gave more and more. But the *[ ]* interview was different; I'd been asked about my "style" and my "prose" and out of all interviews, this is the only one that truly matters to me.

I am thankful to these smart people, a decade younger than me, who ask these questions and run this magazine. I don't think this means I'm cool, even though I've tried to adapt some of the younger writing trends where punctuation is optional and you write things like ha ha to show how apathetic you are and nothing could move you so you say sorry a lot. Sorry. In this interview, I make self-deprecating comments, talk about ennui and pretend to forget what I like, but recall an anecdote from university when I wouldn't leave the house for weeks, which signals a difficult artistic personality, a need to isolate, a bona fide otherness. I say nothing about serial killers, but say I was depressed, which is a lot more acceptable than paranoia.

The constant feeling throughout the years has been one of not quite belonging. Not *not*-belonging—but *not quite*, which in a way is worse, the way all non-committal things are. I've now witnessed four waves of *cool* in my industry. The first was just as Voytek was ageing out of his wunderkind era. I was a mute Polish teenager and he was a man on TV my father called a "fucking wanker" because he talked about the old country like it was embarrassing him. He made fun of Catholics, therefore he made fun of my father, who was outraged not in the name of the Church but about the fact that here was a man his age who moved to the same hostile new land but dared to stand out, a man who didn't buy all the way into my father's story of the immigrant's endless sacrifice, a man who had the same lack of opportunity but ignored it and found a voice nonetheless.

The second wave of cool was when Voytek was a divorced former prof, still a man on TV, when he'd plus-one me into parties where other old hipsters did cocaine in bathrooms in twos or threes like we were in Bret Easton Ellis's New York. The parties would end with loot bags full of sample-sized vials of perfume and glossy magazines that would launch and fold within a year, and sample bottles of champagne and biscotti in crinkly plastic, and someone would be crying in her white stole in a taxi, a woman named Suzanne or Misha in strappy heels, and Voytek saying we should go have some oysters on a rooftop at the hotel across from the big museum.

The third wave happened around the time I published my first short story and got invited to wrestle intellectually in online magazines, with the likes of Sarah Nicole who was professionally cynical, ten years younger than everyone, a high-school dropout who knew all the references to postmodern art pieces and to Laura Nyro. There were kids with artful scarfs and chapbooks, clever Twitter accounts and hand tattoos and joke-bands and inside jokes from the loop parties they'd throw, always the same parties. They all hated people like Voytek, they called them "old" or even worse, "out-of-touch." I was the right age but I didn't have the right inspirations, or the right kind of uneducation; I was writing about myself and bodies and food, yet I made no references to feminists, I didn't watch obscure Italian cinema, I was too earnest and a little cheesy, the wrong kind of European, or maybe I just didn't use my Polishness the right way, as Voytek had—I felt I had no right to it, I didn't live through communism. And I was bad at Twitter. I was invited to fewer parties, I was asked to post my end-of-the-year playlist and then that was that.

I finish reading the Instagram interview cringing the whole time at my own struggle between wanting to suck up and trying to be defiant about *not quite belonging*, mentioning Ruby (always dropping the "mom" bit in my interviews, it's the laziest rebellion on my part), and in the end it reads as if I'm trying too hard to not care, and that depresses me. I would show it to Voytek but I know he'll just make fun of the magazine and its Instagram account of ironic pictures of suburban malls.

I watch him sleep and feel that at least we're in *this* together, this inability to truly fit in, and I feel a new tenderness towards him; I want to tell him about Monster being back and about you and how I'm going to now make it all better. I will not talk about Margot or any other former students, there's no point, we will start anew, we will be a family and we will be happy.

Voytek's eyes are blurry when I kiss him on the forehead to wake him up. I rub him the way he likes it, whispering for him to *show me*, to come for me, twisting his nipples, urging him quietly. It takes less than a minute. After he's done, I kiss him on the forehead again and tell him to take his time. His eyes are no longer unfocused, he searches my face, pulls me in for a kiss. His breath is stale but I thrust my tongue deeply into his mouth, full of hope. My anxiety has dissipated, I can move again and be in the world, I feel confident I can survive this day.

This is the kind of mood I'm in when I wake my daughter up and get her dressed and braid her hair. We skip and slide down the plasticky fibre-carpeted hallway, down the stairs and into the restaurant. We order pancakes for her and powdery egg whites for me, and sausages for Voytek, wait for him to join us.

Later, Voytek leaves with Ruby to go to the arcade and I wait in the waterpark restaurant swathed in a towel, reading other interviews in *[ ]*, including one with an author of experimental poems, all titled after Benjamin Moore's varied shades of white, a pronoun hoarder, which makes me panic because I am boring, default *she* and *her*. I have never felt queer, and sexually I've only ever loved dick and all the trouble that came with it.

The metal chair with our clothes on it buzzes once, twice, startling me, and I pull out Voytek's phone from the pocket of his jeans. The screen flashes with messages, one after another: *I love you too. I can't wait to fuck you again.*

In the car on the way home, I talk too much, I tell stories of the writers I've read in *[ ]* and my voice wavers and breaks, my anxiety is disgusting to me and I can't outtalk it. Eventually Voytek asks me to be quiet, says he wants to focus on driving. I look out the window, an endless, grey highway. Same sort of highway that's been delivering me to various calamities ever since I moved here. Right now the feeling of a new impending calamity has me in its clutch. I can't think of a single good thing, not of you—you are a nuisance. I wonder if I'm getting punished for daring to be hopeful and I am blaming you as much as I blame Margot. Voytek and I are victims, our union threatened by all of you, interlopers bent on breaking us apart.

I place my hand on his and squeeze and he turns to me briefly, What's that for?

It's gonna be okay, right? I whisper and he says, What's gonna be okay? Everything is okay.

Are you sure?

Everything is fine, he says.

I'm feeling funny.

Stop feeling funny, he sighs and adds, Remember, you're not a plate of fish and chips, you're not a plate of fish and chips, you're not a plate of fish and chips—remember to keep telling yourself that.

He's making an old joke, the one he'd use whenever I'd feel paranoid, lost in the doom of my mind, imagining things that weren't there, as absurd as imagining I was a plate of fish and chips.

*I'm not a plate of fish and chips,* I tell myself over and over until I feel some relief at the ridiculousness of the statement, my feelings invalidated, but at least, for now, quiet.

# EIGHT

A FEW DAYS later, I wake up in the middle of the night and leave my husband in our bed and kiss Ruby's sleeping, warm shoulder before taking off to the address I had found online. I write a note about having insomnia and going for a drive, a risk that I have to take, leaving that kind of evidence of my mental state. I will be at Lisa's later, I write, to work on a project. He will never ask, he ignores Lisa and everything about her because she's off-limits, being my friend and all.

I spend a few hours outside Margot's before I see her leave for work and follow her in the ugly silver Toyota that she drives to Liberty Village. She parks in front of a building with a sign that reads *EZ-Consulting*. I eat slimy, brown apple slices from a plastic baggie, apples Voytek prepares for Ruby and that she always brings home. I eat them to prevent her from getting in trouble, but I also pretend he's cut them up for me, that this loving gesture is meant for me. The apples make me love Voytek more. I need to love him to justify this, whatever this is. That's what I keep telling myself. After the apples, I watch a new Ted Bundy doc while I wait for Margot to finish work.

I've never done such a thing before, please don't think this is normal for me, none of this is normal. I've never followed Voytek's women because they weren't real, many of them were just plates of fish and chips.

Once, because of mood swings and delusion, Voytek set up an appointment with his neurologist friend for a middle-of-the-night MRI. Maybe I had a tumour? There was rhythmic clicking noise as the machine took pictures, minimal techno. The machine found nothing, but when I looked at the images later—I was given a CD with twenty-eight jpgs, like from some brain vacation—I noticed a forked tongue, a tiny edge of scales, only clear in one particular image. I said nothing to Voytek who said, since there was no tumour, it was probably borderline or bipolar, he was reading about the disorders on the internet, delusion was a symptom of both.

He convinced me to see a psychiatrist. But first, a woman phoned our house late at night, and it was just someone who needed help with her computer, certainly *not* the essayist who had a similar raspy voice. I was tired, up with the baby most nights. Or manically cleaning and fussing during the day or sitting still for hours at my desk staring at a wall. On the brink of an episode, possibly even in it already. I was imagining things, but he would take care of me, that's what marriage was, taking care of someone when they were sick. I was grateful, mostly for having a person in my life who knew me better than I knew myself, who knew how to protect me from my own mind.

I went to a clinic and talked to a kind middle-aged man about signs and instincts and gut feelings. The more I talked the more I heard myself, heard how crazy I sounded. He asked if I would be willing to come back, even stay for a couple of nights. Voytek had told them I had threatened my life but I had no recollection of saying that, which had scared me, not having a recollection and going so far into my emotions I'd black out. We were all agreeing it would be beneficial for me to stay. Voytek dropped off my pajamas, a toothbrush. I squeezed Ruby too roughly and she cried and I tried not to cry. After they left, I filled out questionnaires about my emotions and whether

I was hearing voices, and I slept in a room with an older woman who at night, scratched her plastic mattress, scratched and scratched. The next morning, she told me she was going to dig a hole all the way to China so I signed myself out worried staying there would cause me to lose whatever sanity I had left. Voytek picked me up and took me out for breakfast, ordered the Ploughman's special and watched me as I sweated and said nothing, Ruby squirming in his sling, and later, he held my hands after she fell asleep and after I broke down crying over the pile of RED-coded bacon. It was obvious to everyone that I was not okay, that signing myself out was a mistake. But in the end it worked, because I had never, until now, dared to admit that there was a real threat, not a delusion, actually another woman.

I wonder what *you*'d think of Margot.

Personally, I'm disappointed. What does it say about me that my husband is possibly in love with a girl who works at a content farm? A girl who owns a khaki skirt and who combines that skirt with wide, brown sandals, and who has a dreamcatcher hanging from the mirror of her ugly, practical car? I come up with those demeaning descriptions to make myself feel better about the situation although the shoes really irk me. I remember Voytek's joke about women closing up their vaginas and in exchange receiving a discount on their first pair of Birkenstocks. I recall too, his jokes about the sort of person who takes his summer class, an in-between kind of person, a retiree, a Linda who has beat cancer or a Gerald who had won a student film award in the 80s and has never recovered from that. And now, a yoga teacher with a knack for writing perfectly unambitious copy for organic lifestyle brands.

I imagine following her home, or to the store, or wherever she drives after work, where I'd watch her shop for oat milk, carry reusable bags. Be ordinary. But I can't make a whole night and day out of this. I have no plan, I don't know what I'm trying to accomplish. Still, after seeing her in the flesh, I fantasize about confronting her for real; in my head I rehearse various scenarios, snappy dialogue in which I always sound eloquent, sharp, my one-liners leaving her speechless and a little bit impressed. I imagine her in some abstract future, telling my husband that he has made a mistake and should go back to me, and although she still loves him, he should be with someone like me because I am so smart and beautiful and the mother of his child. Maybe he tells her to say to herself that she's not a plate of fish and chips, or maybe he realizes he's too tired and too old to take on another project. Now they both feel humiliated by their affair, he says something about how he has to try to save his family and Margot says yes, yes, they cannot build their happiness on my misery. Voytek sends me a long text, or better yet, an email, a letter, about not making any more mistakes ever again, begging to come back. He packs his bags. After he leaves, she calls to tell me. We have a nice chat, I feel generous and noble. But on his way home, Voytek's taxi is T-boned by a transport truck. Neither me nor Margot know that at the time of the phone call, she is full of remorse when she hears how articulate and above it all I sound, she asks for forgiveness.

Has any wife ever reasoned the mistress out of an affair? Won her husband back in a debate? Fantasy is, of course, just fantasy, although in mine I don't win my husband back because my fantasy is not about my husband; it is about my pride. I forgive everyone, whether in their posthumous state or not; it is easy to be generous when you restore the kind of balance I have restored by having this scenario play out that way, in my favour.

But the more I get to know Margot online, the less confident I feel I wouldn't be the one left speechless and impressed. Despite her job, her quiet hobbies, online she seems like someone much more ambitious. I find a picture of her standing at a podium in front of a crowd, she's lecturing dressed in swaths of cotton, a lavender and yellow pie chart on a projector behind her complementing her earth-toned desert garb. Another picture on a yacht surrounded by other happy people. Another one with a backpack, tanned, strong legs, a hand blocking the wide sun-smile, a lush green valley in the background, snow-covered mountain peaks.

It occurs to me the copywriting job must be temporary, and she is probably just biding her time before she catapults back into travel or academia, marine biology or digging up bones in Machu Picchu or maybe even writing, since that's how we got ourselves into this situation in the first place, Voytek's class for losers. Except that she's not a loser. Once I closely investigate all of her social media, Margot as a replacement starts making more sense, her gun of a nose and meaty lips striking and sensual, her personality emerging as I examine her activities, but mostly online discourse, responses to people, her cadence. I even repeat some of the phrases aloud, the ones where she sounds a little tired, or world-weary, like a character from a novel about a rich socialite named Sloane, "We must meet up next time you're in the area—I've heard their tartare is to die for!" Or "We have tried their reds and they were not to our taste, unfortunately, but B. swears by extra-dry if your palate is on the more daring side." She calls her friends "darling" or "precious," she posts moody pictures of old movie posters always with a hashtag #nostalgia. (As for pictures from the yoga retreat to India, they quickly become so familiar that I begin to have memories of the place, as if I went there with her, the wet air, the white fabrics blowing in the breeze, the scent of patchouli and cumin.)

For a couple of weeks, I am consumed by my new appetite for Margot, and she becomes part of my routine. I check in with her Instagram every morning, using a fake account I once set up with Lisa to spy on various ex-lovers or otherwise interesting men. It's a terrible habit but I've never been good at self-control.

But mostly, I'm stuck. Each morning, after Ruby and Voytek leave, I sit outside on the deck and watch the trees. A few months from now they will lose their lushness, their leaves will turn yellow, then brown. Then fall. The sense of loss is ever present. When I try to remember this period later, I cannot seem to put a timeline to it, in that I don't know if it all happens over one day or several. Nothing but the loss seems certain. We wake up, we eat breakfast, they leave, I stay, Voytek comes back, we eat dinner, we go to bed. You text but if you were to ask me now what we text about, I couldn't tell you. The most consistent memory is that of me waiting outside, watching the leaves.

Finally, one evening, something breaks the pattern. Voytek texts to say not to wait for him. I do what's predictable, which is to drive to his secret—not even his secret *location* but his whole secret, if people are indeed their secrets. Our phones are still connected to each other, the secret is at the same address I investigated a few nights prior. *Her* address. I am initiating another act of surveillance, I have to, to save our family. At least that's how I justify it to myself, leaving my daughter alone—I am not thinking clearly. But it's something, it's better than all that waiting. I've become a woman with a dark mission, trying to learn about my husband's other life, the one he always told me I was deluded about.

I don't know how others do it, follow people. And what happens once you learn enough—what will happen once *I* learn enough—will I snap? When do I confront...who first? For now, the only plan I have is to watch, to follow, to observe his car parked in front of her building.

Usually, it's men who stalk, men who wait in bushes or cars, who have telescope lenses trained on bedrooms. Men make the world dangerous, violent, fast. Women are supposed to make the world slow down, catch its breath. I want those two to catch their breath in a different way, catch it in their throats, lodge it in there, make them choke, spit, shake them up, bring them back to their senses.

I am part Monster and I wish for monstrous things.

In the parking lot across from her building, I watch people come home from bars. The bar people seem reckless, stumbling around drunk, away from their homes, all vulnerable to the night and the killers hiding in the shadows. I miss my home, my bed. You never know who is watching and what they could do to you. One man is walking with a woman, his hand wrapped around the back of her neck. Is he going to slip something in her drink later? No. When I narrow my eyes, sharpen my focus I can see that he's holding her lovingly, the gathered fingers massaging her neck. It's a play, a sexy game. I think about how I would like for you to hold me like this one day, but with me on my knees, your hand moving to guide my head. Or your teeth nibbling at my flesh, your hands caressing and kneading first my neck, my ass, your mouth growling orders. You're an insidious thought, but please not now, right now I am busy, right now I am waiting to see about my husband. Different from the waiting I do while sitting and smoking on the deck, watching the trees. Am I waiting for the ending to start, or for some other sign? I'm dysregulated. My emotions don't align—I am desperate one moment and excited the next, spying on my husband while rooting for him to get away, or wanting him gone for good. I've wondered before how starving my body has affected my ability to feel, if the lying to myself and the deprivation of nutrients has caused some kind of brain damage. Think about it. Eating a large meal sends a message to my brain that I am getting full and satiated, only to expel the meal later. The hunger, a confused messenger, trying to plead with the brain. How could I be hungry if I ate such a large meal before? This is what grows Monster strong, the lies, the desires that are unfulfilled. The hunger.

Everything is put on, I can force myself to cry when watching a movie that warrants it. Or when I recall how I snuck around with Voytek in our early days, his delight in watching my delight opening various boxes with ribbons and luxurious tissue to reveal the impractical geometry of lace, silk and eyes and hooks. Or if I recall something from childhood, my Best Friend's Dad. I don't do that one often. I don't do that one and I don't try to think too hard about Ruby's birth either, the opposite of that one. Her face against mine for the first time and Voytek's exhausted face above us—somewhere behind a green curtain my guts all over the surgical table—knowing then, *for certain* we were all home—our bodies created this child. That one would hurt the most because I know now that what I thought was for certain was not certain at all. You can destroy anything if you try or if you hardly even try.

I worry that truly remembering would render me completely dysfunctional. As a teenager, I jumped off a low roof once in drunken self-wallowing and I won't do it again because I know I will probably land perfectly on all fours and scurry off like a cockroach. I have seven screws in my clavicle that hold me together. They will find more screws to hold me together, there's an infinite amount of screws out there, no one really dies until they absolutely must. I worry I'm unkillable. I suppose I could just fall apart in my own bed, let my arms and legs rot off my trunk but people don't die like that and I have a human body.

Around three o'clock in the morning I start the car and drive back through the disinterested city back to my house with the abandoned child inside it. A new text from Voytek comes in telling me he is crashing at Kazek's, whose house is in the opposite direction of the building I spent four hours in front of.

For the rest of the night and the beginning of the day, I am calm, even when Voytek comes home smelling faintly of second-hand clothing. You'll ask me when the first time was that I had *that* thought. I will say it happened that morning and once it came over me I felt at peace. And it wasn't quite a thought, it hadn't yet formed but it was an emotion, the first one that aligned for me.

Later on, I watch the trees. I press my palms against the warm, sun-drenched wood plank of the deck I'm sitting on and feel the pulse of my home.

# NINE

END OF JULY, Voytek has to go to Paris for a week-long conference and I know I will invite you over once he's gone. I have never cheated on my husband. But I'm not anxious about it because of what's been stirring, stirring, stirring inside me and I feel safe in my own home. I'm the middle matryoshka doll and when I think of myself in this way, I feel fortified.

During the week of the Paris conference, Margot will post three pictures: one of them together on a little stone bridge with the Seine in the background, two of decorative tiles. My husband will post one picture, of a table in a row of tiny tables on a cobblestone street, with a newspaper, a half a croissant, *un* café, and in the corner of the frame a thick ankle in a high-heeled shoe, twisting, stuck between two stones. He captions it, "Cliché," which is what he is.

(There will be moments when I'll think of the two of them with compassion, remembering what it was like when I used to travel with him and was bursting at the seams of my secret. When you're in love you want to shout about it, hiding it is torture. I'm in the same situation.)

I text you to come over, on the day Voytek leaves.

Who can I tell? No one. I text Lisa who is as good as no one; I write I'm about to do something naughty, and she writes back, *Details babygirl details.*

Details: Ruby is asleep upstairs. I've dimmed lights, closed curtains. There's the smell of pine needles from a diffuser left over from Christmas. The house is coy and seductive, golden and warm, a wink from behind a curtain.

I've been debating drinking. It's nerves, I'm nervous. I haven't engaged in this kind of recklessness in a long time, not since before Voytek. I run around the house like a little dog, looking in the corners. I eat half a can of pineapple chunks. Too much sugar this late at night.

I dust, sweep, prop, fuss, organize Ruby's bookshelf. It's the books that finally do the trick; handling their various spines, textures, thickness, the soft corners of thumbed favourites, I start to feel calmer, cool, cooler.

By the time you ring the door, I am so cool I'm cryogenic. It feels as if I have no heart, no heart rate. I move slowly, talk slowly. I watch myself from above, from the side, I cannot seem to fall back into my body. And then you say my name, say it quietly, small, like it's a small spell. You pronounce it properly for the first time, *Yoveeta*, you are proud of yourself. I don't comment but this is nicer than flowers or at least more intimate.

I'm trembling. I try not to think of Voytek.

You're taller than I remembered, my house feels smaller with you in it. I let you in, take your coat—I smell it quickly, hungrily—warm leather and tobacco, that minty cologne. We make small talk. We are chummy. I probably say something about the kitchen island because it's been a topic of all my adult conversations lately, people love to talk about renovations. I sit on one of the fancy stools, spin on it. You lean against the island, watch me. On the screen these situations look better, like a dance: she grabs his buckle, unzips it, he kisses her neck, inhales her, she moans, he growls, lifts her shirt, her breasts are perfect globes in a perfect lace cage, etcetera, two panthers fucking.

In real life, we kiss and fumble toward the daybed in my study. I step on a piece of Lego as I start to take my clothes off but you order me to stop as I unhook my bra.

I'd like to ah…savour this. I like this part, you say with a leering smile. A stretch inside me, one opaline eye opening. You reach behind me. I watch you watching. I've breastfed Ruby for two years so my breasts are no longer firm and bouncy but I love their softness and their flirty smallness; you cup each in each palm of your hand, and lower your mouth to my right nipple. Since becoming a mother I've discovered orgasms from having them sucked on. The family doctor assured me my reactions weren't sexual but hormonal, body releasing oxytocin that caused intense contractions of the uterus. It's about bonding he assured me and I wondered what he thought sex was about.

You are a hungry baby, a good baby as you feed on me, Please don't stop, don't stop, please, I murmur like a porno till your quiet *Holy shit* snaps me out of my trance.

What? What is it?

M-milk? you say and I look down and there it is. A pearl drop, creamy white.

I laugh. You laugh with me. We laugh.

That's a bit fucked up, isn't it?

No it isn't, it's normal. You've never been with a mom before?

I have. But I've never—

Stop, I say and pull your shirt up, move my hands against your taut skin, a dark patch of your chest hair, your hard nipples. You are perfect. I kneel down in front of you, I take you in my mouth, my tongue circling, feeling around the soft ridge, my hands stacking up, milking *you* now, you pray to the holy trinity of Jesus God Fuck, and grab the back of my head and roughly manoeuvre your dick so that it fills my entire mouth, I have no idea how. I feel it bend and lodge against the back of my throat.

You run your finger underneath the side of my jaw, press on it, later you'll tell me it turns you on to feel just how far down you've stuffed yourself into a woman's mouth. My eyes water, you tell me to look up and when I do, you shake your head as if you can't quite believe this scene—as if this was the first time you've seen a woman tear up for you. You say, This is so fucking beautiful.

You scratch my scalp, pull small bunches of hair, release, Keep looking at me, good girl, good girl. You pull out of my mouth, pet my head. I think of the priests from my church when I was a little girl volunteering for prayer vigils during Easter Sunday.

You help me back up on my feet, push me gently onto the daybed. You are so gentle with me. So rough. You gather my wrists in your hand, stretch my arms above, press them against the headboard. Keep 'em there, you say and roughly kiss your way down my body, the goosebumps like a million tiny antennae. You tell me to open my legs, to spread, spread wider. That's right, open up. Good girl, good fucking girl, open up, you whisper, your hands on my thighs now, thumbs cajoling till I'm no longer bound by muscle; I'm unstrained, loose and softer than a breath. I shudder, and open, and spread, I am a good fucking girl. I want to come with you so badly, I have never come with a lover on the first try. I want to mark you in that way, I have such a hunch about you, you know this now. I hurl through my mind's catalogue of saved-up clips, real memories and porn, but none of them are good enough, I need something with more impact, a match for the breast milk to shock you into the second *first* of the evening, and then I have it, have it finally, it is not a fantasy, it is the truth in the making. My core contracts, releases, and then once the ascent begins, I put my lips next to your ear and I say out loud: I love you.

A pause, quick breath, and then, you say: I love you too.

That's what you do. You say *I love you too.* You don't stop, don't panic, you plunge right back into me. I levitate, your grip tightens, you slam even further into me, fuck me right through my explosion. I'm a supernova.

Later, we fall asleep mid-kiss, and when I open my eyes that's how we are, our mouths in half-moons breathing into each other.

Shhh, sleep baby, sleep, you kiss my eyelids and I sleep again and this time dream of an alien creature, flashes of lavender and silver, scales, clouds. I don't know at the time that I'm dreaming of myself—I don't have the words to describe it exactly but I just want you to know, it was that first night with you when I dreamt of it as it truly was, its one eye opening inside me, awakening. I didn't understand that any more than I understood what was between us, how we were meant for each other. But I knew we had a higher purpose.

# TEN

YOU MADE ME remember. How I loved being under, how I loved being taken, split open, penetrated, interfered with, invaded, possessed. Crushed. Handled, mishandled. I was once a heterosexual man's wet dream, with my yielding, my cock-worshiping, my devotion to all that is male, I used to love almost every man I'd meet. Their hardness, flatness, muscle, and hair. Their heaviness. Their lines, triangles and no-nonsense feet. Even the word "he" or "him" would turn me on. I'd been able to orgasm with some men only because I loved them, not because they were great in bed. I didn't need much. As long as I loved them, missionary was fine. If a fetish is something one needs to achieve the ultimate sexual pleasure then my fetish is love.

Years and years of fucking and I finally arrive here so effortlessly, as if I've collected enough empty fucks like game credits and now, boom, I climax right from the beginning. You're intuitive, rough but attuned, you know all of that. For me that's only a lucky bonus, I want you that much and wanting you is enough. My emotions are foreplay, I'm wet from the feelings.

You will later tell me how saying "I love you" back was the most perverse thing *you* have done on a new date, it was more perverse than the milk, and how it also felt right, you understood the dare instantly. I explain that I had to say it because once I say it, my body knows what to do. It's an instinct I have about you, about this.

Once, when I was seventeen, I said it to a blue-eyed boy mid-fuck and it ended the way you'd imagine. The boy disappeared. It was fine, I was new, the sex was subpar, fast and dumb; the boy was just a boy after all and didn't know how to work his own body; mine was only a receptacle.

But from the beginning you admire all of me, the flaws, the starved parts, the ropy ones, the squishy ones, the small, soft ones. We're rushing at first, but eventually we do slow down, we start to properly worship. One of the first times we make love, you hold me still, your cock twitching and pulsing inside me and I am so attuned, that subtle expansion is enough to put me right over. I wonder if together we create some particular chemical combination, something off the Periodic Table, two undiscovered elements that respond solely to one another. For example, when you ejaculate inside me I experience a powerful contraction that often surprises me with another orgasm.

I also have visions. I look at my legs like slim pale calla lilies sprouting on the sides of you, my cunt an open shell, with its pearl swelling; I shudder, shiver as we breathe against each other's necks, ears. The first hours of our lovemaking are contained as if in a cloud, the time is spent on elevations and slow dips, and falling apart and putting each other back together, we never ever untangle, I am always holding onto a part of you and you a part of me.

I am not a spiritual person, but with you I become spiritual. I experience euphoria.

After we say goodbye, you turn back around, cup me between my legs, and look into my eyes and just from that, I gush all over your hand and we both pant, Oh God Jesus Fuck, we breathe, we tumble back inside. You hoist me up, press me against the wall and I wrap my legs around you, my body slo-mo down onto you, my hands flailing and holding onto coats, or the coat hanger that predictably falls out of the wall.

You screw it back the next night. After you're finished, I stand behind you and put my arms around your shoulders and tiptoe up to whisper a little wish. You turn and grab me by the waist, hoist me up with your other arm, and again, I flail my hands and the fucking thing comes out of the wall again, the noise waking Ruby up—she calls for me—and we laugh that particular laughter, the haven't-slept-all-night laughter, Shh, shhh, you put your hand against my mouth as you drive harder and faster into me (mummy, mummy, I'm gonna climout! I'm climingout!), I'm pushing you away, there's more noise upstairs, some grunting and then a loud thump and slapping of feet against the wooden floor and rattling of the baby gate (mummyopenmummyopenopenopenmummy) and you say, Open mummy, open for daddy. I shudder against you hard, I bite on your hand, you hiss, Fuck, fuck, and it's 6 a.m., Tuesday, the day is yawning a big, summer-morning yawn, the sun falling in through the open windows, shattering against the polished wooden floors.

I miss you from the instant you leave. Everything seems wrong. I walk around, Ruby toddling behind me. The house becomes a museum, or a stage, somewhere that's familiar but no longer a place where the status quo makes sense, where Voytek makes sense, that diseased love, now a parody of what love was once there. I need to make this a home again. I pat Ruby on the head, shush her, pass her snacks, turn things on and off, pass her things, all while keeping one hand cupped between my legs, I praise things (That's nice, Look at that!) as I replay the past few hours, how you possessively held my face in your hands, how you didn't look away once, how you made me levitate so many times.

After I put Ruby down for her morning nap, I calm myself down by watching a new TV series about a serial killer. It's slow-paced, set in the 70s. The TV screen smells of B.O. from all those polyester golf shirts. The air fills with smoke from Marlboros. I wonder if there are any serial killers around these days. Or was it something that bloomed in the last century and tapered off in the more recent years?

(You don't know yet that I watch television like that, or that I have dreams and specific nightmares of violence and assault. You know about me and food. But you don't know about my appetite.)

Voytek calls once a day and we talk to each other through the time and space between Toronto and Paris. We say things but we're not really there, we are taken with our lovers so we say words we're supposed to be saying, How is Ruby? How is Paris? Paris is Paris. Ruby is Ruby.

During the day, I follow the script: a husband on a fun work trip, a wife at home waiting for him, spending hours on the child and chores and folding laundry, whites to whites, and colours to colours.

Voytek doesn't know about you and I am grateful for not having to deal with that yet, our story is still so young, fragile, I don't want to apologize for my desire, I don't want to blaspheme against any of it. Whenever the pain of Voytek's latest betrayal surfaces, I wave it away. I understand I have no right to it now that you are here, taking me every night. But that's precisely why I summoned you, so that I would have the strength to leave. I wish I had that strength on my own but women never leave, not even when their lives are in danger, or especially when their lives are in danger. Because what if he changes? What if he stops? But he will never stop. The easiest way for a woman to stop a man is with another man.

Every night in-between our lovemaking, we bring each other up to speed. We summarize each other's history the way all new lovers do, trying to catch each other up on all the pieces of our lives that seem to have made no sense because we've spent them separately. We are astonished that we've made it this far without breathing each other's air. Were our lives just rehearsals? Yes, we are a cliché, but when it's just the two of us we truly believe that our feelings are big and none of this is cheap; this union between us is sacred, and before it was all chaos and pointlessness. I wonder out loud if this is perhaps unfair towards Ruby, whose existence should be the only thing that makes sense in my life, and you pull me close and press my face against your heated chest, and say, You should've had her with me, as if Ruby was inevitable and I chose the wrong parts to assemble her.

You laugh, And how did *you* get assembled?

(Disassembled, I think. My father hit me in the face and my mother called me fat. I starved my body to prove her wrong but I let men violate me to prove him right.)

Nothing special, I say, I was born to a mother and a father, who met when they were twenty-one and stayed together until one of them died. They were good with dogs but not with children, they were not good with me. Something will happen sooner or later, they used to say. It's like they couldn't wait for that something. And then something happened. But it wasn't the guy's fault.

And then what?

There was therapy, of course, I say and start kissing you, your slightly salty skin.

I think about that time, bland couches, pastel drawings, flat shoes, blouses, Hold this rock, what does it remind you of? Eyes trying to meet mine as they darted around their offices, their ringed or unringed hands, them smiling, me trying to figure them out by crystals on their shelves and titles of books or their paintings of pastel landscapes. Dreamcatchers. Inspirational posters. Empty walls. If you're thinking of suicide. M.S.W. M.Ed. Ph.D. M.D. E.T.C. Bleeding cuticles.

I was the one who initiated it. My Best Friend's Dad. Is that a common thing? I mean it is a porn trope. *Oh, no! You gonna get me in trouble. Ohhh you're bad. Are you a bad girl?*

He picked me up in his car without a roof. What do you call those cars without roofs? I said to him and he said I was adorable. I wore an oversized sweater and we got a hotel room. I had fake ID. He had a wife. He was friends with the owner. There was a bar downstairs and I drank vodka shots. I sat with someone's bored girlfriend and she said I was like a duckling. She said, Feel my boob, it's silicone. I wanted to stay with her, have her mother me, but I didn't have the courage to beg.

I had only been kissed once before that night.

The hotel room had a low ceiling.

Afterwards, in the bathroom, I looked in the mirror. I was still developing. My left breast was bigger than my right one. I looked in that mirror and I looked and I couldn't tell what changed. But men could. They've followed me ever since.

There is a high correlation between girls developing eating disorders after suffering sexual abuse. Maybe there is a high correlation between girls developing sexual abuse after suffering an eating disorder, too. A girl has a body and the body betrays her, so she brings a man into the body. He doesn't fix it. The girl punishes the body. And so on. The therapists were pleased I understood.

I've never talked about how much I enjoyed myself with my Best Friend's Dad. But I really did, everything we did, I asked him to do. You're the only one I share this fact with.

Are you okay now? That's all you want to know.

I'm okay now. The most patriarchal thing you can do is let a dick ruin you, I say and you laugh and run your hand up my leg, wedge it between my thighs, say something about wanting to ruin me just a little bit. We fuck, you try to leave, we fuck again, you leave, Ruby wakes up, the day continues until it is over and I can finally see you again.

# ELEVEN

YOU SAY THERE were drugs. You had a problem but you don't any more.

Are you sure?

I'm sure. I still party. Rarely. Never.

What kind of drugs?

No, forget it. No drugs. Not like that. You shrug.

I drop it and ask about the women before me. I ask you to tell me good stories, I am not interested in teenage fumbling or quickies in public places.

There's nothing wrong with teenage fumbling, or quickies in public places, you laugh.

Like this? I whisper and rub you with my hand, gently, my thumb massaging the most sensitive skin on the underside of the penis, the delicate frenulum, which every girl knows is a spinal-cord pathway that sends signals to the ejaculation centre, upwards of four thousand nerve endings.

Does every girl really know that? you say, your voice hoarse.

Uh-um, they teach us this stuff in girl magazines. When I was a teenager. How to look pretty and how to suck dick.

And what did they teach you about pussies? you say, your hand between my thighs now, prying them apart with your fingers.

Oh, not much, I purr and writhe a little bit, rubbing myself against your hand like a kitten. I say, Maybe they do these days. But I was reading the other night how in some medical textbooks a cross section of the female pelvis tends to omit the clitoris altogether and back in the 80s there was still this view that pussies were underdeveloped cocks, a failure of male genital formation... I close my thighs, trap your hand between them, remove my fingers from your four thousand nerve endings as if to punish you for all that bad education. A clitoris has at least twice the amount of nerve endings and most of it is buried under the surface, two teardrop-shaped bulbs, arms and a shaft, the little tip of it that you can see is much like the tip of the iceberg. (Another monster of sorts, beautiful and cloaked in mystery.)

You tell me a story about a B-list actress you met while hitchhiking in the desert in your twenties, how she invited you to spend a weekend with her, nothing sexual, she said she was clear about her boundaries, she just liked your face. She showed you a picture of her girl. You smoked weed and listened to vinyl records, she danced in a crop top and old man jeans and you thought she was so sexy, the vinyl scratched, it was like a snapshot from the 1960s. On Monday, her girlfriend came back and walked into the guest bedroom where you were and she climbed into bed with you, reached into your pants and sighed, "Oh thank god," as she freed your dick. The girls asked you to stay for a week, a week during which you lived out every straight man's fantasy in every configuration possible.

Then there was the persistent younger sister of a friend, a teenager who drank too much, and who wouldn't stop taking her clothes off; you once picked her up and she let you dress her as if she was a floppy doll. She was staring at you the whole time as you pulled her pants back on, stuffed her breasts into her bra, buttoned up her shirt. And then like a toddler, she took everything off again as soon as you were done. Another time she followed you into a shower, snuck in, demanded you wash her. You resisted, but a few nights later you gave in, and this turned into moving in together for a few weeks, your only live-in relationship. She brought home stray cats, thrown-out leftovers from fancy restaurants and eventually other boys—boys her age. She called you "Daddy," the first time any woman called you that. You were twenty-three.

Keep talking, I tell you and I slide up and down your thigh as you describe another girl asking to be tied up and driven out to the countryside, re-enacting a serial killer fantasy. She asked you to put her in the trunk of the car. You drove slowly and when you politely half-walked-half-dragged her out, her body pretend-lifeless, you couldn't get hard. You were too scared to say that the fantasy didn't work for you. She got mad when you peeled the tape off of her mouth to ask if she was okay. Now it was all ruined and she screamed and hit you in the face.

I reveal then how taken I am with serial killers. You admit you find it confusing.

Many women are into it, I say, Like your ex-girlfriend. It gives us the illusion that it won't happen to us if we study them. There was research, I say, aware that I'm losing your interest.

I tell you how I watch and rewatch their interviews. You tell me to maybe find a different hobby.

Is this our first fight?

No, it isn't. It's just not my thing. It's even worse than those reality TV shows. You shrug and say, I'm a little disappointed in your entertainment choices.

I'm a *wettle disappointed*, I mock you. But isn't it fascinating how normal they seem? Richard Ramirez looks so polite. Dahmer just looks perplexed and eager to please—and he did an interview with his fucking dad. And Bundy is so goofy, obviously a class clown, look how he flirts with the crowd.

(Their voices are so measured, their efforts to please and entertain all those wide-eyed, hair-sprayed interviewers.

Did you always feel you were different somehow?

Yes, I've always felt different, ever since I was a little boy.

Did you feel like you were perhaps possessed by Satan?

I felt as if there was something or someone inside me. I heard voices.)

Baby. Stop. It's disturbing. My *wettle* freak, you say and touch my breasts, pinch my nipples. You kiss the insides of my elbows, you lick my neck but I'm in it now, I won't shut up. I squirm and defend, try to explain some more. I need you to know and love all of me.

I maximize the YouTube window, Look at them! Listen to them!

You blink. You don't get it.

It's so satisfying, watching those men caught and placid now, with their hair brushed, their eyeglasses clean, their neatly arranged hands in laps, no strangers' DNA behind their fingernails any more, no more undigested body parts in their stomachs. I could watch them for hours, trying to navigate the normal human exchanges of various *60-Minutes* or *20/20*s or *Oprahs*, having to stoop down to our logic and morals with clarifications that defy morality but not reason. The reason was there. It made sense to them and I understood that on a certain level—when I was pregnant, I was complete, one with Ruby, her skeleton and skull a part of my anatomy, her little orb of a liver, her perfect toes. I know now that I should've left Voytek then, that there is one other thing besides cock that makes women leave and that is a child. When Ruby was inside me, Voytek didn't matter. I was powerful, a lifegiver. I was content, the bottomless mouth was shut, it wanted for nothing. When I expelled her, the mouth started to open up again. I became hungry and incomplete. Trapped. I could not protect Ruby but it was still me who had to give her a home, now that my body evicted her. *I cannot do this on my own*, I decided, while staring into her squished screaming face. I became weak. I didn't leave. I inserted my husband, his cock a plug that would keep me from spilling out and dying. It worked and then it didn't because eventually, like every man, he would turn flaccid, slide out of me, no permanent solution for the hollow.

Dahmer said he kept his victims' parts and ate some of them because he wanted to possess them. He had to kill them even though he couldn't explain that in a way that would justify his actions according to our human laws. He didn't want his lovers to leave. He ate a heart to feel the heart, he kept a head to preserve the beauty. The head was a lover's memento. He didn't say he was sorry till later because being sorry was beside the point. He wanted to make an altar out of the parts, but he worshiped them even before he finished building the altar; he knelt in front of his macabre bounty in the same way I was kneeling in front of you.

I like worship and I'm sentimental. For example, I don't replace the stained table cloth after you fuck me on the dining room table for the first time. Once my husband returns, for a week or so, every morning, and evening, I will eat there with my family, the little stain delighting me secretly while my husband will ask me to pass the salt. The stain reminding me that I am no longer alone.

After you leave on our final Paris morning, I am inconsolable until 8 a.m. when Ruby's quiet chatter reminds me that I am who I am. Not a tragic heroine, at least not yet. I get her up and dress her and feed her and then I sweep and dust and cry. The house is quiet. My daughter plays in her corner, silently. She doesn't ask me to turn things on or off or to look at anything, or to get her snacks. She senses my distraction, my mood as I sweep and dust and cry. I do this until 11 a.m., which is when I check Instagram to see if Margot has posted anything. She has. It's a picture of a forearm, an elbow on the table, undoubtedly it is my husband's forearm and elbow. The hashtags are #waiting #longing. The picture calls for a reaction but I don't let myself be provoked.

Voytek texts from the airport. His stupid *Home now, my love* irritates me. *I brought you a present,* he texts and sends what looks like a picture of egg yolk with tiny red veins and what will turn out to be a little silk scarf that he says goes with my *colouring,* forgetting perhaps that he used to buy me purple and blue when we were first sneaking around, claiming the same thing.

Why the performance? What home now, *my love*? Do they share the cab together? Or do they go through a tearful goodbye at the airport? Voytek is not the tearful type, he will pat her on the back, tell her to be brave. He is proud of being practical, he has always made fun of sentimental gestures. Every Valentine's Day he'd get me a box of chocolates and five red roses and a cheaply made stuffed bear and a Hallmark card with some ridiculous inscription, from the nearest drug mart—it was all meant to be understood as a joke, of course, we were better than that. I've saved up some of the bears, six cheap identical bug-eyed chihuahua bears.

Restless, I feed Ruby again, carry her upstairs to her room where I lay her down in her big-girl bed, pat her back, press her down, insist she rests. She squirms and whimpers in complaint—her body's routine is regulated to the minute, suspicious of this too-early nap—but I press harder, I rock her back and forth, gently but firmly at the same time. She finally gives in, exhales loudly.

I walk around my museum-house and imagine it different. I would strip the dark paint and throw out the heavy furniture.

I would paint it white. I would install a glass door in the front to let in more light—the house is dark because it's the middle worker's cottage out of three in a row and there are no side windows. I've thought about this many times, often before falling asleep. In those fantasies Voytek isn't here. Now that I think about it, I've always fantasized about the house without him in it.

In the bathroom, I powder my face. I change into something white and geometric. I am an origami, complicated and pure. I go downstairs and sit on the leather sofa and wait.

I'm almost excited about the argument I'm about to start.

# TWELVE

VOYTEK AND I do what every couple does before they separate, which is go to therapy. Neither of us wants to save the marriage but we go because neither of us has a plan for what to do when there's no marriage. He has changed his passwords again so I have no access to his emails but he's distracted and not unhappy so I'm assuming he's in touch with her. Just as I am in touch with you, we text all the time and see each other twice for furtive, quick loving in your box condo, and you always ask me when you can see me next.

I've called Lisa and told her about Voytek's Paris trip and about Margot, but I don't tell her about how I can't stop thinking about you. You are my only good thing, my precious secret, better even than whatever you've awoken in me, the one eye open. Before you came along, not even Ruby's pudgy cheeks and happy chatter were able to distract me from often feeling like I keep missing a few small but crucial steps in following life's instruction manual.

The couples therapist has a round Eckhart Tolle face, he wears a green short-sleeved shirt, khaki pants, never a tie; his uniform is nice, calming. He's younger than Voytek but authoritative with his quiet yet decisive voice and firm handshake. He's someone a friend recommends, someone who she said had saved her marriage. He's not cheap but she said it'll be a lot cheaper than a divorce and nobody wants a divorce.

Why are we in therapy if nobody wants a divorce? Did I demand it? I can't remember.

I mostly remember the outfits I wear that summer, how it is always hot. I wear print dresses with nothing underneath them and one time I bend down to adjust my sandal and when I look up, the therapist is looking away and his face is red. But he hates my husband even more than he hates me, at least that's what I think when I listen to the questions that to me seem skewed to favour me: Why does Voytek think he needs validation from those younger women?

What women? Voytek says, his right leg pressing an invisible pedal on an invisible sewing machine. His eye twitches, he coughs into his fist once, says, Her jealousy has always been an issue. It's *pathological.*

Before I have a chance to answer, the therapist throws another one at him, What is it about his relationship that makes him want to step out? What is it about marriage, what is he running away from?

I'm not here to entertain my wife's delusions, my husband says. This isn't helping.

For those and other reasons—problems with authority, and an ego the size of a beachball—Voytek hates the therapist too, and so the three of us power tensely but politely through all that hatred, three sessions in one week, one where we're all together and the other two one-on-ones.

Finally, during the fourth session, Voytek says calmly that he wants to separate, and equally calmly, wordlessly, I get up and walk out of that office, walk right outside onto the dusty sidewalk and noise of the city enveloping me instantly, my armpits wet, my skin steaming as I keep walking and walking until I see a frozen yoghurt place. I get myself a large-size sour something with red and purple fruit and I sit outside on a cheap metal chair at a table that is chained to the ground, scraping loudly as I move it. I don't know what to think so I don't think.

After a while, Voytek shows up, points to his phone. We left the share-locations setting on, an oversight on our part.

It's not that we've never tried to break up, it's that he has said it so clearly, as a matter of fact; the dispassionate plainness made me understand this was serious. I'm not ready, I need a plan first. It scares me, being unprepared. Not in control again.

Why did I get up and just leave? He wants to know. It's that unpredictability, your moods, that kind of impulsiveness that… He composes himself and lowers his voice.

I say, What was there to do? I didn't think saying anything would make any difference. How are we going to do this?

We look at each other like two people sharing a problem, which is not a wrong way to think about it. Inspired, I point to my phone, unshare, untether my location, which makes me feel untethered in general and like I'm dissolving into fatter and fatter pixels until I'm one with the chair, the table and the air around us.

He smiles a pained smile, We'll have to get lawyers. I've already spoken to Brian.

(Now I feel truly duped.) I say, How long have you been thinking about it?

A couple of years, to be honest.

Since the rat in the ravine?

What?

The one with the weird rodent face.

Who?

The essayist.

It's not like that.

What is it like? I say and then he says, That's the least of our worries, and I say, The least of your worries, and then we say everything you'd imagine would be said but maybe because of the heat the energy is low, our voices never rise, nothing in our demeanour matches the drama that is happening in our lives. A series of random images flips through my mind, all the things I will have to miss and cry about soon: An antique praying bench isn't just a praying bench, it's a sweltering July afternoon and an estate sale, and a sexy photoshoot on it, my belly between my legs like a giant balloon, the week before our daughter was born. A jet chandelier, a reference to the jet necklace that broke and spilled on the hardwood floor of Voytek's office, on the night of the second time we had sex. We bought the chandelier because I said it made me think of that night. Laughing into each other's shoulders, a hand squeezing a thigh. Trips, elbows out windows, wind in hair. Ruby's chubby feet being dipped into the ocean for the first time. The rickety glass sink in the upstairs bathroom that fooled us into thinking our new house was fancy, the frozen pipes bursting and the wall behind the sink collapsing, and us with our "we're in this together," and a pile of blankets, and an old dog bed—when we first moved, the dog, Rocco, was eighteen years old and blind and skinny but he loved napping by the floor-length window in my office, and my office, of course, pictures of Ruby's drawings on the wall, all the prosaic and not so prosaic stuff, a shuffle of memories grabbing at me as I try to formulate the next words.

I should beg Voytek to think about it, to take it back, to stop it. I should demand he tell me he's joking, that he's just overworked, that this is just a midlife crisis. But joking about what? I wanted this, no? I feel betrayed, but mostly because he surprised me in the therapist's office. But it's fine.

(I will have one more meeting with the therapist who emails me to say how sorry he is and would I like a free Exit session? An Exit session. In the Exit session, he will tell me my husband is not to be trusted, and...but confidentiality won't allow him to divulge more. In his practice, he's only ever fired one other client. I will stare at his calming green outfit and will hate that I feel like a jilted wife, a co-conspirator and my husband's mother. The way the therapist talks about him makes me want to defend Voytek.

No, no. The way he just sprung the separation on you, The therapist will say, and I will wonder if the therapist wants to fuck me, if this is his way to buy my trust. I will remind myself about being a strong, independent woman who wrote a book about being true to herself. I will say, it's fine.)

It's not exactly fine. It's not good. It's not losing Voytek that I feel despair over, but my future. Even with you in it now, possibly, it is still nothing like the future I knew just a few months ago when I still played along with my husband's double-dealings in my role as the wife of Voytek Tak, as a first-time author and a mom to a sweet berry-cheeked girl. There were little plans, little ambitions, and that was comforting and it made me feel safe. I suffered from love, boredom and only sometimes food. Nothing big, no bones were broken. And you *can* live with a broken heart for a long time. Until you die.

We renovated half the kitchen. We talked about opening up the attic, putting up a staircase, making it into a rec room; we joked about Ruby coming home from various concerts and clubs in the hormonal future, and sleeping off her hangovers there, the air filling up with vapors of inexpensive perfume, hair product, stale cigarettes and cheap booze.

I don't know how to talk about this with *you* because how would you ever understand? You're my age but you're only a man and you've only lived a little bit—school, girls, hitchhiking once, too many drugs once, a journalism gig you fell into because your uncle ran a local paper where he let you write about cool gadgets, your first apartment, your first condo. You fucked lots of girls, but you've had only three semi-serious relationships, one with a girl who made you role-play a killer, and one with a sad girl that made me wonder if you were developing a pattern of going after broken women. You've described that relationship as traumatic, the word "traumatic" made you laugh when you said it and, truthfully, it made me laugh too, how you thought I was someone who would be shocked by a story, how you thought I was normal, not like her.

Even though I am tired I understand that I'll have to come up with a new future, that I will need to want to do it over again—with you? I will have to repaint the walls. This is what I believe is known as hope.

Voytek asks me why I'm smiling, what is there to smile about, and I tell him that this is one of those things, like smiling at a funeral, a hysterical reaction. Voytek likes the word "hysterical" because he's old, uses words like that for women, and he smiles too. Probably because he appreciates that I admit that he's been right all along about me being a certain way, hysterical.

# THIRTEEN

THE BAR IS nothing special, dark and empty. Its name is fitting, No Name Bar. We sit in a dimly lit corner and slowly get drunk on beers. I normally hate beer but that's what you drink and this is where we are, nowhere, no name, and I have no idea what will happen to me now so it's all fitting. You ask me about Voytek's indiscretions and I tell you whatever story feels freshest, most painful, I suppose it's the Margot story, I talk about her priggish way of corresponding, her being a former student, Voytek having a joke how he'd never fuck a student—at least not until he's handed in the grades. You are outraged but I've intoned the story to cause outrage, in another mood I might play it for laughs.

Has he fucked a lot of students?

One. Me. Not many. I don't know. Once, a . . . protégé, I try to make it sound better than it was and tell you all I know about her, a short, curvy redhead, who was the opposite of me in terms of appearance—I looked her up—and who apparently came onto him. She showed up at his residency, it used to be something he did every fall up until that year. The girl accused him, wrote about it in her blog, but then withdrew the accusation. She was obsessed with him. He was supposed to take her author photos, she had a book of poetry out.

Wait. Why is he taking photos of girls? You want to know, and I feel myself tense up, trying to explain, He's helping out new writers, he has a good camera. I used to get mad at him, It's just a free way to get women to be pretty for you; but it's just something—I mean he studied film, he's a great photographer. Anyway, he told me the crazy redhead took off her clothes when he wasn't looking, he was adjusting the camera—

And I can't finish the story, I want to take those words and shove them back into my mouth, but since I can't, I shut up.

(I remember how he told me that another time, at a faculty party, she supposedly handed him her phone with a nude selfie "accidentally" left on the screen, how he told her to leave, how she had a certain history. How she tried to later take him down and how she couldn't even remember her own lies so in the end, no one believed her. I remember how he complained about some young women closing doors during consultations, young women writing emails asking how to get into publishing or talking about li-te-ra-tu-re, and/or attaching photos of themselves without bras, etcetera. He would be dismissive of it, of course: so-and-so has a crush. Some of that is true, maybe it is all true and Voytek has been a victim of all those nymphs all along, I mean, wasn't I one of them, going on his work trips, carrying organic meat in my suitcase during his keto diets, waiting for him in g-strings and thongs in hotel rooms all over the country while his wife nursed small dogs in New York?)

I'm sorry, you say.

It's actually fine. Let's just drop it. Can we…talk in private?

You raise your eyebrow. We're in a booth, the only people in the room.

I mean *more* private, I say and you smile, Ahh, yes, we can talk in private.

My phone buzzes, another message from Voytek wanting to know how long I'm going to stay out. *Forever,* I want to text back but instead I get up and gesture for you to follow me. We will talk in private now.

In the bathroom, I get down on my knees and you gather my hair, sweep it into a ponytail that you let go of. Then you do it again: sweep, let go. You keep doing that throughout the whole thing.

Somebody knocks on the door but I don't stop, I wrap my arms around your thighs and press you even closer, I hold you like that, not loosening my grip, and you fill up my mouth, my eyes water, mascara running down my cheeks, the knocking starts and stops again. You say the prayer: Jesus God Fuck. You yank my hair harder, pull so hard I yelp, you mush the altar into my face, the wiry hairs scraping, the musk of you intoxicating, Body of Christ, Amen.

I swallow and hug your thighs, touch your buttocks, I feel so much love for you that I suddenly burst into tears.

Hey, hey, you say, wipe the tears with your thumbs, your beautiful cock retreating, shy now. You help me up, you pull up your pants. In the tungsten light we're frazzled and olive-green, my mascara, my hair, I'm like one of those dozens of scribbles on the walls, *Go home mom ur drunk*.

A man with a crewcut is outside the door, telling us to get the fuck out. So we get the fuck out.

The night is chilly but I like the cold, it snaps me out of my drunken haze. We walk towards the park and smoke cigarettes, my voice sounds stripped-off, raw. A bar voice.

You tell me a story about your father driving you to school drunk one time and making a violent turn and the door opening and you rolling out right onto the street. Because you laugh, I laugh along with you but I am in shock—from the story and from this night and from my life taking its wild turn and me rolling out; it's impossible to know if I will survive this. Tonight, it feels as if I might live; another unexpected surge of happiness washes over me as we walk and laugh about our traumas and I am back again, the feeling of being myself with you, authentic and here, flashes and zaps me into the present, the feeling of loving you is a strange, troubling joy.

We don't enter the park. There are signs warning about coyotes all along the way.

We find a bench and debate trying to find another bar. You list your deadlines and ask me about mine. I think it doesn't matter, what deadlines, what kid, what schedule? But I'm done drinking for the night.

I say two things: One more cigarette, I'm falling in love with you.

The air snaps, the night gets darker, colder. You stiffen, take a drag, exhale. You say, I don't think you are. It's just booze. But I *am* in love with you.

There's a strange, loud, echoing howl in the woods. It sounds serious, bigger and heavier than a coyote; perhaps it's a werewolf.

Why don't you believe me? I say.

You shrug, The way you talk about him. It's a strong bond. What if this is just a distraction?

Now I am angry. At myself, at you, and at the moment being wrong. *Please don't disappear on me,* I beg you in my mind. I look away from you but you pull me close and wrap your arms around me, I'm sorry. It's fine, it's fine, don't worry about it.

You say other things, you make a joke, tell me another story of childhood negligence, this one involving a radiator, I reply and make my own joke, something about Voytek's students again. I tell you a Ruby story, you tell me about your boss, and we banter and tease and dance around each other sweetly until another text from Voytek reminds me none of this is mine yet.

When my Uber arrives, you jump in at the last moment. Sorry, I just need to touch your skin one more time, you murmur in my neck, your thumb brushing the inside of my wrist.

# FOURTEEN

SOMETIMES I AM exactly the person I said I am in my book, excited to be in my body, having gained back control, no longer a slave to my appetites, satisfied, a woman with no holes that need filling.

I slept well and dreamt of being somewhere hot, oiled and naked, some kind of a dream beach with other oiled, naked bodies in the distance and I awoke with an unearned sensation of softness and sex. I've been sleeping on the daybed in our guest bedroom that doubles as my office. The light in this room is the best in our otherwise dark house, the vine leaves covering the windows filter the sunshine into a happy, lush green, an extension of my garden. The backyard is actually tiny but I've planted various climbers, grapes, and berries, and small bushes around the fence to create the illusion of a space, as if it all led to a big secret garden, hidden behind the walls of branches and leaves.

The house is quiet, Ruby out with Voytek at the library or perhaps both of them dead upstairs—anything is possible in this not-yet moment. I stretch and yawn exaggeratedly, like a cartoon princess, I run my sharp nails over my legs, enjoying the sensation, pretending those aren't my hands. Whose hands? Not yours, but maybe another cartoon princess, maybe some lusty Frazetta girl with a round ass and pouty lips, and full, heavy breasts so unlike mine. I close my eyes, conjure her in my bed, dive under the covers, inhale myself. I don't know if I'm ovulating—I don't pay attention to times, cycles, moons—but I am deeply myself, turned on, full and swelling everywhere. I am the Frazetta girl and I am me and I am now touching myself all over. I think of all those pillow-to-pillow conversations of university years with awed boys, variations of all those *God if I were a woman I would just play with myself all the time,* as they would cup and squeeze and marvel. And I would squeeze, and cup and marvel with them, I would feel myself to be in the body but also outside of it. I would, only in those moments, understand what all those you-go-girl girls meant when they would call other women goddesses, I would finally understand the looks that I'd feel lingering on my ass, my thighs, my lips, I would be convinced I'm indeed a miracle and they're all lucky to see me, to be with me, to have me. To have me! That's the ultimate luck, such privilege to touch and feel and then dive inside all of this wetness and softness, to inhale my salt and flower smell, to have access to those intimate places only I have access to at all times. To have access to my drippiness, my cuntiness.

I caress this body that I've punished and starved, now all that seems like a complete misunderstanding.

This is the mood I was in when I wrote the book, when I felt I finally made peace with what had been bestowed on me by the virtue of having been born a beautiful, briny, swollen woman. I too, could take pleasure by being inside the space that caused all these sensations for my lovers. I could be their hands.

When I wrote my book, I tried to remember those moments. Thankfully, there were enough of them to form into some kind of a story. I was able to describe it and vouch for it with little essays on having found myself. I would clear my schedule and write and rewrite as much as I could because it was the only time my job didn't feel like lying for a living.

On bad days, I would sit, immoveable, poking at Monster, the old thought forming and reforming, *Let me die.* I used to repeat it endlessly, back when all the days were bad, before I learned *I'm not a plate of fish and chips.*

Regardless, I sat at my beautiful acacia tree desk, heavy so heavy, imported all the way from Africa, a gift to me from Voytek's older sister. Voytek will ask for it during the separation and I will intend to give it back because I'd sat at that desk and said, *Let me die* and I scratched inside myself, a little wedge at first, just a paper cut, just a tiny groove. I scratched. My fingernail poking in, opening it, riding the groove mindlessly, back and forth, scratch, scratch, thinking of Voytek and the women, then not thinking once the fingernail pierced through. Then I just drilled and drilled. Made circular motions, worked out a circle, a phantom tube. One more place to shove some kind of a dick, another hole to plug.

When Sada Abe killed her lover Kichizō Ishida, she cut off his penis and kept it inside herself for days, until she was found after a country-wide manhunt. She did it to preserve her favourite part of him after she choked him to death during a sexual act. There was some indication that Ishida consented to his own death. They played increasingly more dangerous sexual games that included asphyxiation, were madly in lust with each other, and unable to be together as a proper couple because he was married to another woman.

At my most despairing, during my postpartum, I had a recurring thought about cutting off Voytek's penis. But not because I wanted to preserve it, or even stuff it in the new hole I'd worked out in my mind. At first, I truly enjoyed being a new mother. I liked the baby smells and I liked all the routines, even the boredom that everyone seemed to complain about. It didn't bother me to sacrifice myself to serve this new human being. I finally had a purpose, I could see the results of my work every day as she grew fatter and more aware. Voytek didn't take to childcare, he spent even more time out of the house. Some nights he would not come home till early hours in the morning. It hurt even though a part of me was relieved he was leaving me alone with the baby. I put spells on his penis, cursed it to not work unless it was near *my* hole.

As time went on, the routines formed a contained loop from which there was no exit. I could not imagine my life past the baby. Intellectually I understood that this would not last forever but in every other way it seemed to me I was trapped in some kind of a labyrinth of interrupted sleep, colic, shit, rashes, dressing, undressing, endless walks, afternoons in front of a TV on mute. If there ever was a time when I was genuinely crazy, it was then. I saw things that weren't there, the baby dying and the baby being alive, neither discovery being a happy one. There were times when I questioned if I was a part of an alien experiment, if I lived in a vivarium where I was being tested and observed by celestial creatures. I started dreaming of cutting Voytek's penis off, as if that would keep him at home. And then, he suddenly came back to me. Seemingly randomly—I said nothing, there was too much to say—but I secretly believe it was my curse, he could sense something, maybe his dick ached in unexplainable ways. We put Ruby in daycare. She was ten months old. I slept through the night. But the ghost tube inside me moved like a worm, curled, grew, grew scales, eyes, teeth, pussies. I petted the new hole, I caressed it, I loved it. I said *I love you, you fucking loser.* I kept not doing anything about them, the women. *I'm a plate, I'm a plate,* I said, a woman who's never dared to eat chips. But I didn't yell, I said it quietly, to myself, all the time. Or, I said, *Let me die,* as if that would help. As if that would shrink the new hole, prevent me from making it bigger. I had also run out of curses, or, more accurately, the violence of them scared me. Every child and witch understands that there are no free curses and I had no way of knowing that the next one wouldn't cost Ruby's life—now that she was here, I finally had something to lose.

Now I see that the book was my first escape from Voytek. I wasn't strong enough to physically leave, but I could hide in the book. And yet, the book let me down—I wrote lies. The only truth would've been leaving for real. I worried about that, worried about being found out, and called out on my lies. I worried there was a woman out there who would see what I was doing, that I was trying to find a place to hide from my real pain. A woman who could fact-check my emotions, expose my cowardice.

But is any memoir ever truthful? A few months before publishing, I talked to a writer friend of Voytek's, a woman with a new memoir about alcoholism, about how she was still drinking while caring for her new baby. We were at a dinner party. She said the burden of her memoir was too much and she relapsed, while still on tour, talking about overcoming addiction. She gave interviews under the influence, nursed a buzz while pictures were taken of her thoughtful, supposedly sober face next to headlines about the secrecy of being an alcoholic. She always carried a small flask in her purse while she smiled sadly for the camera, and said quotable things about the love for her son being stronger than the urge to drink. I remembered those pictures of her, her big, knowing eyes. It doesn't matter, the memoirist said, You're just a writer. People will project their truth onto you either way. Your book is a separate entity. You are not your book. You owe them nothing. So just do the thing and get your money and run. You might feel guilty or like a hypocrite but we're not our stories, and I promise you that this dichotomy is sustainable—I don't plan on killing myself over any of it. Besides, you can get better when it's all over. I did, she said and took a sip of her ginger ale. I wanted to ask her if she had mixed it with anything, if she still carried a flask in her purse.

I try to remember her advice, and, on good days, I am reassured that I am not my book and what other people think about me, about my book, my life, is not my responsibility. And today, despite my husband leaving me or me leaving him, I wake up the way I wake up and the dewy morning sunlight is on me and the house is beautifully empty and I am full in it. I am *this* more than I am my book, being in the moment like a monk or a serious yoga person, maybe even Margot—the hell, it's not Margot's fault she's a real talent and my husband is a talent scout.

In this generous, optimistic mood, I walk around the kitchen naked, I squeeze my own ass, I pinch my nipples, the quick pain energizes me even more. I walk on my tippy-toes. There's no flesh hanging lustily around my hips or off my ass but I grab myself as if I were a winding road of a woman, the goddess, the fertility one, the Frazetta girl, again. I run my hands over my belly, touch the delicate insides of my thighs, graze my labia, scratch over the Venus mound.

I imagine I am being watched—by you most of all. I send you all those images of myself in my mind, will them into existence, suspend my disbelief in other dimensions and decide that indeed you are seeing me, my body, in some ESP realm. You are waking up in your bed and you're struck by sensation after sensation: sight, smell, sound—my elusive wetness, my sighs—and the umami of the almost-touch every longing lover is familiar with, the nostalgic memory of a particular person's skin on skin that seems so painfully recent, still warm, like a fresh kill, how is it possibly not real?

I allow myself to bask in this strange self-love, I know it's only momentary, I know that it comes with a crash. I have no right to feel this good, I should be small, shrivelled and folded into my depression. I should wait for what's coming next, the lawyers, the sadness, the angry emails, long silences that are deafening all the joy. And yet, inside me, Monster shuts its eye, lulls itself, calms itself down, collapses back into itself.

I strut back to the daybed and I find my phone, the empty field where I will now punch in the text asking you to meet me somewhere, soon, now, this afternoon, sooner, when is good?

You text back immediately: *Now*.

I nod at the text and run upstairs to shower, shave, rush to be able to carry this feeling, even a sliver of it, some whiff of its essence, to you. I want to show you how good I am and I want to feel good when I show you, I want both of us to fawn over me.

# FIFTEEN

MY LIFE IS on hold, Voytek and I are sharing the space but not living together. The house is patient, waiting for one of us to claim ownership. *It will be me,* I tell the house. The house doesn't believe me. I think about its future walls, visualize buckets of white paint, a dripping brush, and minimalist decor, pale slim tulips in glass vases, wicker and birch. I press my forehead to the walls to pass on the message to the house. All women can cast spells, but with my Slavic grandmothers I've a whole legacy of knowing how to hex.

We've divided Ruby's time with us as if we've already separated and have gone through a few custody agreements. We don't fight over her—at least not yet—although Voytek likes to email me reminders of her activities and appointments as if I didn't know what was what. Some nights Voytek claims to be staying with Kazek. I have half a mind to go and surveil but what would that do? I know where he is and I know what he's doing, I don't need any more humiliations. In the beginning, I write him emails asking to talk, to *rethink,* but this seems like something I'm doing to simply play this out, a script I feel I should be following trying to rescue what is in shambles, a family. He doesn't answer, he's cold and efficient, he has produced adapted schedules and mediators and has sent listings to condos. His unwavering stance scares me but I am impressed by it too. (I myself am wavering, unsteady, I still don't really know how to navigate any of this, I don't know what to do with all the residue that keeps leaking out of me, I mean tears, I mean that I'm crying, but there's other moisture too—the slick that coats the tender inside tops of my thighs sometimes when I wake up and you were in my dream. Always you, in different forms, sometimes just as you, other times a woman; in one dream I am your mother and we are running away to hide our incestuous relationship.)

Now, I have stopped all attempts at reunion, and we've both pulled out our tax returns. The pandemic has made me apathetic, I took to isolation too well and now I have no one I need to tell, no family member who would rally for me. The fear of the uncertain future overwhelms me but still, I am unable to connect to the drama I'm supposedly living through. More than once, Voytek sends an empty email with a subject line: *Please stop stalling.*

I check Margot's Instagram but the only update is a group photo from a new yoga studio featuring sweaty, grinning Margot holding another woman's leg. I zoom in on her grin, try to read my husband in it and I swear I see him, this is a woman in love, this is a woman who has somewhere to go after the picture is taken, someone to tell her she looks beautiful even when she's sweaty like that.

I take a selfie, grinning to see if I can see *you* in it and I can't, my eyes look haunted. If there's one thing I'm truly jealous of, it is their certainty, and yours—how the three of you seem so sure about your love.

I get a break from this peculiar misery when I have to go to New York to promote my book on NPR and do a reading in Chester, Connecticut, which is a two-hour drive from Manhattan. I'm also going to meet my publisher and the PR woman who I can tell doesn't like me by how she emails (*I'm a little confused*) and I don't know why until I see her in the flesh. But I could be wrong, maybe she is perfectly happy in her body, doesn't need my starved self to tell her how she should feel, or maybe this is because I'm Canadian, and a nobody. I'm not even on a level with my husband, who is an old kind of darling, a no longer trendy Communist Defector, but who at least has a Wikipedia entry.

The entire time I'm in New York, I will be checking my phone obsessively, waiting for you to text. I feel feverish and filthy as if I am covered in soot. When my phone buzzes and your name shows up on the screen—the tiny circle with your picture—I have to stop whatever I'm doing, take a breath, my body buzzing from the electric shock of it. Maybe it's the distance but I keep imagining you're messaging to tell me you are leaving me, that this part of the experiment is over. I delete the message without reading it and feel terrible but also relieved.

The PR woman is cold and polite when we meet, and she tells me she has a sister in Toronto, and then she tells me about her other authors, who she *actually* (emphasis hers) can't wait to meet, one a bestselling YA novelist who writes about sexy wolves, and the second one a hipster with a snarky Twitter account. The PR woman is squeezed into a tiny red dress, her body trying to escape at every opportunity whenever she moves. She waves and jiggles, she is glorious. I envy her, envy that she is perhaps free, unlike me. I couldn't help but stare when I first saw her walking towards me in the airport. She noticed me staring and I felt my face grow hot. I quickly asked her where she got the dress to which she said, I don't remember. This is not the kind of dress you wouldn't remember getting, it's a deliberate kind of dress, a fuck-you dress.

I'm dropped off at my hotel and given an itinerary. I sleep well and dream of nothing. I eat nothing. I go to the MET, sit in front of *Unique Forms of Continuity in Space,* the famous Umberto Boccioni sculpture, its paused motion, and think how I'm the same way, moving but paused. I keep wanting to text you and every hour that passes that I don't gives me a strange sense of accomplishment. I'm not sure what kind of game I'm playing.

The NPR interview is a blur, and I worry about saying the wrong thing. I'm too nervous to be charming and when the interviewer asks me how the readers know I've really overcome my eating disorder, how do they know I'm not lying, I am unprepared and giggle like an idiot and ask what the point of lying would be—and that's really the strongest answer I'm capable of giving. I think how the interviewer is exactly the sort of a woman I'd imagined would call me out, I wonder if I'd conjured her.

Afterward, I walk through Manhattan but without enthusiasm, I'm only walking because I feel guilty about not taking advantage of the free trip, blocks of the city recognizable from movies and pictures I've grown up with and not a place I could participate in. The buildings go up and up and up. Everyone shouts and there are sirens.

I sleep during the two-hour drive to the Chester reading because the PR woman is busy on her phone and I'm too shy to interrupt her. I know she has a daughter Ruby's age but we've exhausted the topic of raising little girls during our lunch and I can tell she's not interested in becoming friends. Neither am I.

The reading is held in a beautiful, old library and every attendee is female and some of them share their stories of struggling with food and body image and I press the autopilot button in my mind, like I do back home, and continue sleeping.

I spend the second night in New York dreaming of nothing in my fancy hotel.

In the morning mirror, I notice the barest edge of a shard of something ugly I seem to have swallowed during the night, its tip poking out of the corner of my eye. I blink and blink until it goes away. I don't want to admit what's happening, maybe it's only anxiety but no, the now-familiar uncoiling and coiling inside me says I know exactly what is happening. I bite my fist, push it into my mouth as if it were someone else pushing it. I have to quiet it down, all of that, the open eye, the hissing I hear sometimes long after I turn off the shower—*it*'s getting closer. And this time, I don't know how I'm going to appease it, I don't know what it wants. *I don't fucking know*, I think to it but this is not a thing I can plead with; that's like screaming at myself and expecting I will calm down.

The publisher is a nicer, grey-haired dandy version of Voytek; he gushes over my book, I gush over him gushing, we talk about his wedding in Canada during the Trump era and problems at the border, and clothes, and maple-glaze doughnuts, and health care, and dental implants, and small dogs. By the end of our meeting, I'm fantasizing about us in the future, our husbands and boyfriends and children and small dogs spending weekends in country houses. I see a vision of myself laughing on a sun-streaked white porch in a gauzy dress, he's passing me a tall cocktail with three different herbs and a sugared rim. You are there too, just a blurry sketch of you, maybe you are showing Ruby a butterfly that you release back after the two of you marvel over its fragility.

For the two hours that I meet with the publisher, I can almost feel what I should be feeling, which is accomplished and stoked that I get to do this unusual thing in New York—he even asks me questions about books that I'm reading, he says my Instagram is dark and edgy and he could put me in touch with some marketing friends of his who could help me get more followers. This is one of the only three times where I feel alive on my trip.

The second time is when your next text comes through after lunch, which inspires me to walk around Manhattan again. I feel claustrophobic as if I were in one of those snow globes; the world is somewhere outside, its solar system sneaking in through the openings of the larger streets. What would it be like to live here, to have to navigate this space all the time?

The third time is later that evening, when I leave my hotel room and go to the airport. I have held off from replying to you and when I finally give myself permission to do so, I feel enormous relief and then immediately regret not enjoying myself more. I might be the only person who's ever travelled here and left without any sense of the place; all of it seemed staged as if someone was merely providing a background for my mediocre dream.

I get sick on the plane and throw up and as I do, a neon sign flashes in my head screaming WARNING in response to what you've asked me to do as soon as my plane lands. I really shouldn't, I should be responsible. I am a mother. And a wife, still. But I think we've established that I don't do what I should, more often I do what I shouldn't. Yet, I'm disappointed when the plane lands smoothly, doesn't crash.

# SIXTEEN

WE ARE TOGETHER for three nights and three days. Another small eternity to be later dissected, packaged and stored into forever memories, lingering looks, touches, deep fucks, kisses, snores. This is one benefit of our short affair—that I get to parse it endlessly, the days like years, each gesture an artifact I can study and analyze.

The more we make love, the more I want to make love. It's compulsive, as if you were releasing a secret nutrient I never knew I needed, as if I lived my entire life without this nutrient that is vital not to my survival but to my well-being. This hunger doesn't feel like murder. I'm only satisfying a nutrient deficiency. I will be whole. At least it seems like that in the beginning. The first impressions are almost always wrong because they're rarely based in reality; there's no reference, only the blissful abyss of the unknown—I haven't cried over you. Everything is perfect. If we were to die after these three days, I would die happy.

I don't charge my phone until the last day. Three nights and three days is how long I can afford to believe that this is my world, here with you, and that I don't have a daughter and a breakup to attend to. I reply to Voytek's alarmed email saying only that I've decided to stay longer in New York and that I'm okay and to please not contact me unless it has to do with Ruby.

For a few moments this feels good until I get an email threatening to change the locks if I don't return sooner. Something about obligations, work and a conference he has to go to and how I've known about it for months. I don't remember a conference and before I met you, I would've come back, tail between my legs and all. But now, I don't want to deal with reality; I want to immerse myself in this trance. The only thing I regret is not being able to send a message to my house telling it not to worry, if the locks are changed I'll hammer the doors down to reclaim it.

We can pretend this is our life, I tell you the first night during which we get drunk on tequila that I picked up at the airport.

Do you want this to be your life? you say.

One version of it, yes, I say and it's as if we've exchanged vows.

Your eyes are yellow-brown ambers in the candlelight, your mouth is supple and red like a girl's. You are a poet, a romantic hero, a vampire prince, your curls fall over your forehead as you lean forward to kiss me again, I inhale you and it's something soapy but sharp too, like lilies soaked in diesel.

I play along but more than that—I suspend logic and reason, and you don't ask about Voytek or Ruby, you don't question my spontaneity, you're happy to build this grownup version of a pillow fort with me. You've cancelled your own obligations, took two unpaid sick days and all that is left to do is indulge in each other.

I've been in love before. I've lived in that intoxicating bubble where only the object of my love mattered and everything that we did was extraordinary. The parameters of this feeling are familiar but, of course, it only truly hits when one is in it—in my dopamine-starved case, it's wave after wave of euphoria. I revere each moment of our seventy-two hours of bliss. Eating—yes, eating—and showering, and going to the store, reading the news, and going for a walk—we cannot manage being away from fucking for too long but we force ourselves to take walks—and smoking a cigarette on the balcony.

I never talk to strangers but now I do, I get into conversations with corner-store workers and dog owners and other couples, I even smile at babies. Or maybe it's that everyone seems to talk to us—we attract eyeballs and nods and everywhere it seems people approach us, intrigued by our magic dust. We feel superior to everyone, unfortunate loveless strangers who try to rub against us. I've walked through the same park so many times with Voytek and with Ruby, trying to catch someone's eye for a friendly nod, and it was the opposite of this, as if our little family was cloaked in invisibility. I used to say all those cliché things about Toronto—how cold, how unwelcoming, how expensive. But now I find it to be the friendliest city on earth and I cannot imagine being anywhere else. Maybe Bali, or Costa Rica, or Columbia, one of those places where lovers go to lose themselves even more. For our honeymoon. Or we could stay, raise a family. I calculate. I have at least six more years left to give you babies.

(Ruby's sudden and insistent face is an inconvenience, a glitch in the delusion, and I ask her in my mind to *please leave mummy alone*. At least for now. In my house on the beach, there's a dark-haired boy and a dark-haired girl, starter children, starting over.)

We get home from walks and eat but I don't do any math, the codes don't apply. I'm not my usual famished or overstuffed, dysregulated self. With you, I eat like a normal person and I wish I could share the sense of pride I feel over that. You make poke bowls and a niçoise salad and a vegetable soup from scratch. I actually taste the flavours, I'm not rushing to get it over with, I don't feel anything other than gratitude and delight as the food lands in my belly.

Undressing for bed, I catch a glimpse of myself in a large mirror on the door and for a moment I don't understand how I'm in this borrowed skin of a woman in her late thirties. Whose eyes am I seeing through, mine, yours, Monster's? I don't know. But there's a glitch in the system when I'm with you and I cannot decode this, cannot decide what I look like. Yet, it is fine, all I need this skin for is just to receive you, to please you and to serve you.

We try to watch movies on Criterion, slow Japanese movies, charmingly disheveled French ones, gritty and bruised Polish ones, Scandinavian ones, gruesome and austere. But every time my restless hand travels towards you, or my ass starts grinding into you, and you react instantly, your hot, urgent breath, *What a wet slut, look at your dripping cunt,* you whisper in the crook of my shoulder and we never finish a single movie. Soon you're holding both of my wrists above me, against the wall, as you drill into me, halve and quarter me. I splinter. With you I become a pillow-biter, a screamer, a whimpering little girl taking her punishment and loving it. Inside me, Monster waits, alive and forming itself, opening and closing its slits, a whole row of them, luscious, wet, sticky.

On our final day together, we drive to a mall and it's as if I've never been to the mall before, I'm an alien mesmerized by all the objects and people and decorations. We run around and shoot little videos of each other on our phones. I try on outrageous clothes and we take selfies in mirrors, you scowling and me beaming, unworried about my hair not being the right way. I don't notice if there's anything wrong or right with me, an out-of-body feeling, like I can't quite connect, not that I want to connect—I'm content in this state. In this state I have no responsibilities or motivations other than being with you.

I wish this was enough but even wishing might burst the bubble of this illusion—wishing will lead to introspection and introspection is dangerous; it destroys dreams. I've spent a lifetime unsure of myself and questioning my right to be happy. *I deserve this, I deserve this,* I chant inside my head like a crazed self-help addict whenever I remember that this is a fantasy.

You buy a cotton scarf for your mother, a soft leather belt for me, and a jar of clay bears for yourself. You put them in sugar to keep the crystals from coagulating, you explain.

You're my sugar bear, I say.

I want to spend all of my money on a dress you say looks beautiful on me, a long, slinky black tube with a raw silk skirt by a cool Asian designer who often gets in trouble for touching unwilling strangers. When I put it on, your mouth opens in a childish caricature of shock. It's only $2200, I say and you shake your head. I repeat the price again, find it to be even more acceptable. In my euphoric state I don't bother to subtract Ruby's daycare and upcoming dental appointment, and neither do I add imaginary royalties from my book or from some sad grant that is taking months to clear because of an administrative mistake. I have no money in the bank, what's left of my savings will probably be spent on lawyers, I've never been one of those people who has maxed out her cards—maybe I am now, a woman who's crazy in love and takes crazy risks?

I'd rather see you out of this dress, you say-kiss my neck and squeeze my waist. I've now pictured us at various dinner parties and openings and launches, me in the dress, you next to me, smiling and touching each other's hands, being fabulous together.

Well, at least shoot me, I say, and you make a little film of me dancing in the dress around a mannequin, the shiny skirt reflecting, sparkling in the pot lights as I twirl.

Later, we sit in a Tesla inside the mall, you pretend to drive it. I cannot stop giggling, I am high from giggling. Your hand slides between my thighs and you squeeze and growl under your breath, Open your legs, and when I do, you say, You're so wet. Your pussy is dripping. My giggling subsides, and yes, I *am* wet, I've soaked through my panties, the thin fabric of my skirt. I leave a tiny stain like a stamp on the leather seat.

We walk to the food court but there's been a change of plans as you pull me into a hug and grind into me. Our drive back to your place is torpedo-fast, we make it there just in time to avoid crashing into the lake or a wall.

# SEVENTEEN

I'M WAKING UP at Lisa's, where I'm staying after my disastrous return home. Voytek has changed locks and left for the conference. He has desecrated my home, made it unsafe. After I charged my phone, I read the series of increasingly threatening emails. Seven warnings and then the final email letting me know he would be back in three days to let me in if I haven't abandoned my daughter yet. He's forced to bring her to the conference. I wonder if she'll get to meet Margot. He hasn't filed a Missing Person report because he didn't believe I'm actually missing, he wrote that he knows I'm playing a game, but he misinterpreted the game's objective; he believes I am trying to get him back.

After that email I took an Uber to check if he was bluffing about the house. My keys were useless. We were definitely at war. I pressed my forehead against the front door and whispered my apologies. The house whispered nothing back so I pressed my body against it, my breasts. I pressed and rubbed my pubic bone against it. My neighbour, a hateful, old Italian woman—she hissed and shooed at Ruby whenever they crossed paths—came out and stared, before pretending to pick basil from a clay pot on her front porch. I stared back trying to read her face, looking for clues that could tell me that she had seen another woman here, one with a big nose and a chin, if she'd seen Margot come over at night while I was away. Over the years, I made half-assed attempts to be friendly with the neighbour but she ignored my attempts to talk, responding angrily in Italian or not at all. Now I wished I had tried harder, wished I had baked her a Polish cake, or offered to watch her shut-in grown son whom I could hear through the basement walls sometimes, wailing. Her eyes remained impenetrable. If she had seen another woman come over while I was away she now had the satisfaction of not telling me, the secret was hers and for once she was even with the universe that had made her son the way he was but my daughter an absolutely perfect child.

At Lisa's, the windows look out onto another condo across the street. Instead of the sky, it's walls of green-tinted glass reflecting each other and nothing else because there's nothing else here. I wonder how many women are standing in these windows, looking out at nothing.

It's unclear if Lisa is paying for the condo, she has a wealthy grandmother and seems to make good money. It's a nice place, with tall ceilings, William Morris wallpaper, a massive bed, and a dramatic chandelier that belongs in a ballroom of a European palace. Lisa is seeing her subs in another space in the building, which she shares with two other women in the complex.

When I arrived, we got drunk on red wine given to her by a man who pays to suck her toes, and we took photos of Lisa in her new blue gown, her freshly dyed bright red hair swept up into a carefree tower of curls. Her nipples poked out of the top of the gown and her mascara was smeared and yet, she looked incredible and intentional; everything about Lisa is like that, she's a walking editorial. She's also drunk all the time, but it's not really a problem, except sometimes when she gets belligerent and accuses me of stealing from her. It's like she's playing a girl in a gang, when she demands to know where I hid her *smokes*, her *dope* and her *pills*. I don't know how much of that persona is authentic; Lisa didn't grow up rough but sometimes she forgets that she doesn't need to lie to *me*.

The second night of my stay is gnarly, no more gowns and pictures. Lisa accuses me of hiding her Adderall before going on a date with a man who pays her to witness him hold rubber objects up his rectum while they dine, and I spend the whole night texting with you.

I haven't told you about my situation. I made up a story about Ruby having a cold. I miss her and the missing comes over me like a giant wave and doesn't let go. I send many texts to Voytek who tells me to stop until I get upset and demand to speak to her on FaceTime. He calls me hysterical. I'm blocked till the morning. He texts to come back the day after tomorrow. Don't dare go to his mother's house. Don't text him till I'm in a cab on the way home.

You send links to DJs you want me to listen to. I fall asleep crying into my pillow.

On the third morning at Lisa's it all really gets to me. The many hours of the day seem impossible to scale. I rap on Lisa's bedroom door and she groans to come in. She looks like a smear of herself in the middle of a mountain of baby-blue sheets and pillows. There's the blue silky gown on the floor and a pile of heels. On the night table an envelope with cash spilling out of it. She gestures for me to join her and I do.

We order UberEats brunch, waffles and Danishes and a whole box of freshly brewed Starbucks and a plate of fruit salads. We're done for, Lisa says once she confirms the order. I nod grimly.

Lisa admits to finding her Adderall in the pocket of her coat but doesn't apologize. We watch TV, a show about drugged-out teenagers fucking each other in pools and motels, and then another show about Recession-era grownups prancing in wisteria and trying not to kiss for five episodes.

In the afternoon, we order sushi and wine. This time I say, *We're done for,* and Lisa falls dramatically into the pile of pillows shrieking and laughing, *Yes bitch, yes.*

By the evening, we are stuffed with takeout, and trashed and I cannot remember which one of us panics first but soon I find myself in Lisa's concrete bathroom, throwing up and slobbering over to the sink where my bloated face looks back at me, recognizing the familiar thing that's been close to the surface the entire time.

All the lessons, all the ghosts of past therapies and groups flash and disappear: waiting five minutes, counting to one hundred, distracting myself with physical exercise. I have no defenses against the thing and now that I'm here, I know it's always just a question of *when* not *if*. I've been slipping. I can't control this side of Monster, the side that hurts me. I don't know what the antidote is but, just like that, all my old tricks come back as well—drinking warm water, tickling the back of my throat with only one finger, clenching my stomach muscles—and for a moment I even feel proud as if mine was an athlete's body, remembering the technique for an elaborate athletic feat. Muscle memory, emotional memory. I don't need a psych degree to know that I've been making myself vulnerable to this full relapse for weeks now, starting with you and our extravagant dinner, the pizza in Niagara Falls and all that sitting around in the house, waiting. The only consolation is that soon, I will be beautifully empty and spent and nothing will matter, not my torment nor apathy nor the uncertain future. I will have to attend and nurse my body, make sure I replenish it with liquids, lie still to avoid fainting, chew gum to avoid eating again.

It's Lisa's turn and she empties her stomach of calories, and her mind of her client. Waiting for her, I read an article about my book, a woman claiming that it's helped her to arrest her orthorexia and find a new perspective; she praises my "radical honesty" and "unwavering self-judgment" and "maintenance of self-love," some of the stock phrases I've come up with to make my book more palatable to bigger audiences. In reading this article, I am hoping to be reminded how I wrote the book in the first place, what the incantation was—of words, of actions, of events—that brought me to the place of starting. Now, I can't come up with a single memory of actually *writing* it, I'm as new to it as if I was one of my own readers. I open the book in Kindle and search for words like "change" and "turning point" but I don't find anything particularly revolutionary, it's all just filler words, empty calories on a page, none of them feel like they came out of me. I cannot convince myself that there's any actual wisdom in the text. It's surreal, looking for my own advice to advise myself.

When Lisa comes back to the bedroom—paler, taller, slimmer—I tell her what I've been doing and she says it's like trying to rescue yourself from drowning, it's just as delusional. We reminisce about the group where we met all those years ago, where neither of us was telling the truth while trying to differentiate ourselves from the rest of the women. Lisa talked about running to stave off her compulsion and I talked about being a new mother and finding my purpose in that particular vocation. I remember that version of Lisa as even more elongated, white like a stem and her lash extensions casting lovely shadows onto her pale face. I hated her refined beauty and I recognized her bullshit, called it. After group was over, she lingered outside with a cigarette dangling at the end of her hand dressed in a white, lace glove; these details irritated me even more, next to her, I felt like a smudge, my dirty hair in a bun, my vague body in a mental-illness-regulated hoodie and sweatpants, my Fat Clothes. She pulled on my sleeve gently but firmly before I walked off and said, So you think I'm full of it, is that right? Well, so are you, she smiled sadly.

I fell in love with her at that moment, the relief of being read correctly flooding me; I didn't try to defend myself. We never went back to the group.

Now we lie to each other effortlessly, she ensuring me that she never does this anymore, what's come over her, it must be the booze, and me agreeing and saying I can't imagine ever doing it again after such a long period of abstinence, it must've been booze indeed, too much booze, we should quit drinking, that's what our problem really is.

Maybe *your* problem, Lisa sighs and puts on a documentary about Richard Ramirez, *The Night Stalker*. She is also fascinated with serial killers, thinks she can avoid getting murdered by getting to know the ins and outs. We're both instantly calmed by the footage of crime scenes and the brutal descriptions of chunks of flesh missing from bites, pools of blood coagulating in the carpet, purple faces, rigor mortis.

My fascination started back in university. Every other night there was a taxi parked in front of the liquor store across the street from my place. One evening, I was smoking on the back porch, accidentally staring at the parked cab. The driver smiled at me but his eyes stayed still. This happened again, a couple more times, we never exchanged more than those awkward smiles. I was reading paperbacks about murderers, devoured them in-between boyfriends, unable to be alone with my thoughts for too long.

I studied at the kitchen table, feeling exposed by the bank of large windows that looked out onto the liquor store parking lot. I called that space "the aquarium." I was the fish inside of it. The taxi driver continued to park in front of the liquor store. I stopped coming out onto the porch and drew the blinds. I decided the taxi driver was a murderer. I phoned some friends and described my circumstances. Female friends suggested I stay at their places. Male friends suggested they come over. One came over and didn't leave for six weeks. He sold me on the idea after he pointed out that he was bigger and more tattooed than the taxi driver. He drove me to my classes and as time went on, I grew resentful; I didn't want to be protected. Perhaps, I thought, I wanted to be annihilated after all. I didn't know how to escape my situation.

When winter came around again, I broke up with my protector and read about serial killers some more. It was the only thing that engaged me. I was still afraid to leave the house and for two months I would go for days on end without groceries, eating out of cans before arriving at a new pursuit: Not eating. Different from bingeing and purging, not eating demanded a militant degree of control and its rules were unforgiving but simple. Water, lettuce, Konjac Ramen Noodles, sugar-free gum. Stand, don't sit, fidget, water, jumping jacks, water, pushups, exercise bike, pushups, lunges, water, water. Don't. Don't. Don't.

Even though I was afraid of the taxi driver, I didn't fear sexual intimacy. I still needed feedback from the external world and to me, the external world was men, and has always been men. As my body started to shrink, I felt an intense desire to test it. I noticed how men responded to me during the odd times I would leave the apartment. They were again following me with their eyes like when I was a teenager, they would make comments, they were *seeing* me. When I finally emerged from my apartment in the sexual wetness of a new season, I ditched the sweatpants; I bought a short skirt, Hugo Boss, with a tight stitch.

I took my new body out to clubs, bars, alone or with friends. I brought men home. Their reverence for my body was confusing, complicated, but always secondary to how I felt about them.

Once I'd find a suitable lover, I had to consume him, and have constant access. Playing house was only a pretext. Moving in was so easy then, everything was IKEA furniture you could put together, take apart, three garbage bags filled with clothes. I took the men apart, put them back together, moved them out and in. Some cooked, others cleaned, all bent me over. But even moving in wouldn't be enough. As it was with food, in the beginning my man-hunger begot hunger. If I had boyfriends, I had affairs, strangers took me in fire escape staircases. In taxis. Ravines. Passing soaked panties under tables in pubs. Holding boys' heads in my lap as they lapped me up in toilet stalls. The more they wanted the more I wanted them. And always, another cock at home, unaware, tucked in and waiting for me. We all knew who was really in charge.

Lisa says I'm no fun because I'm spacing out. She's right. A reminder on my phone announces I have to do a podcast interview. It's only been a week since my New York trip but now my author persona seems completely foreign, a cosmic joke. I have no recollection of writing my book, and I have no memory of healing. But I pick up the phone when it rings and talk to a journalist who asks me for "tips on loving our bodies," and my decision "to write unapologetically."

What was I supposed to apologize for? Maybe for describing the ugliness of wanting to be wanted. We're not supposed to admit to wanting to be wanted so bluntly. I destroyed and rebuilt my body.

In the book, I never talk about Voytek and his indiscretions because I thought I was solely responsible for my damage. Now that I am here I accept the danger his infidelity brought into my life—I *was* harmed and I said nothing about that. But to say I was harmed, in print? In my book? It would put me in a Victim Narrative, the bad girl being bad because of others, asking to be redeemed. Instead, I asked for no excuses, I detonated my own minefield. But in not saying anything, I was complicit. I didn't rage and scream and I used food to stuff the leaking hole and when I no longer did that, it wasn't me being healed, it was me giving fully into denial. I chose not to see and I told myself there was nothing to see, the problem was only with me.

The journalist is chatty and friendly and confesses at one point to having struggled with anorexia. She says my book was more than just a self-help book—it was never that, I try weakly but she ignores me—because it was so raw and honest and it didn't try to hide the fact that mental health is ugly and that it preys on ugliness.

Desperate and wanting to perform well, I feed her a few quips about being attractive and owing the world, and I know this isn't going at all as I planned but I also cannot recall what I planned at all.

Once I'm done, Lisa and I drink more wine and after our purges, neither of us has the energy to get up and go out, so we stay drunk and eventually pass out in bed. You send me a text saying "Send me a video of your pussy." Instantly wet, I make myself come by reading the text over and over—repeating the words in your matter-of-fact voice—but I don't record anything, unhappy with the lighting.

When I wake up the next morning, I collect my things as quietly as I can, daylight hurting my eyes, my head pounding as I walk, ever so gingerly—I'm reminded of the Little Mermaid getting her feet for the first time, feeling as if she was stepping on knives but soldiering on for love and to fulfil her human duties.

# EIGHTEEN

**YOU WANT ME** to leave. You say, Now. Tomorrow. I say, Look at this moon, it's almost full.

The words spill out of you, Fuck the moon, I don't want to talk about the moon. You say I'm the reason you feel excited to wake up, I'm the most intriguing woman you've ever met, everyone else is boring, we are not boring, you're not trying to pay me a compliment. Even me being a mom, you love that I'm maternal—well, that I take care of Ruby, it's such a lovely bond. Sacred, all of that. It's just different from—well. How I turned out to be all of those things you've always wanted in... your person (you cringe here, take a deep breath) and more, none of which you've been able to find in anyone else. You didn't even know you were looking! You *were* looking. For me.

You're so breathless, as if you've done cocaine, the words fall out of you machine-gun fast. Why do I think we met? Why do I think you fell in love with me so quickly? Why?

I don't—

You cut me off, say you thought you were insane at first because you didn't think a person could fall in love so quickly. You thought you should be embarrassed for falling for me so quickly. As it turns out, this, us together, is the most pure thing you've ever felt; you've never had to doubt these feelings, a first for you.

I don't have the context, I don't know what feelings you've had to doubt. It sounds like there's a story and maybe she had similar eyes, a similar walk. Similar Monster.

I want to stop you from talking but you're not letting me, you grab my hand, hold it in yours, squeeze it when I open my mouth—

No, please. Please let me. Because I don't like who I have been all these years, and, at the very least, I know for sure now that I'm not going to be that same person anymore because I fucking despise him, and because you're the one person I've ever met whom I've loved this strongly—so as cheesy as it sounds, I want to be a better version of myself for you more than for myself...Maybe I'm not like what you're used to, I don't write books or sit in galleries—

Nobody's sitting in galleries—

That's not what I mean. You know what I mean. I'm not at your level, I know that.

I hate that you're forcing yourself on me like this. I told you I will leave Voytek eventually but I need time, I cannot afford to be stupid about those decisions. I need him out of the house and out of my life and then we'll see.

You close your eyes, wincing, Okay. I *am* impatient. Okay? I want to take care of you. If you told me today that I could spend the rest of my life with you, I'd jump at the opportunity and I would.

I sit stunned, unable to respond. You tell me what I should want to hear and yet what I hear is an ultimatum, a deadline that I won't be able to meet. I'm embarrassed for you. For both of us. Your childish confession sounds rehearsed, you've thought about this, possibly wrote it out, memorized it. But this is not a play, and we are not children.

The evening is warm, soft, the lake reflecting the city's spark; there are people everywhere walking along the waterfront, happy dogs and bike bells, the maniacal shrieks of children up way past their bedtime, crystal laughter of girls on dates. I should tell Voytek about this place, we could take a family walk. This random thought scares me, it scares me that there are hiccups like that where I cannot stick to my reality.

I'm mad at you, mad at how easy this is for you—no child, no house, no history that you have to reassess; it's just you and your feelings. It's selfish. You're like all those contestants on reality dating shows who within hours of meeting choke on each other's tongues and confess drunkenly to feeling *vibes* and *energy* and *connections* with near-strangers.

I just need you to be patient with me, I say. I don't know what untangling from Voytek will involve but it's not how it happens in movies, instant and straightforward.

You say, Just cut it off. Now. What about his yoga teacher?

That's not fair. I didn't give you that information so that you could hurt me with it.

It's *you* that's hurting *me*, you say. *This* is hurtful.

But I don't even know you, I blurt out, because it's true. I've made assumptions about you, and I'm making them now. I take a breath, say, We have time.

(I'm offering this consolation to myself, as much as you. Maybe I'm not as lucky as I think.

No, I am. I am lucky. Luck is instrumental to survival; I have to be lucky to survive. I am a certain kind of a woman and women like me don't live, we survive. I have survived my own slow murder, Voytek making me mad, calling me crazy, the MRI scan for what he called my delusions. I have survived worse.)

You're a hypocrite, Yoveeta. How can you say you love me if you don't know me?

I just had a feeling about you. I said I loved you so that I would grow into loving you.

You say, A feeling about me. You need to make a decision. This is not good for anyone, not even Ruby.

Her name in your mouth sounds wrong, inappropriate. You have no right to say my daughter's name. Or even Voytek's name. But you like to say his name, tell me how you fantasize about running into him and punching him. Your loyalty is admirable and it is also misguided—Voytek, the man and the problem he poses, is mine, not yours.

This is my fault. I've invented a prosecution, a setting for our tragic romance, I've cranked it up. My husband the student-fucker, the fucker. I don't know how to explain to you that one wrong move and it will be *me* getting eaten because Monster is hungry, dripping with gasoline lust, iridescent slick gathering in its folds, pulsing, waiting. A real thought slips in: I'm really afraid. Of how this could unfold; I don't want it to unfold yet.

Let's talk about something else, I say.

You clear your throat but before you get a chance to speak, I say, Please. You can do it. (You can, you're a natural socializer, I've noticed you chatting up strangers, asking them about their dogs and strollers and where they bought their cool Adidas jackets.)

You excuse yourself and when you return, I force myself *not* to look at your nose. And we talk about something else, anything else, jumping from topic to topic, fashion trends and TikTokers and music and what's on the news but only the safe, familiar news that everyone else is talking about these days, the impending end of the world. We spend some time debating whether con artists are becoming the new darlings of popular documentaries. The lockdown. There will be more of it, in and out. In and out, Omicron, rhododendron, pocket full of posies, a tissue, a tissue, we all fall down. This month we're allowed to sit on this patio, next month the patio might not be here.

You tell me you miss being able to go to clubs, you miss drinking with your friends in pubs, the jukeboxes and clacking of pool balls and clouds of smoke in alleys.

See? We are two different species. A Man and a Mother.

I can't remember that clearly—or maybe I don't care to—what it was like before Ruby, before Voytek, before anything serious. It's like one of those junk drawers in my head, vacations in Europe, drinking on trains, dancing on beaches, endless airports, long, depressive nights after boring days at the university, living with forgettable roommates, boyfriends. I was looking for a home but I didn't know it, I thought I was liberated, unattached. There was a slog of part-time jobs until I saved up enough to write for a while, then the year I wasted editing what I wrote, sitting in various dives with various drummers or small-time drug dealers reading what I'd written as I drank and listened to them telling me I was good at it, writing, in exchange for a cop or a quick hand job. It was all romantic and chaotic before I became a slave to things like credit-card debt, organic products and the garbage-sorting rituals of a homeowner.

God, you say, You make it sound so sad.

It's not sad.

I thought you loved your house. What did you write?

I do. Love my house, it's one of those things that I didn't appreciate until it was too late. And listen, it wasn't sad. Just different. It was beautiful. Nothing ever came out of that writing. Not until *the* book.

We watch the scenery again, in silence, fewer children but more couples and groups of young men and in the distance the sound of a skidoo or some other water machine. Despite the late hour, it's still hot and for a moment this almost feels like a vacation.

I check my phone for texts and there's one from Voytek telling me he's going to bed and to please don't stay out too late, I need my "beauty sleep." That's something he'd say to me in the past, when he would play father to me before he became an actual father. It makes me feel loved but then I feel sorry for myself and then I resent him for not really caring. We've separated but our old habits haven't. It's hard to break old habits, etcetera.

I think about your weight on me, the thick arms, hairy thighs like trees, your insistence. I'm looking at you, you're looking at me, our eyes diving into each other. I gave you a cleaned up version of my past, this time, I said nothing about my obsession with serial killers or the hunger that would keep rearing its head back, I don't know how to talk to you about it yet.

I need you. But I need more time, I say again and you shake your head.

Or you—we could just leave, you say.

You're breaking the rules, I say.

What rules? I can't with you.

Then *don't* with me.

I can't do that either.

This morning there was a series of images from my iPhone memory bank. I usually ignore the iPhone's "For You" bait but I was defenceless, and strangely optimistic, in bed with Voytek whose arm lay across my stomach. We fucked the night before, the way we've been fucking occasionally, in some way saying goodbye to each other, or as if meeting on another plane, a parallel life where he had never slept with the essayist in the ravine, where I gave birth to a baby girl and went to an office job every day and didn't cry at my desk, where I made proper dinner and a dessert every night, where I never developed a tic of watching my husband's fingers enter new passwords on his phone, where he never had a password on his phone because there was never anything to hide. There it was, his arm across my stomach, and I thought how it was not like him to cuddle, I wondered if he cuddled with Margot, if she was bringing that out in him.

The images on my iPhone were portraits of us as a family, me, Ruby, Voytek. "Together Over the Years" the phone announced cheerfully. *This is what's at stake*, the images said but then, as I looked, they suddenly took on a different meaning. I remembered every moment being documented, the forced smiles betraying me, my eyes telling the actual story: On this trip, I found a lacy thing in his suitcase. Before this one, we fought in the car, the baby screamed for so long she eventually fell asleep exhausted. We kept fighting. In this one I hadn't slept for three nights, I threw up all the time. We woke up in the middle of the night to go to the MRI and on the way back, I kept thinking the lake looked like black lava. Ruby's second birthday, and the weekend I relapsed after two months of peace. I ate soft food. I got an email from *Anonymous9876* telling me Voytek slept with someone named Anette. I ate soft food because I could feel spikes in my throat every time I'd try to swallow. Noodles, ice cream. I drank gallons of water.

Etcetera. The pictures were nice, we looked younger, happier, but we were only younger.

Well, I have to go, I say and get up.

You spring to your feet, eyebrows knotting, mouth twisting in protest, you say things but I can't hear you, I'm already gone.

If you leave now—you say, and I leave.

# NINETEEN

RUBY STAYS HOME sick and I pull down the blinds. We get back into bed and watch cartoons all morning and nap, buried into each other's warm bodies. She smells of milk and spit and very faintly of sweat. Sick, she's clinging onto me, her hair in my face, her arms wrapped around my neck. I miss her early days when she was always with me, sleeping in a sling I wore everywhere, her mouth constantly rooting for my nipple, her sticky hands, even her heavy diapers that I loved to relieve her of because I loved helping her.

In the beginning of her life, I was convinced I lived to care for her, felt proud of being so essential to her. Her need for me was what I needed, I was terrified of her leaving me as she grew older. At first, I couldn't even remember what interested me before motherhood, I had no idea how I would fill my days once the world would take her. But then, by the time the world took her, I wanted nothing more, I was ready. I understood the biggest lie fed to women was that children were happiness, motherhood fulfillment. I was not happy, and not fulfilled. I couldn't say anything to anyone, and especially not to my husband who always joked about getting trapped into fatherhood. I became obsessed with wanting to follow him out the door every time he'd leave at night. I fantasized about surprising him in a restaurant with a woman laughing into his shoulder—the woman's appearance changed but she was always leaning into him, laughing and he was always sitting back, looking around, proud of making her laugh and then spotting me, his face falling.

After my daughter started daycare, I felt enormous relief. In less than a year, it was all revealed to me, the lie, but I was too exhausted and besides, who would I complain to? God?

I loved reclaiming myself, my body, and I became resentful of my daughter's demands, I took my breast away even though I had planned on feeding her till she would stop requesting it. The breasts were for Voytek, I didn't want him to continue looking for breasts elsewhere.

I joined the gym and briefly took up boxing to deal with my rage, I lost all the curves and nooks of belly folds Ruby loved to snuggle and kiss—there were moments when I wanted to slap her little hands away, scream in her little face, *Tricked ya,* when she would reach for what wasn't there any more, the comforting fat of a mother. I became territorial with my body and banished her, refused to let her cling onto me and accepted only some of her affections. It didn't take long for her to learn that she didn't have the permission to touch me just because she was my child, I never had to deal with hitting or biting or any other acting out, her hugs were brief and respectful.

I was proud of my composed girl, I looked down on other mothers who couldn't seem to get a handle on their offspring. This is why her need for me today is fine, I can handle it because it happens so rarely and I'm comfortable in our little nest, I am able to give her the attention she asks for. A sick day is a special day and so this is special too, although briefly I worry that she's going to learn to fake feeling unwell, but then she already understands boundaries and my withdrawal has never caused any bigger distress—

not that I've noticed. Sometimes Voytek would put her on my lap and order me to hug her. Her arms would wrap around me briefly and we would come apart. Today she is too weak to fend on her own and I make the effort to show I'm here to protect her and love her.

I know that my methods seem selfish and cruel even but I don't want my daughter to grow up like me, dependent on attention and affection, unsure of her own body unless someone confirms it with theirs. I also can't risk Monster sniffing her out, finding a new host. For the same reason, I never look at her for too long, I blur my eyes if I'm forced to—during birthday parties, her first Christmas performance—because my judgment isn't pure, with Monster, my eyes can become a rifle scope.

Voytek texts that he'll be staying at Kazek's again so I shouldn't wait for him, should order takeout. Although we're no longer a family, he still treats me like his older child—a child he can rely on to take proper care of his other child. He's usually the one who cooks because he likes the control it gives him. When we met, I'd been a vegetarian for ten years. Once, he took me to a party where he urged me to try a certain appetizer, little orange-and-brown lumps of fat, and I stuffed three in my mouth, one after another, wanting to impress him and show him that I was the carefree type he thought I was and that he hadn't made a mistake by leaving his wife for me. I knew before he started to chuckle openly that I was eating something animal. I was not angry and laughed along with him—I understood the cost of being with a man who desired all women but whom I desired all to myself.

*Fois gras,* he said, proud of himself when I asked to reveal the prank. He explained about the torture it took to produce the delicious morsels I gorged on.

His cooking for the family was ostentatious, a performance of aprons and oven mitts, and seven different spatulas and a spice rack; it was a sacrifice he had to make, one of many that he'd made when he upset his life for me.

My publicist emails me with more interview requests and links to interviews that have come out already and she forwards messages from women telling me that I've helped them. There's a lot in there about me being brave and raw and unapologetic, again, a lot about how my honesty allowed them to be honest. One woman writes that she'd attended three different rehabs and it was only my book that made her understand that she was not the monster she thought she was, that's the word she uses, "monster." My own Monster is quiet today. Sometimes when I try to give it a shape in my mind, I see an exhausted alien creature, stuffed into a small space, the door closed but not locked. I think of the cartoons I watch with Ruby of big, friendly furry beasts that love children, that are walked around on a leash, their soft pelts blue and green, and fluffy, their scariness fake once you get to know them.

It's hot and the AC is broken. I wake up through the night from sweating too much, move Ruby's sleeping form, feel her pants for wetness, kiss her, get up and go to check downstairs. The house is quiet, content to be our cocoon.

You send an email telling me how you can't stop thinking about me. This is not the first email I get from you at 4 a.m. in the morning. I know they're fueled by cocaine because you've confessed to that, and for that reason, I cannot take them seriously. This is just drugs talking, no matter how gutting some of your confessions are. You write you missed me so much, you took a day off work to stay in bed and fantasize, and you were able to imagine everything, even the way I breathed when I was nervous. I had no idea my breath changed according to my moods. I'm uneasy about this revelation, I think of men who watch women breathe, obsess and build shrines to their victims, who spy, who want to violate their victims' bodies, wear their clothes, their skin.

Your attachment, your obsession, worries me. I don't want to be indebted to another man, I don't want to be fed food I don't eat, I don't want to have to steal your passwords to check your phone, look over your shoulder as you punch in the numbers quickly and try to guess them later. You must understand that at this point, I am still torn between this life and the one that we will build together. I'm not being cruel, I am being careful.

In the morning, Ruby feels better and Voytek doesn't answer his phone. I didn't think he would but I call him anyway, mainly to disturb him and Margot. I think of it ringing, or buzzing, my shadow presence shrinking and softening his dick, her getting upset that I'm on his mind, maybe even getting out of bed in a huff to do some angry sun salutations on a mat in the kitchen where I'd murdered her in my mind.

There's another email from you, also sent at 4 a.m. I delete it without reading it.

# TWENTY

VOYTEK'S SISTER ARRIVES from Vancouver; she shows up as a negotiator, she's my husband's negotiator. Her clipped hair, no-nonsense wardrobe of a bucket hat and Patagonia vest are no longer quirky, charming. Her unsmiling mouth holds firm. She's an accountant. She's always been devoted to Voytek, and I am not like the first wife, who she much preferred, who understood experimental theatre but also private clubs, who played tennis and wore white. Briefly, after Ruby's arrival the sister and I became close, exchanged emails and pictures of dogs, being a "dog person" she loved Rocco, our old hound, like he was her own. We recommended books to each other and TV shows; she loved serial killers, even though she didn't move through the world in a way that suggested a fear of men, perhaps because she mostly dressed like a man. We visited her in her country home for vacation. She witnessed Ruby's chubby feet being dipped into the ocean for the first time, the summer before my daughter learned to walk and still had to be carried everywhere. The sister took a turn and held Ruby under her armpits and I snapped a shot of her looking back at me, her face younger with awe and gratitude.

When she looks at me now her eyes are cold, impassive.

The images of our house flooding or on fire are ever-present whether I'm asleep or not, my low-grade panic increasing with every family meeting. Voytek and his sister are not panicking, they are cool and reasonable; a look frequently passes between them, one that suggests I'm a person who needs to be sent to the mental hospital for good and locked up, given another MRI, and then deported on the earliest plane back to Poland. The sister has adapted even better than Voytek, she is every inch a Canadian now. She refuses to speak Polish, even with Voytek, and her accent is almost non-existent. She paid a tutor to rid her of the hard consonants, she has never had any trouble inserting syncategorematic words where they belonged.

In the beginning I rant and explain and ask for explanation, the two of them watching me side-by-side on a little loveseat as I squirm. I say things I don't mean but I am gripped by fear and blather on to outtalk it, Please, we are a family, we could do more therapy, this is just a rough patch, my first book is out, I'll be nicer, I'll clean, cook, take care of the baby more, I haven't been depressed in a while, I'll contribute—

Please, go on, The sister says when I run out of words and a corner of her mouth goes up ever so slightly. No, no, just let her go on, She shushes Voytek who sinks back into the seat and sighs.

We sit in silence for a bit until the sister smiles, Are you finished?

I'm suffocating, Voytek declares and the sister squeezes his hand.

I say, We had plans. The attic and Ruby—

Do you want Ruby to grow up with us like this?

Like what?

He sighs.

The sister has written a Pros and Cons list and has brought with her notebooks and folders, and even a calculator, and more apartment listings for me. The house was purchased with their family money, just as were their studies, trips, their move to

Canada and the English-style wedding to the first wife, with her pale blue eyes, pink lips, and the wife's tiny dogs like royal ermines, nestled in her elbows.

Voytek and I never got married but one day we signed a will binding us to each other in the event of death.

We could just elope on our way out, I pretend-joked as we left the City Hall building.

Feel free to call me your husband, Voytek said. Is that good enough?

I forced myself to laugh along. I didn't want to ruin our special day. I said it was good enough. (From that day on, I called him my husband.) Afterwards, we drove to the Bluffs where we had a picnic on the edge. It was a warm fall day, a cloudless sky. The lake was tropical blue, a skidoo tore through the flat surface of the water in the distance. Voytek wore a linen suit, wrinkled as always. His hair wasn't all grey yet. I wore a short-sleeved light-pink dress that Voytek had altered before the event to fit my shrinking frame. Back then he took such good care of me, bought me clothes and paid for my nails and hair and called me a "doll" and I felt like one. It was a nice feeling. I wanted to be his doll. At the Bluffs, we ate cold eggs and salmon, drank wine and kissed like teenagers. We looked around for a place to fuck but in the end Voytek couldn't get hard; he was too afraid of getting caught despite the fact that fucking in public was his one unfulfilled fantasy, and despite the fact that we were in an isolated spot. Instead of fucking, we looked at the lake and the rocks below and Voytek made a joke about me pushing him.

I didn't say that I was mostly thinking of jumping myself—I had those kinds of lemming urges near tall edges or high up above the ground, bridges and skyscrapers. Instead, I admitted that pushing him crossed my mind.

See? he said, I only have a fantasy of fucking you in public. But you're a woman and all women have two fantasies, white and black. The wedding and the funeral.

Right now it's the funeral I think about. I look from Voytek to his sister and I don't understand how those two who were my family became enemies. I am rattled by the sister's turn. I realize that to her, I was only a vessel that carried her niece—her bloodline and last name—into existence. She was nice to me because I took one for the team and reproduced so that she wouldn't have to.

I don't know what the sister will think of Margot, her hirsute beauty, those eyes even darker than mine. I imagine Margot moving in, replacing me, sitting in this chair, in the office, at the table, being in my bed, sucking my husband's dick, or in Ruby's room, tickling my daughter's armpits and feet, perhaps even wearing my clothes, riding my bicycle. A wife upgrade, a newer model. Curvier and smarter and more importantly, younger, less depressed and more invested; a mostly blank canvas Voytek could paint a whole new life onto now that he's learned from his mistakes.

I don't share those Margot scenarios with Voytek or his sister. I reach deep inside and find a lump of calm that I knead until it spreads into my limbs, numbing me, letting me sit through these negotiating sessions without raising my voice. I cry, but I haven't shouted yet. The sister presents me with numbers, with logic, with documents—the will, the house deed, receipts for repairs—that she hints would probably hurt me in court, were I to go after the house. She says "mental illness," "instability," and "track record," often enough to ensure that I understand the threat.

He mentions the affidavit he's writing, how I've abandoned Ruby after my trip to New York.

I burst out laughing at the ridiculousness of this but my laughter dies abruptly after the sister tilts her head. Voytek stays mostly passive, adding occasionally, "because we're separating," as if he had to remind me in order to stop me from trying to convince him otherwise. Yet now that I have a witness, I feel emboldened to bring up his infidelities but the sister waves me off and says, No, no. That's private stuff.

I have my own pitiful puddle of receipts, three years of paying for Ruby's activities and daycare which was my financial contribution to the family, and the sister looks away as if I've presented her with a turd. Right, right, she says and pulls out another notebook, more meticulously recorded columns and lines such as, "Call lawyers again. Try mediator. Prepare financial statements."

Over the week, the time zips but it also drips, like tar, as we sit and discuss, taking breaks to participate in our regular activities, Voytek going to work or perhaps a brothel, or to Margot's rickety bed, who knows; and me, writing a newsletter about feeling amazing in my body, answering interview questions, and napping. I'm more tired than I would be from a physical activity, but I've learned from my depressive years that sleeping ensures I can sometimes curb my *hysterics* so I let myself do it. The sister retreats to the guest room where she buries herself in documents and papers and numbers like some kind of a mutant mouse. When Voytek comes back, he leaves again to get Ruby and I lock myself in our marital bedroom.

Before my naps, I kneel on the pillows at the head of the bed, and place both hands against the wall. We own an actual piece of furniture designed specifically for this activity, prayer, but there's something about being on the bed—the bed I used to share with my husband—like I'm trying to channel the energy of years of lovemaking and of heartbreak, this, here is the nucleus of my marriage.

As a child, I attended church all the time. I was obsessed with the rituals, the rules, the wrath of God that could be brought on by simply having wrong thoughts. I volunteered for vigils during the Easter holiday and I said litanies to St. Tadeusz (the patron of children and miracles). I had a rosary that I carried with me everywhere. When my mother got sick with cancer, I prayed every day after school. There were treatments and the prognosis was good but there was no way I could rely only on science when I had God to ask for grace. One time, I prayed so hard, for so long, that I fainted. I came to with a priest's cool hand on my forehead. He walked me out of the church and told me I was special and that only a child or a saint was able to carry a pure prayer, that God listened to children and saints. He was handsome, with a thin face and heavy-lidded eyes. His long habit smelled of candles and something else, an earthy, slightly sweet smell, myrrh or frankincense, I wasn't sure which and was too shy to ask. We sat on the church's steps and he talked, looking straight ahead, as if reading words in the air. I wondered what it would be like to kiss him. I wondered that about every man, even my own father. I knew that I could never ask God to let me kiss a priest. I came back the next day and there was a new red cushion on the kneeler. I thought of it as his secret love message and I fantasized about the priest watching me, convinced myself I could sense him, sense his presence all around me. But I didn't see him again. Eventually, I was able to bring my focus back to my mother. And my mother's cancer went away.

I stopped praying, worried that the next thing I would ask for would eliminate the wish I had been granted. So you understand how badly I want what I'm praying for, on my bed with my hands pressed against the walls of my home, badly enough to sacrifice my own mother's life.

Evenings are a play we all put on for Ruby where we pretend we are still a family and her auntie is visiting, a nice auntie who even reads her a book, her body stiffening subtly when Ruby tries to kiss her. Since Ruby understands physical boundaries she doesn't seem fazed, she rests her little hands on her knees and listens attentively, smiling politely until the nice auntie is finished.

Voytek cooks: pork chops, borscht, potato pancakes; he makes cucumber and sour cream salad with dill. The food of our respective childhoods. I throw up whatever he's cooked, and I wash. I wash the toilet, and I wash the dishes, and I wash floors, shelves, everything, towels, blankets, curtains. I find all the dust and I annihilate it.

When we're done with our chores, we put on cartoons, we do bath and bedtime as always, it's a whirlwind of activities.

You write and plead to meet and there's so much to say to you I don't know what to say so I come up with excuses that have nothing to do with being in a house on fire. Ruby has a cold again, I have a cold, Ruby has a playdate, a visiting family (the only true one), soon though, soon. Truthfully, I am so panicked about losing the house I don't know how to explain it to you and your faith in things working out because now, after this week, I'm losing *my* faith. I'm not a child, not a saint; I worry my prayers are futile. But I don't know what else to do. I want to write to you how when we moved in, the backyard was barren and filled with rubble and how I turned it into an oasis. I want to tell you how I keep talking to the house, how I keep promising it I will fix its *darkness*, a little hex I've come up with that I repeat throughout the day whenever I touch a wall. I'm afraid that still none of it would be enough to convince you what is at stake here, to keep you waiting till I have enough of me back to be able to withstand the unknown of the future.

I wish you'd just go and lay on the train tracks, Voytek says calmly on the last day of the sister's visit.

And with that, the negotiations end. The sister doesn't comment but they step out to go for a walk together and when they come back it is decided that since I won't move out, the house will be sold.

Or you could move out, I suggest. Let Ruby grow up in a house. You have enough family money to buy a condo.

The sister rolls her eyes, slams the notebook shut, says nothing.

Voytek says, I'm not moving. This is my house.

(Margot wearing my dress, fucking in my bed, cuddling my child, working in my office, gardening in my garden.)

Voytek, The sister says softly.

They exchange that look again, the one where the sister simultaneously scolds *and* sympathizes with Voytek who tried to make it work with a wild, untamed animal and made an unfortunate choice of a womb. Unlike most immigrants they don't consider our similar backgrounds a preservation of culture or values but a step back. But what's done is done. I remember a little joke from when we were dating and Voytek compared me to his *English rose* of an ex-wife and called me his *chwast*, a Polish word for weed.

Have it your way. We'll be back in apartments, dealing with neighbours and landlords, coin laundry, all over again, Voytek says, But fine, have it your way.

I put my hand on the wall, unsure if I am consoling the house or relying on it for support.

After Ruby goes to sleep, upstairs in our bedroom, I plead with Voytek one more time—therapy, therapy, therapy—and he sits in the corner chair staring at me and sighing, waiting for me to finish. I need more time. I need him out of the house organically, out of his own volition. I need him to acquiesce. I don't say this part, the part that will enrage him more but I plead all the same.

You don't want me in your life. I'm like a tumour in your life. You don't want a tumour in your life, he says, misunderstanding what it is that I'm asking for; not him.

I try to remember if this is something I screamed at him in a fight and no, it's not, but I recoil from an old memory of blocking his entry to the house when he'd stayed out all night, my fire mouth hissing in his face to get the hell out, the baby wet and hot, screaming too, in her sling, stiffening, tensing her body to get away from my angry one. I've only done that a couple of times, it was as pointless as not reacting at all.

Oh for fuck's sake, don't cry. You're going to play a victim now? You shouldn't be with someone who makes you cry. He gets up sighing and starts to undress. He is right about that.

Our goodbye fucking is the last place where we still find some kind of a residue of us as a couple, we are two nostalgic ghosts stumbling around in a fog with their genitals glowing, coming together, clinging onto each other, coming apart, immediately apart, once the sex is over.

Before it ends, I ask Voytek to hit me. I don't know what I'm hoping for, a release, but also punishment. I know well that what I'm asking of him is far outside of his comfort zone. I'm asking him something a wild, untamed animal would ask him—I'm not even asking, I'm daring him.

We make out silently, going through the motions, twisting the erogenous-zones dials that we both know exactly how to twist to elicit a response. He spreads my labia, gently circles my clit, and I grip him hard and harder, move my hand up and down. I am not turned on. But I am excited because I know he will do it, this new forbidden thing, it's how he moves, too slowly, reciting his shaky fingers through their repertoire, biding his time, hesitating before we get to the next part. I watch his Adam's apple move rapidly up and down as if he can't swallow properly. Since he doesn't look at me I have to tell him,

I whisper, Now—and in an instant, he climbs on top of me, holds me in a vice-like grip with his knees, and hits me right in the face, not quite a punch but harder than a slap. The sound reverberates in my head, lands somewhere on the bottom of a well, shoots back up, then explodes behind my eyes. I see stars, just as you do in cartoons, the whole Milky Way. I am shocked. Not because I didn't think he would do it but because I didn't expect him to do it so confidently as if he'd been preparing for it and—and then he does it again and—and then again, and at this point I am scared. I feel his cock bouncing against my belly.

Does he like this? The punches land with the same force though they feel increasingly harder; is he reviving himself up, is this just a beginning? The thoughts clamber and cluster in my sore head, the punches slamming them further into what's left of my reason.

I know about snapping, I know that not all killers grow up methodical, preparing by pulling wings off of flies, setting fires to dumpsters, planning a menu of torn limbs. Some grow up nice and normal—a loving dad, a loving mom, two siblings and a van—and then something happens, and suddenly, they explode out of their human form in fists and guns and knives and severed throats.

I know that Voytek won't kill me, but it's one of those ideas whose absurd premise suddenly makes sense. He has lived his adult life in beautiful spaces, in libraries, universities; once he gained fame, lived it slurping oysters and drinking good wine and sleeping with elegant women. He has a cleaner who presses his shirts so that for a whole week he's not crumpled, a barber who once a month tames and coifs his wild tuft of hair, and he once had a maid who would regularly clean his first marital home. He'd spent most summers in his first wife's Muskoka cottage or on boats, sometimes in Italy, in Monaco and south of France with other émigrés, directors and writers and thinkers. His wife decorated their apartment with fresh flowers and made elaborate salads on a marble kitchen island; there was an original Chagal in their living room and Charles and Ray Eames chairs, and antique Chinese vases.

And then he met me, a child of a factory worker Polak who disrespected him, called him a pansy, suspicious of his highbrow lifestyle, his pursuit of his daughter, who then eventually told him he could have me, I was his problem now. And I became his problem, along with my student loans, my once sloppy drinking and shoplifting habit, my now-dormant propensity for pouting and demanding, my assortment of mental illnesses. He didn't use me for play like he should've—no, he planted a baby inside me and moved me into his house. But now he wants me to lie on train tracks and die. He *is* capable of surprises, maybe he's capable of killing me too.

I have never been afraid of Voytek. No, correction: I have been afraid of what I would find out next but I stuffed that with food, I held off. I have never been afraid of him like this. I've never known him to be violent except for a couple minor instances, a rough push or once grabbing my wrist and twisting to pry keys out of my palm. This is different.

And now we are here, me offering myself like this, at a new level of depravity and Monster likes it, it likes the danger of it.

I watch as he stiffens, his hand raised above me, then coming down fast and stopping right before it makes contact with my skin.

He is looking me in the eyes now—the first time he's ever looked directly at me during sex. His eyes say, "What now?" and I hold his stare, "Do your worst," Monster full of bravado; it will sacrifice me just to win this round, this dare, it will swallow him into its cloaca, spiky on the outside, velvet and wet silk on the inside. It will shit him out, a man hollowed out by murder and hatred. I tense, clench, try to push it to the front, try to birth Monster, push it out of my body to do its work, but we've still got a ways to go, too many membranes. I am not good at birthing, I couldn't even do it with Ruby. But then, suddenly, you! You show up—your ghost, your feelings for me—pleading with me to get a grip, to snap out of it. You don't want me to get hurt, you don't care about whatever this is with Voytek, you want me out of this bed but not in a sling or worse, in a body bag.

I try to soften, relax. Despite myself I have to relax, force myself to loosen every muscle in my body. I must.

Voytek seems to relax too, as if I'd poured molasses into his bones. He starts stroking my cheek—not to reassure, not to comfort me. His touch is charged, letting me know he can lift his hand and bring it down again. Instead, he puts the hand over my mouth, shoving back the dregs of my laughter.

I shake my head wildly, finally ready to speak now that I can't, I need to stop this, I will stop this, I want to see *you* again, I don't want this anymore, I don't want Voytek anymore or for Voytek to hurt me or kill me. It's as if I'm finally coming to, waking up to what this is, an angry man straddling my chest, threatening me or playing being threatening, none of this is okay.

He moves his hand from my mouth and I say through the clenched teeth, Get the fuck off of me.

He starts to move his hips, his cock still hard, probing between my clamped legs, trying to open me up as I fight him a little bit, that old move we used to love so much when we'd role-play and I'd let him dominate me.

I don't. Want. This, I say and he stops as soon as I say it.

He moves away from me so fast that I only barely catch a look across his face. Still, I know he meant for me to see it; Voytek likes to perform, he's a stage-whore who loves public readings of his own genius work, always conscious of being watched. The expression is that of disgust. I brought this out in him, no one else makes him crazy like this, no one else makes him lose control like this. And in that way I have won, I have humiliated him. He starts getting dressed, his back to me. In the past, I would beg him to stay, to talk, to explain but I already used up all of those words and I don't have any left.

Once alone, I get on my knees and press my palms against the wall. The house finally speaks back and it tells me that I have no choice.

# TWENTY-ONE

VOYTEK MOVES INTO Kazek's place. I don't do anything about that—I'm bored with all these indignities of my own domestic drama—although occasionally, I still check Margot's Instagram, which she doesn't update ever, nothing since her group yoga photo. I try to imagine the two of them, Margot and Voytek, but all I get is some fucked up version of me and Voytek from ten years ago, her face sewn onto mine as I-she writhe on the floor of his office, my backpack underneath my-her lower back to prop up my-her pelvis, to give him better aim, more depth. What do we do afterwards? What do they do, do they go to the rooftop patio overlooking the museum and order a dozen oysters and a bottle of white and do I—does she—tell him gushingly, instantly feeling stupid for the cliche—that she can taste the sun? Do we look at the city sprawled in front of us, containing all of our uncertain futures? Does he call her my name by accident in the beginning? Probably not, he rarely called me by my name, I had many nicknames, stand-ins for affection that were interchangeable. Doll, baby, kochanie, misiu, chwast. Monster says to dig deeper, to find out more, to go back to her house, but what for, I tell it? I know what I know and knowing more won't change a thing.

On his days with Ruby, Voytek brings our daughter to his mother's. On my days she stays with me. When we have to be in the house at the same time—him picking up his things, me never leaving—we pass each other politely, we are vicious only in text or emails: *Please submit your financial records or I'm going to have to get my lawyer involved.*

When I tell Lisa about this arrangement she says it must be hard to be missing half of my daughter's childhood and her comment seems unnecessarily mean but that's only because it's the truth. As long as I stay in the house—with Ruby's toys and clothes and her big-girl bed, her essence like her shadow always present—I can pretend that this is not the case yet.

When I'm alone during the day, I sit on the stairs to my backyard and smoke and watch the leaves turn yellow in real time, inhaling the sharp bite of a new season and the sweet rot of the old. Inside, the house is waiting, tense, impatient. I light the cigarette, take a drag. It makes me think of my grandmother, a devoted smoker, a subscriber to the gruesome *Detektyw* magazine with its crude red and black illustrations and gratuitous descriptions of bodies decomposing in plastic bins or in shallow ponds, and vampiric killers on the loose. I spent every summer with her as a child, playing near the *dacha* where she'd sat on the steps to smoke and read, a mysterious adult ritual I now understand, that back then was tinged with feelings of dread and discovery.

After my grandmother would retreat for her afternoon nap, I'd pull out the eared newspaper-print tabloids from underneath a pile of *Przyjaciółka*s and *Przekrój*s and read about murderous men. The trees around me were tall and skinny and white—shimmering birches—and the air was heavy, quiet save for an occasional bird sound or rustling of leaves. It was rarely windy; the forest seemed still, waiting. So many corpses I'd be reading about in *Detektyw* would be discovered in forests just like the one around me.

And now I am here, sitting and smoking and watching the leaves, the outline of my family becoming fainter and fainter, a photograph left out in the sun. My grandmother was the family's official nutcase, her smoking and sitting too intentional to be just a pastime. As family lore had it, her husband's mistress made a scene at his funeral, weeping loudly in a fur coat identical to the one worn by my grandmother. My grandmother's silent rage punctuated for years by cigarette ashes, her refuge from men in monsters from tabloids.

In sitting here the way I am, I am fulfilling some small prophecy or legacy, I'm not sure which, maybe both. What I do know is that my grandmother became sane one day and quit smoking and laughed again, as I remember it happened overnight; she had finished a pack of *Sporty* and finished grieving for good. I'm not there yet. For a while, I am so paralyzed by my new situation that I can't bear to be around you, I can't bear to be around anyone. A family has died and I need to mourn it. My grandmother would understand.

Meanwhile Monster is starving, begging to be fed. I try to hold off. When I can't sit and watch my backyard anymore, I ride my exercise bike to tire myself out. When my hunger still won't let go, I watch increasingly disturbing clips on porn sites and make myself come to men brutalizing women, or other men. Ironically or not, this particular theatre of porn is the only honesty I understand these days. This seems to do the trick most of the time, it quiets Monster down.

The evenings alone are quiet and dark; in fact, I don't turn the lights on once the night falls and stay in my spot on the daybed switching from disturbing porn to watching serial killers on my laptop. It's comforting because it's familiar, the danger of cocks and the danger of hands, captured on camera, contained. I feel suspended in my formaldehyde life.

On Ruby days, I am twice the mother that I used to be. At first, my daughter is confused about my sudden affections, my invitations to keep me constant company. I'm growing dependent on her, her soft warmth being the only pleasure that doesn't make Monster angry. Eventually, she yields to me and we develop new routines of closeness: baths together, reading, watching cartoons, falling asleep in the big bed I used to share with her father. I don't miss her father, but I miss having someone breathing next to me. I've shared a bed for most of my life, with good and bad men, but sleeping at night they were all absolutely perfect.

Some nights, I wake up with my heart pounding in my chest as if something or someone was chasing me, the image of my face being pummelled by a man's hands flashes and disappears as soon as I recognize my reality, the sleeping child next to me. When I can't fall back asleep, I wake Ruby up, pulling her close to me and kiss her all over, whispering for her to open her eyes, *mommy loves you* over and over until she groggily mumbles *I wow you too*, and I feel grounded or at least that I've staved off madness for a few more hours. I don't want to become one of those mothers desperately attached to a child, I don't want her to think she's responsible for my happiness, but I am too weak to resist this simple and readily available comfort.

Our new-found closeness makes me aimless when she's at the daycare or with Voytek. I can't seem to remember what I did before. Some days I turn my laptop on and sit in front of the screen waiting for words to form into a story but the stories I end up writing have no beginning or end, only middles, scenes from the past, all of them grotesque or banal betrayals of various men I gave myself to. Starting with my Best Friend's Dad and ending with you, all I'm capable of writing about are moments when I felt panicked and abandoned, my Best Friend's Dad threatening me with police after I keyed his car, or you, demanding I move when I need to stay.

To placate myself more, I make trips to the nearest mall and buy bags of food that I know will be easy to consume and expel: croissants, pudding, cereal that gets mushy instantly, pasta, pierogies, cheese, ice cream. I read message boards for people like me, for women like me, who feed and starve their bodies at the same time, and I follow their tips: drinking lots of water while eating, eating marker foods that stain a certain colour to know when I've reached the bottom. This is the only way I know to trick my insides into thinking that I am not hungry.

When I have you over for the first time in weeks, you're gentle, timid, at first. You can sense that this is a battlefield now, a space that's being occupied, not lived in. I don't expect you to be sympathetic but I am angry about your attitude when you again and again ask me why I don't just pack up and leave.

Because of the house, I tell you even though what I really want to tell you is to shut the fuck up.

It's so fucking toxic, you say somewhere below my head before you suck on my nipple. Your breath feels desperate against my skin, I've forgotten what it's like to be wanted like I'm oxygen. Voytek used to want me like that, he worshiped my body, part by part, took photographs of it, talked to my pussy as if it was a separate entity. But your want is somehow greater, more anguished.

I respond with enthusiasm, I don't hide the pleasure I feel the way I do sometimes if I'm worried about making myself appear too vulnerable, my body moves like a wave, undulating, arching under your touch. My anger dissipates. Your timidness disappears. You fist my hair, you growl when the tip of you hits the back of me, my throat. (You're not wrong, it is toxic. But there are ways to decontaminate a house.) Still, our lovemaking is distracted, your mind on alert for a trap. This isn't a trap. And I *do* need you. I need you to fuel me for another week, or a month or however long it will take. I know you don't understand because how could you, nothing has ever been taken away from you.

After we fall apart, we are silent. You get up to put your clothes back on. You tell me that you don't believe me that this is only about a house.

Let me fucking spell it out. I've left everything that mattered behind and it wasn't my choice: my language, my friends and my home. It happened to me and I couldn't do anything about it. The worst part is the longing didn't kill me but it made a way for all of the hungry holes that opened within me whenever it would hurt for too long. And now, I cannot let it happen to me again, I need to be grounded and I worry that a man—yes, even you—will never again be enough to ground me. I need to rely on myself, just as I said in my book. I lied in my book about all of that but now I am making myself come true.

As you get dressed, with your back to me, you rehearse another emotional speech, tell me how you've memorized me on an exhaustive level. The ends of my hair are like tips of a flame or something about electricity. A mole on my shoulder in the shape of a star. One corner of my eye is longer than the other, something about an elongated tear duct. You say you could recognize my pussy—its lines, the exact way my hips curve—even in a line-up of a thousand curves. A thousand pussies all lined up, and mine special, glistening, glowing. My thighs are like a highway leading you to the...source. You say you could drive all the way off the edge.

Don't drive off any edges, I say softly, hoping you won't see this as me trying to dismiss you, and you say, Then I can't help you. You say this standing up, eager to get out and go back to your life. Your eyes are somewhere else already when I look at you, they are impatient and the ambers are cooling coals now, setting sun.

The emails from Voytek's lawyers arrive more aggressively, like lasers tracking to shoot down whatever sanity I have left. Each one is a threat or a demand, the formal language freezing the blood in my veins. Ever since becoming a dirty immigrant who had to apply to be considered a human being in this new country, I've been afraid of administrative, officious language, specifically articulated to make the reader feel stupid and worthless. I'm reminded of Margot's pompous response to my pathetic email and the photograph of my family. I toy with the idea of sending her an email encouraging her to stop fucking around with yoga and go to law school.

In the emails, Voytek is referred to as Mr. Tak. He is my acerbic and charming professor all over again and I am a lowly student with sleepy eyes who's not even a real talent, whose only actual talent is how snugly I wrap my holes around Mr. Tak's dick.

On Lisa's advice I too retain a lawyer, a no-nonsense middle-aged woman with a severe ponytail and horrid polyester blouses, who will soon send, on my behalf, more violently condescending emails back to Voytek. On the phone, she reads me the first email in which I'm referred to as Madam Jagiello.

I tell her that my husband is a writer and an English Professor.

Well, I hope I get an A, she says. This is the only joke she makes the entire time she represents me, and it's also how she convinces me she's the right one for me.

Soon, I fall into a new pattern. Meetings with the lawyer to talk about financial statements and assets—the chandelier, the acacia desk, the Persian rugs—and long walks with Ruby, museums, playgrounds, splash pads, malls, benches. I am restless. Waiting for emails back. Chewing on the insides of my cheeks. Monster is twitching to get loose, trembling under my skin, little claws clawing, closer and closer now.

You come over on evenings when Ruby's with her father. We fall back into our trance, our lovemaking is all vibration and play, you asking for things I told you would cross my boundaries. At the same time the more boundaries I cross with you, the easier it is to stop bingeing and purging and so I let you push me. I can't tell if the cure is you or what we do or is it just the novelty of you. Perhaps all three.

One night, you beg me to let you take my ass. And then, right after you pull out, I take you in my mouth, my tongue circling the head of your cock slowly, the smell earthy, deep and taboo, filling the air around us. There's a bit of blood too. I gag and my eyes water. There is power in debasement, of course, your eyes are full of admiration when I look up at you. I've cleaned you up perfectly. This is a sexual sacrament, devoted and satanic, an intimacy so deep that I imagine only death could bring a similar kind of breakthrough.

You tell me you've never…but I don't let you finish because this isn't about getting some kind of new sexual-repertoire badge. I let you have me this way not because I want to impress you or because it's kinky but because for you I will do almost anything. I want to trust you with my blood, shit and tears. And you understand this so it's besides the point that you've never done anything like it. I know you haven't and neither have I because I've never loved anyone enough to risk being this vulnerable and ugly. There's more ugliness to me, you haven't seen it all but this is close.

No, not ugly, you reassure me, Just the opposite.

After this, Monster is satiated, you've tamed it, there's no trembling and nervousness, no rumbling and hissing, all the gills shut close after the encounter, stay that way and keep me full.

Later that night, when our filthy joy should be enough to make us fall asleep in lovers' bliss, we have a fight. You ask me, again, to leave my house, to move, to abandon this. The gills open back up, grow sharp little teeth, threatening to snap.

It's like you're married, still. Like you hope you will get back together with him. And I'm just some kind of a distraction.

It's not like that at all. You have no idea what's sitting in my Inbox, the latest a new cruelty contained in one sentence like this: *Although Mr. Tak is the sole owner of the home and the parties are not married, he has not yet sought to remove your client from the home in an attempt to maintain some level of continuity for Ruby during this transitionary period post-separation until the issues arising from their relationship breakdown could be dealt with comprehensively.*

I feel like I'm stuck between two glass panels slowly moving toward each other, threatening to squeeze me to death. I know trying to prove to myself that I don't need another dick to leave one behind is silly, but I'm a woman who's belonged to too many.

When you begin to cancel, I do nothing, because truthfully, as much as I need you, I'm relieved.

You text asking for some space.

Fine, I'll give you some fucking space, I text back. I know that I love you for sure because you have the power to hurt me.

I wish I could explain to you why I need you, how you keep Monster in check but how would you understand? I would have to explain everything, I would have to show you *all* of my ugliness, the bloated awful face I see in the mirror, exorcising myself after a meal. I would have to disassemble what we've created together, the seductress Yoveeta, the hot mom, the authoress, the detached wife of another. I would no longer be the goddess you worship and now rage against.

Unlike most people, I don't want to find someone who finally understands me—I understand myself perfectly and what I understand isn't anything I wish to share with anyone, I am not looking for absolution or compassion.

So I do what I can to make Monster stay staved, curb my restlessness, I indulge in small excesses that keep me at a baseline. I can't dip, not now, not with the lawyers. I get a haircut, I meet once with a personal trainer, start getting my nails done again, and facials and massages—I miss your hands on me so I pay strangers to touch me. On one occasion I orgasm discreetly while getting my ass kneaded by a masseuse named Rose.

I get matching bra and panty sets from Fleur du Mal, tiny luxurious constructions that hold my small breasts in teacups of lace, the sort of lingerie that is prettier than breasts themselves, panties that should be framed if only for how much money they demand for how little fabric. I throw out an old robe and any towels that have even a bit of fuzz of wear-and-tear on them. I finally manage to max out one credit card on an online store that sells real silk, painted kimonos and cashmere robes. I change what is in my power to change, which is my outsides. The changes feel urgent and necessary, correct; I get dopamine hits with every visit to a salon, my mood elevates with every elegant package that arrives with ribbons and little cards from designers—at this level of spending, brands put a lot of work into relationships and all products come with stories. I feel special reading that the new Suki & Ono line was inspired by spring in San Francisco, and the result is the short robe I, Dear Customer, am holding in my hands. The soft, white cardigan from Echoecho arrives in a box of chocolates, *sans* chocolates, with a handwritten letter that informs me the sweater was created with romance in mind and that it pairs best with champagne and a new companion. A black Minx cami and shorts set is even more provocative and arrives with a little booklet with naughty adult games divided into three categories: Lick/ Suck/ Touch.

The newer brands I order from on Instagram are all like new lovers, asking me questions about my routines, about my lifestyle, if I'm single or alone, do I like it slow or more naughty?

I gladly participate in giving out private information to algorithms that parse it all later and target me in the way that makes me feel chosen. I'm being courted and seduced, "Oh, you," I think as I fill out an online questionnaire declaring that I'm a beach person and that I enjoy the sound of rain on a warm summer night.

I also set up a dating profile. I don't tell you about it because as it stands, I only have you to gauge my newly single attractiveness, and Monster needs more than that, especially now that you're away, having your space. The appetite has always been bigger and stronger than me.

I put up three pictures and write something about spending a lot of time alone. I list mango as my favourite food and write "fridge" under "favourite travel destination." I pick "moderately" for working out and "socially" for drinking and skip the religion part. I don't lie about my age, but I lie about being a mother. It doesn't matter. None of this is real, I'm a thirty-seven-year-old woman who likes mango.

It doesn't take long. Now, every time I have an urge to send you an unsolicited text, I log into my profile and exchange flirtatious messages with strangers. There isn't that much difference between them and the pretty products that I buy online: They all come with a cute little story and have preferences to be either on the beach or in the mountains, to stay in or go out on Fridays. The men list famous dead people they'd like to dine with, and talk about hockey, two truths and one lie—I was in Boy Scouts, I have a twin, I'm related to Robert Downey Jr.—and jumping out of planes, riding camels, going out for beers, eating seafood—preferences and activities meant to hint at their personality. A few sound as if we're in a fight already announcing what they don't want and warning about being shallow and having no sense of humour, which I find funny. They volunteer and they spend time with their grandmothers, and they watch Italian cinema. They want to run away together. They sleep in, love brunches, they go to the gym, hang out with dogs, see concerts. They play guitar. They have three things they can't live without and for some of them one of those things is air. They don't take themselves seriously and I shouldn't either. They watch what they eat and want me to do the same. They value intelligence and stimulating conversation. They drink wine. They prefer Scotch. They have a daughter who is their entire life.

I screenshot the ones who interest me and make a folder on my phone with little notes about each because I treat this like a job and I don't have a lot of time to waste. That's not exactly true, I do have a lot of time but I worry about wasting it just the same.

When not talking to strangers online, I watch my shows about murderers. I'm running out of English-speaking productions and have now moved onto Scandinavians and Eastern Europeans. Every story seems to happen in that in-between time of the year with no leaves on trees, mud and wind and rain. Men with three-day stubble, women with messy ponytails, everyone holding styrofoam coffee cups, eating food while standing, driving around in dirty, grey cars. In dramas, no one murders people in the summer—the opposite of real life.

Voytek emails about renting a sublet nearby, to be closer to Ruby. I read this as a threat. In three weeks, he will become my most problematic neighbour.

Your silence makes me more and more nervous as time goes on. I try to get rid of you, see if I can fool myself into unloving you. I delete all of our emails and messages. You've never given me any gifts except for one. A soft leather belt you bought in a mall because you had a vision of wrapping it around my wrists. It didn't work, but the theatricality of it made us laugh; our violence was best when it was spontaneous.

I put the belt in a yellow envelope and address it to you. I write slowly, each letter calligraphed; I want you to think of me when you read your own name in my careful cursive. You've commented on my handwriting before, you found it amusing that it was something I learned in school back in Poland, as a little girl. Your own handwriting is no-nonsense, no curlicues, no Os that look like open mouths; they're just letters that exist only to deliver the message, nothing more.

The purge doesn't do much, it only intensifies the feelings. I look for you in the absences now, I remember every word I deleted; the words are sharper. I mail the yellow envelope out, kiss along the ridge where it closes, fourteen kisses in total. The young, dark-haired woman behind the counter at the postal office arranges her face into indifference when I pass her the envelope.

Other than that, I don't contact you because my mother taught me never to chase a man, but since I want to chase you, I've all this pent up energy I need to do something with. So I clean the house obsessively, I star in a film inside my mind wishing you could telepathically see me carrying boxes in and out of the basement, my arms so strong, my face brave. I divide my clothes into Summer, Winter, and Fat Clothes, stuff them into black garbage bags. I wear a bandana, a white tanktop, too-big jeans held together with a rope instead of a belt. I've outlined my eyes in black. I strain, rest, hands on hips, scratch my left ankle with the tip of my sneaker. Salty droplets above my upper lip, lick them off. Planned and stylized all for you. Monster is taking big gulps of air. I pleasure myself often, quickly, to my mental porn-clips, which only enrages the squirming inside me. *I've got nothing*, I tell it, *you're on your own.*

# TWENTY-TWO

VOYTEK TAKES RUBY away on vacation and now I am really alone. It's not that I am unable to be alone but also, it absolutely is. I have no experience with it, not really. As soon as men got a whiff of me, I was never alone, even well before my Best Friend's Dad gripped me briefly by my hips—my Best Friend hunched over a school project, a diorama we were preparing at their kitchen table—and told me I was a little tease.

But it started even earlier, one afternoon with a snowman. We were eight, my two friends and I, and a man stood in a doorway and took something that looked like a newborn bird out of his pants. I stared and tried to figure it out. Then I figured it out. We ran. The snowman was left unfinished. One of my friends dropped her mitten but we never went back for it. The man tried to block our exit. We ran inside an old building, fast, two stairs at a time, our faces stinging from the change in temperature, our breaths steaming, hot. When we got to the top, we ran back downstairs, squeezed out past the man, waiting there for us—his arms stretched abnormally wide and catching and catching us forever, till this day, in my mind—and ran home.

The next year, another man stood behind me in the cashier line at the Polish hard-currency shop, Pewex. I had a little koala stuffie in my hand. The man pressed against me and I felt something hard rubbing against my back. Even without knowing what it was, I knew what it was. I quietly walked out of the lineup and found my friends, waiting for me to buy the toy. We have to go, I said and placed the koala back on the shelf. My friends' little faces fell all around me, one chin trembled. I was the only one from our group with a real US dollar, mailed to me by my dad—who tried to make life better for us abroad—and they had accompanied me on my shopping trip for the cool, foreign toy. My friends demanded an explanation. I wasn't sure what to say.

When I was eleven, a camp's counsellor's boyfriend played a guitar and sang a song he said he dedicated to me; the lyrics involved little tadpoles swimming toward an egg and he stared at me intensely when he got to the egg part. Another time, he asked me to sit on his lap. I refused. Near the end of the camp term, he caught me and tickled me, his hand sneaking under my blouse brushing against my tiny nonbreast. He called me his "little girlfriend" and my friends were all jealous. He had a beard.

You get the idea. It was my Best Friend's Dad, however, who showed me that you could tame a man, he was the first one I wasn't afraid of. His wet kisses left goosebumps all over my thighs, the translucent hair raising and swaying—in my mind the hair was seven-feet tall, a whole alien forest of it—as he moved his mouth closer to my core.

So, I never learned what it would be like to be only with myself for long periods of time. Before Voytek, I had an Excel spreadsheet where I would input the names of men I had slept with. It sounds psychotic but it wasn't. I loved all those men. Each man was someone I had decided to be with, to tame. After a man would exit my life—whether because it was morning and too bright outside, or because we no longer could agree on which TV series to rewatch—I'd register his name. Each time I added a new entry, I would read all the names, beginning with my Best Friend's Dad. It was a reassuring litany; even in their departure they were still with me.

But you can only do so much with spirits, ghosts, names; soon I would become aware that my own company was not enough. Sometimes it would get so stark that I didn't know what to think about. I'd have no real thoughts, just obsessions, eating something and then getting rid of whatever I'd eaten. I read and watched the killers because I wanted to understand something about human nature, in general at first then maybe in particular, maybe I would understand something about myself. I didn't understand the girl in the mirror, how she was put together, which is why I tried to mould and tweak this body to fit some kind of shape I would recognize. I was sure that once I saw the correct shape, I would know it instinctively but I am here to tell you that I still don't know it. The closest I came was with Ruby inside my belly.

I feel Monster throughout the day, it exists in my ankles and elbows and my cunt and my ass, my tail, all those scales forming, the sharpness and the slickness too, just swimming in my bloodstream, pouring out of all the holes and pouring back in, endlessly finding its way through me. I'm at peace with these visions; a woman's life is a life of bleeding. And life is a vampire but always, women are its source, we exist so that life can feed on us; men are its teeth. Occasionally, a woman bites back. I can feel my teeth now, and your absence makes me want to bare them more and more each day. Without your love, in this house of waiting, I am growing angry.

Female rage. Are you going to make fun of it, dismiss it, put it in a category, like my husband used to do? Female. Rage. That time of the month. That time of the year. That time of the end of beauty. That time because she has no more time, poor thing, because she can no longer buy time with her tits and her eyes and her hips. Thank you for looking at me. I need you to come back and look at me again.

# TWENTY-THREE

IT'S BAD FOR a woman to scare a man. At least that's what I was taught as a girl. My mother was stupid. She was the one scared—of men. She taught me the lessons that were taught to her, to not bother men, to wait for men to come back on their own, make them think she was unavailable. If you show a man too much interest he'll run.

A better lesson was when my Best Friend's Dad taught me how to hold and steady a BB gun, look between the front sights and aim. At first, my arm would shake, but with time I learned to withstand the discomfort. Tinny metal smells, and cologne, sharp and musky, and grown-man sweat, salt. He held my waist and whispered in my ear, Like that, good girl.

I developed a fantasy of having him watch me put the barrel of the gun inside myself, sliding it in and out, its hard edges tearing at tissue, making me wince, never breaking eye contact. I once asked him if he could bring the gun to our secret dates, but he had sold it. His wife made him. I didn't like hearing about his wife.

My second gun fantasy was to shoot the wife in the face. I'm telling you this so that you know that violence, anger, aren't new to me; they've been foundational, starting from my first man.

Are you my last man? I wish I knew but I'm in a state that's neither awake nor asleep and nothing is real. It's as if I've been missing days, just pouring myself from one night into the other. On my phone there are notifications, missed phone calls and texts from my husband, pictures from their vacation, Ruby's radiant smile against many different backgrounds, whatever background you'd expect from New York—that place again! The Statue of Liberty, a pretzel stand, the Atlas, rows of flags, *Mamma Mia!*, a yellow taxi cab, a billboard with an android stand-in for a flawless woman in a matching red bra-and-panty set, a giant M&M and Spiderman. My husband in an integer sequence of appearance. Such perfect pictures of a perfect vacation.

What if they haven't really gone anywhere? What if it's all Photoshopped, decoy? What if he had moved to Switzerland to take her away from her insane mother and this is all done to placate me—or no, what if they are dead and I am in shock, what if I had only imagined them, what if all of this is an experiment, and Monster is really just a tell-tale sign that I can no longer be and breathe on this planet, I'm running out of whatever gas keeps things like me alive?

*I would like to die*, I used to say out loud sitting at my desk, my husband unsure about my whereabouts although I was right there. *I would like to die*, I say now, because there's freedom in death. Falling back into darkness, going inwards, inside my insides, and dreaming your tongue vibrating against my skin, your lips sucking the poison out, the weakness and the pull in my inner thighs, I shudder against a whole constellation, I come to, shards of me strewn around the kitchen floor. I'm curled up in the corner and the fridge door is open and I welcome the cold breeze.

I should try to accommodate. I should try to fit the world into my vagina, make the world a drink, rub its shoulders. But when I try to be nice, I become a deep, black hole with no teeth.

I fall into it and crawl out of it and it goes on like that forever. If I had a friendly vagina and a good soul, there would not be an extra hole.

Now you're gone and it's just me and that hole, that hungry mouth.

# TWENTY-FOUR

I GO ON dates to get over you but also to hurt you. I can't seem to do either. I save my dates in my Excel sheet. None of them make me feel love but each encounter is an opportunity to, I hope, psychically disturb you somehow, as if you'll sense my promiscuity and want me back. Each encounter is food, also, a story for Monster to feast on. There's the romantic nephrologist who takes me to a Mediterranean restaurant, where he orders a tower of bitchy pincers of crabs, and virgin dollops of scallops, and glistening pussies of oysters, and tiny baby cock shrimps, and two bottles of white wine; he chooses for us, he's comfortable in this restaurant, he has taken dates here before. I don't retain the name of the place, this is not a sensual, careful meal I would have had with you. Everything is still colour-coded, RED, YELLOW, GREEN and the number "800," never seems to fade no matter how much alcohol I consume. But I'm forcing myself to be someone else—I have to be someone else because otherwise I'd be a woman who is in love with you and you don't want me. I eat because I am a woman who goes on dates and eats. The nephrologist talks about boats, a woman he misses—*used* to miss, he corrects himself—who is older and has a yacht, and a teenage son. His brow knots, he strokes his beard, waves his hand, She's in the past now. He wants to fall in love again, his eyes burn into mine and I look away, suck a long white tendril from an orange claw, bite baby cock's red tail off.

He wants to hold my hand in the taxi. His apartment is sparse, the building is cheap, his stipend, he explains. He lives in a sea town in Italy, he's in Canada for a year, teaching. He shows me a picture of himself on a boat, behind him a woman in a striped sailor shirt, her face obscured by black curls.

A bit of grappa, some Venchi chocolate. Books everywhere, a simple table, two chairs, a mattress.

His penis is enormous and he fucks beautifully, my body underneath him and then above him like riding waves, his thighs are an entire forest of hair, his chest is burly, thick, he grunts and when he drives that cock balls-deep into me I inhale sharply, suddenly aware of a whole new unexplored layer.

He stops, lifts me and says, Are you okay, bella? His voice is soft. He smooths my hair, runs a finger over my cheek, his cock buried deep inside me still and waiting for me to adjust. He is gentle but not too gentle, he fucks again and comes, and then he licks me clean and we sleep for a short time and then he tells me more about the sea and the clouds too. He says something in Italian. I say, Say something else, say something else.

He says to say something in Polish.

We talk in Polish and Italian, he rubs me and with his huge hand moves my knee, holds my thigh in place with his arm and we're still talking, me catching my breath, panting, him ramming back into me—this one is a lot less gentle but that's fine because I'm soaking wet, his entrance is timed perfectly, my body is elastic. Inside me, there is a roar and claws, an open hungry mouth. Inside me, a row of gills, tiny cunts, open and close, open and close again, in tandem with my pussy clenching around him.

In the morning the Italian tells me to stay in bed. I stay in bed, shallow-nap, until he calls my name from the kitchen and on that sad, little table there's a checkered table cloth and freshly baked bread and flowers in a vase, heirloom tomatoes and three different kinds of cheese. There's smoothies in two jars, and classical music playing quietly in the background, momentarily overpowered by the percolating Bialetti.

He apologizes. He says he will make me a proper breakfast one day. He will take me to his boat. Do I like Satie? Everyone likes Satie.

I eat the bread with the cheese and leave the coffee alone because I can feel my anxiety buzzing softly in the pit of my stomach, threatening to spill further. I don't know what's wrong. What's wrong is that this man is wrong and this romance is wrong, this aftercare, the food, the way he's looking at me as we sit and eat, like he's happy to have me there with him, like this is a start of something. But all I can think about is how I'd much rather be with *you*, in your soulless condo, or even Voytek and Ruby in her high chair, in my home. I don't think about the food that I'm eating, all the problematic sustenance I pollute myself with.

He wants to know why I'm sad.

I'm not sad, I say and start to cry.

He gets up and walks around and then lifts me from the chair like I'm a child, and carries me back to the bedroom, the mattress, and he undresses me gently and he licks and fingers me until I forget that I'm sad and I want one thing only, which he gives me.

The sense of loss returns as soon as my body calms down and I whisper for him to call me a cab, no he didn't do anything wrong, I'm just overwhelmed.

I get better at hooking up with strangers after that one—that one was a lesson, I remind myself whenever I feel badly about how it ended. The Italian is a gentleman and makes only a couple of attempts to see me again. He stops after I tell him I went back to my husband.

In between hook-ups, I see my daughter on my days with her and this, more than anything, feels like a double-life. The men make me feel less alone, or less inadequate. They're not demanding, my currency is sex and since I give it to them I'm already giving them my best, in their view. I don't have to worry about their futures or their mental health. With Ruby around, I am too acutely aware of the house. Neither the house nor my daughter ask for anything but more and more I have the sense that I am failing both of them. The guilt is overwhelming.

Lately, I've been picking Ruby up from daycare to go to a park till it gets too cold or too dark or both. In various parks, I watch my daughter play on various structures, slides and monkey bars and swings. I watch her talk to other little girls or little boys, sit in sandboxes and conduct complicated transactions of exchanging sand sandwiches for sand money. I talk with other mothers and fathers about what our children are doing, I tell them about Ruby's daycare and I tell them about Ruby's independence and they tell me about their Oliver's and Olivia's daycares or nannies and their lack of independence. They all ask me how I got Ruby to be the way she is and I tell them truthfully that I'm just not a very good mother. Everyone laughs and says, *I hear you, I hear you,* but they never ask me to explain further. It's still warm outside, the fall this year is gentle and awash in all its usual shades of orange; I love the walnuty, deeply earthy smells of death. I love sitting in sunny patches, catching the last rays of this year's second summer. I love the chill too; I need all the help I can get to be present.

A coyote with a mange has been spotted in the neighbourhood and sometimes when we walk home people tell us to cross the street or to avoid a certain front yard. I push the stroller, thinking how the animal will be too scared to attack, but if it does attack how I could use the stroller to slam into it and scare it off. Most of the time, if the sidewalk is empty and wide enough, I push the stroller with one arm and walk beside it, my eyes straining to see, it, in the darkness.

When we get home, we go through our routines: dinner, books, bath, bedtime. Now that I'm sharing my body with strangers, I don't let Ruby into my bed. She fusses the first night I refuse her, but not for long; she is asleep before her anger can take over. I kiss her wet face, then lick the saltiness of her tears off of her cheeks.

There's a forensic psychologist I see mainly to ask him about his patients and he tells me about the high-security building I didn't know existed in my city where there are people locked up for murder. He loves his job but doesn't know what made him interested in psychos, he had a good childhood somewhere in Norway or Denmark. His hair is so blonde it's almost white.

He orders a virgin margarita.

He kisses me delicately, but grabs the back of my head the way I like, the way you do it, and I melt into his heated front car seat and ask if his children are at home; they are not. I tell him about Ruby, how I'm going to have her this weekend and how we've planned a trip to the island where she loves going on the swan boats. This isn't true, Ruby doesn't have a particular affinity for swan boats but I want to sound more involved and familiar with my child's life than I am. From my park visits, I've learned that a lot of parents attribute their children's behaviours to various personality traits instead of just regular stages of development. This one is stubborn, that one is artistic, another one hates movies with Robin Williams. So I give my daughter swan boats and independence and a few other quirks and the psychologist laughs when I describe her fictional tantrum when in the car on our way home one day she saw Lake Ontario and screamed, Swans! and she was unconsolable until she elicited a promise that we go to the island.

The psychologist and I are both terribly sober, but already, inside me, there's a pink, foamy slick, Monster opening its gills and mouths, electrifying its tail, standing to attention. My nipples harden when the psychologist reaches over to the glove compartment to show me a printed photograph of his children, two blonde clones.

His house reminds me of a sauna, it smells of fir, there are evergreen trees in the backyard visible through the back wall which is all glass.

He grabs my hand and we walk upstairs, shyly, ceremoniously and he takes my clothes off slowly, marvelling over the softness of my skin.

We slide under the blue, silk sheets and he gets on top of me and rubs against me to no avail, he can't get hard.

He sits up in bed and holds his head in his hands, Rodin's *Thinker*, and he tells me he is not over his ex-wife, it's a recent separation, it's embarrassing, he is very sorry, he really wants to, it's not that he doesn't—

I don't mind, I tell him, and tell him I understand and that I miss my husband too but I mean *you*, not my husband.

The day after the psychologist, there's an English professor who says he's heard me interviewed on the radio and why do all women write about themselves and their experiences? Can they not come up with anything that they haven't necessarily lived through? It's all relationships and bad men and body positivity and mental illness. Everyone has PTSD and everyone gets triggered!

The English professor orders pint after pint. And don't ever get him started on the transgender agenda. He'd probably get cancelled if anyone heard him, ha! Ridiculous. Am I gonna cancel him?

He's not terrible-looking, a sharp beard and wet eyes. I've never been with a bigot.

He fucks me in an alley, or tries to, because when he makes a second attempt to enter me, I simply push him away, pull my skirt down and walk off into the humid night, the alley stinking of garbage but in that pleasant way that just suggests dead things, creating live things, moss and mushrooms and worm food.

The whole time I'm with these men, I try to tap into Monster believing it's my psychic energy, my one super power where I can reach you. At first I wanted to provoke you, punish you—later all I want to do is summon you. You text me a few times, *How are you doing?* and I don't text back because I'm overwhelmed by wanting to be honest, explain everything and how to explain everything? Here we are in this story; this is me explaining.

A guy I call Landmark reminds me of you, he has the same physicality, thick arms and he asks me to pronounce my name for him, the way you did, before he fucks me. The cult he belongs to holds weekend-long workshops during which people call their loved ones and apologize for things they did and didn't do, after hours of sleep-deprivation, chanting, berating and self-flagellation.

The Landmark guy answers every question with a question and asks me why I ask questions but he says to ask myself that, he doesn't need to know.

Arriving at his condo, I turn my eyes into camera lenses. I hope you can see the black pantyhose Landmark asked for, how he rips them off, asking me at one point somewhat angrily if I've ever been with an alpha man, which I'm not sure how to answer because I don't know if we are role-playing or what.

I point out that this is a question and ask him why he's asking. I don't want to tell him that this is probably not a question an alpha man would ask.

After the sex, we watch Bill Burr on Netflix and laugh at jokes about Hitler and child soldiers. I wait for a signal from you, some kind of telepathic jolt that'll tell me you're receiving this transmission. I don't know what I'm waiting for. I'm giddy from all the craziness so I laugh too hard at the crude jokes.

Landmark invites me over again and I feel strangely happy about it because now I associate him with you, in my memories you are there with us, and also, I like the sex, his energy and the fact that he demands different outfits. The second time, he asks me to wear long boots and no underwear and I keep the boots on the whole time while he bends me over the kitchen island. He has the same Plexiglas stools Voytek installed in our kitchen and after the sex, we talk about chairs and what makes a good chair versus a bad one.

That night, after he sends me home, I finally see the coyote with mange. It's much smaller than what I expected, a thin, uneven body like it's wearing a fur stole with holes in it, which is exactly what's happening. The animal weaves in and out of a couple of front yards, a grey patchy arrow, then I can't see it because it's too dark. The internet says coyotes with mange are not dangerous to humans although contact with them could cause contamination. They appear in human areas because they're too weak and sick to hunt so they look for scraps. They don't want to be caught although the only way to help is to treat them with sulfur and lime. But the animals are too crazed with itch and later, pain, from festering wounds, to slow down or stop, and as they start to rot alive, they try to outrun death.

The hook-ups become boring and mildly troubling. The only good thing about it is that I'm not hungry—just as I predicted. But I'm still lonely. And when I'm alone, all I do is miss you. And the more I conjure you, the more every man I've touched, fucked and left becomes distorted, their faces and gestures and cocks and bodies, and voices indistinguishable, like Ruby's Lego guys;

they could switch their heads, pants, bodies, and it would all be the same—the same in the way that they're not you.

Voytek announces he will be selling the house. The news brings you back to me. I suddenly can't remember why it was so important that I ignored you, or what kind of a grand gesture I'd expected from you. I suppose there was some vague idea of you barging into a man's house—Landmark's condo?—and punching him in the face and dragging me out by my hair.

I call you and you pick up on the first ring. Hearing your voice makes everything instantly better and I don't feel like I've capitulated, I feel as if I've won.

What are you going to do? you say, our bodies steaming, our legs intertwined, your foot slowly running up and down my calf. We can't completely fall apart, now that we've reunited it seems our bodies are afraid to separate again and there's always a point of contact, hands, feet, mouth, knees.

I loved getting ready for you this morning. With my dates, I was reminded again how much I used to enjoy getting ready for a new man. And now that I have to impress you and possibly trap you all over again, I've paid extra attention to this part of our encounter. The preparations; the ritual of bath, hair, masks, creams, nails, fabrics, lace, hooks, shoes, straps are as exciting as what happens after the man finally arrives. As I slowly rolled stockings over my soft-hard legs, my hand caressing the heel momentarily, tickling the sensitive part of my arches, I could see Monster, like a kitten arching its back.

The stockings are ripped now, something I asked you to do to see if it'll jolt something in your subconscious that would prove to me you *were* there with Landmark. You wrapped one of them around my wrists, pulled on it lightly when you entered me for the second time, your eyes on me, loving and kind. You unwrap it gently now, your fingers brushing my skin, then your mouth, again, hot against my neck, your scratchy kisses that make me shiver, Hmmm, have you figured it out? you murmur into my neck.

Yeah, I have. I'm going to fix everything, I say. Because I am going to fix everything. I move my hair away from the nape of my neck to give you better access and you know what to do.

# TWENTY-FIVE

ON THE WEEKEND, I meet with Voytek to hand over Ruby and he says I need to be out of the house for a morning showing the next day. Do I have somewhere to go? He keeps giving me a once-over like a boy in a club. I look away, stretch quickly, elongate my body, arms above my head. It's a gentle display, intentional, innocent. I haven't eaten in days. I feel pure, crystalized, I'm surprised that no one can see the light that's pulsing inside me at all times.

It's a welcome feeling since I've spent the past three days skulking out of the house first thing in the morning, adding more activities to my schedule with my daughter, including a morning coffee at Starbucks. Now it's the end of the week, you are on an important deadline, you send me updates like I'm your boss and you're on probation. I believe you, I tell you and try not to feel abandoned. In one message you tell me you're struggling but when I ask with what, you write it's just work, don't worry about it.

Yeah, I have somewhere to go, I tell Voytek. We are in the park where we do Ruby handovers on days she doesn't have daycare.

Oh. Where? Lisa's?

No, another friend.

A guy?

Yes, a guy friend, I say and watch his face. Blink blink blink. He shakes his head. Shakes again. Exhales loudly. It's a whole performance except it's not a performance, he is genuinely disturbed.

I am wearing a thistle-purple dress I got on a whim on sale at Saks, hair up in a high pony the way Voytek likes it. The dress is not the kind of dress I would buy for myself these days but it's the kind of a dress Voytek would buy me in the beginning when he loved to show me off like a prize cow at his various dinners and launches. His divorce was still fresh in everyone's mind. People didn't bother introducing themselves to me, I was just some young thing Voytek brought around—everyone knew he loved his ex-wife very much, she had real class, he was just in pain. The women stared and looked away, the men just stared. After their ties would get loosened and everyone's laughter would get louder to compete with the music or speeches, the men would turn friendly, speaking in conspiratorial whispers, telling jokes. They wanted to see if they could charm a thing like me and I flirted with everyone aware of the fact that Voytek was watching and liking it; he had the thing they all wanted and I went home with him.

Right now the dress and the look is precisely to let him know I am still the thing but I no longer go home with him. I have a mysterious guy friend whose house I can stay at. For the past few weeks, during the handovers, my husband has seen me in a rotation of grey or beige garb, long heavy dresses like habits, even if they are designer they signal that I've given up, that my sex appeal has disappeared along with him, the only man who could inspire me. The thistle dress and the hair up and my announcement are, I hope, a shock to the system.

He says, Is it serious?

He says this like you're cancer and not a guy friend. I shrug. I watch Ruby in the sandbox, playing by herself in the corner, lining up plastic containers according to size in a meticulous, focused way as if this were a job.

Not that serious, I lie.

I don't know what to say, Voytek says. I suppose I'm surprised. I thought—I miss you, he exhales. He is staring at me, the look I recognize from a long time ago, the pained expression that is intended to show me I am really in charge here and he's at my mercy, at the mercy of my feminine power. He is a slave to women and I am a woman and therefore I can hurt him but I can also save him.

I believe he is honest, with his confusion, hard dick, mixed-up nostalgia. I throw him some scraps, say to him, I know you do. I miss you too.

There's a chill in the air that is unmistakably of winter, the future of short, brutal days and snow. I'm one of those idiots who likes to pretend that the seasons don't change, trying some dubious spell meant to arrest the summer by wearing wrong outfits that signal it's still warm and friendly. Now I'm freezing in my dress and my little leather jacket, sacrificing comfort for seduction, suffering for beauty. All around, people are wearing warm coats, even winter hats. In the corner of the baseball diamond, there's a teenage girl in a red parka and a hat with a pompom. She has a large, fluffy puppy and a stick, the puppy barking happily as it runs to retrieve it, and her throwing the stick again, laughing like they're in a commercial. I think of the coyote with mange, more specifically how its suffering radiates through our neighbourhood like low, slow smoke, close to the ground, filling those cute front yards, wrapping around porches and whooshing away as the animal runs and runs trying to mindlessly outrun it. And then there we are in our jackets or inside, in our beds, unaware, tucked away safely with good skin, warm and asleep.

I'm aware of my own mange eating me away from the inside but it's different now, it's something that I understand that I can tame with its own specific treatment that is not my own skin.

Yoveetka, you okay? Voytek is saying something, has been saying something for some time and I can't figure out if it's important or not, he still has that pleading look in his eyes but that could mean anything, him telling me that he's decided it would be best for him and Margot to live in my house with Ruby, and I shouldn't be jealous, or him asking me to suck his dick one last time. I hear him, asking me if I remember.

Remember what?

Our—thing. Anniversary. It'll be eight years, he says. Or nine.

Eight, I say.

Jeez, we couldn't even make it a decade, eh? He sounds chummy and I nod in a chummy way. I can't believe my luck or coincidence, everything lining up. Him asking me if I remember. But that's one of those Voytek contradictions: not being sentimental but absolutely being sentimental.

Should we do something special? I say and we both laugh, me first to show him that I am a cool, non-threatening soon-to-be ex-wife.

He looks grateful, relieved. He briefly grabs my hand but lets go as soon as I give in to his touch, a conditioned response.

He says, Sorry, sorry.

Don't be sorry, I say. I'm not.

When I think of our early days, I always think about that rainy afternoon in his office, the first time we didn't rush or hide, the day we count our anniversary from, even though we'd been sneaking around for some time, and I'd travelled with him and pretended to be a wife in Saskatoon or Halifax. But that afternoon was our first real—not only sexual—intercourse when it was obvious that this was not just an affair. Every couple has their own rainy afternoon.

The memory is a real one but over time I've added various fantasies to it, my little tropes that turn me on because of my own sexual fixations. In one, he is simply My Best Friend's Dad. And I am me as a kid. In another, I imagine myself in his office and I am a little older, wearing a short kilt and long over-the-knee socks and a white dress shirt with a tie. He's my tortured high school teacher or maybe a priest, some combination of both. He rolls my over-the-knee socks down my legs slowly, holds my foot in his hand and kisses me, starting with my littlest toe, all the way up to my knees, my thighs, my pussy. His hair is dark the way I've only seen it in pictures. The door rattles. I run my hands through the hair, feel its softness. I love running my hands through men's hair, their vulnerable scalps and undyed textures of their serious or silly haircuts. In this fantasy he also looks a little bit like you, he has your essence, or maybe it's that you have his. Outside, the rain gets more intense, the windows become blurry with all that water sloshing down and there's thunder and it's nighttime.

On the playground, we're watching our daughter climb out of the sandbox and join two little boys pushing a large, plastic truck. In her usual fashion, she is polite and standing to the side, the boys are ignoring her but their energy seems to go up a notch once they sense her near.

You could visit me at my residency, Voytek says. I will make dinner. You can even stay over. There's another room. Or not, whatever you like. Just an idea.

I told you I have a place to stay, I say, carefully.

Yes, I know, he sighs. I mean another time. On Thursday.

He is leaving for the residency in a few days.

I need to reclaim it, he says.

I wonder if this is more about going back to the scene of the crime. A couple years ago I tried to do my own investigation, tried to find the redhead student. I examined all the evidence—what I already knew and what I could deduct—and I dug around on Reddit and social media, found some stale threads that mutated into side stories or died. I subscribed to her blog, which she stopped updating. I read my own old emails from that time, surveyed Voytek archaeology as I tried to piece a story together, but soon all the leads became fainter and fainter. There was never anything new, the girl's Facebook remained private and locked, her profile picture never updated, always the same cat in a red Santa hat, looking melancholy and dumb.

Why do you want me to visit? I say.

Why not? We can be civil with each other.

He has never invited me to visit him there, not even when we were together. And I never wanted to go, afraid of what I might find: a scarf, a condom in a waste basket, a box of tampons underneath the sink. I never visited because I knew I would look, knew the ensuing argument: It was the previous artist who left it, am I snooping, why am I snooping? Are my delusions back? You're not a plate of fish and chips!

If you ask women like me what they knew and what they didn't, or how did they know or how they found out, you'll learn that these are not the right questions to ask. We *always* know but we can't always take on the burden of that knowledge. We have to bide our time, we have to have strategies.

What about Margot? I say and he winces.

Don't worry about it.

I'm not worried. But what is *this*?

What is what? Please, there's no pressure.

I want to ask if I'm about to become Margot, more accurately if I'm being demoted, invited to become The Other Woman (again). As it turns out, there are more ways to humiliate your wife than just having another woman.

Voytek says, Margot is fine. We're breaking up.

Aha, I say. Another story. I don't believe it. I know Voytek's breakups because in the beginning we went through many of them—first over him and his wife, and then over me and my so-called delusions. The breakups were always final and sometimes dramatic—but mostly they were just us leaving restaurants in opposite directions in two different cabs—but no matter what was said, they were never actually final. Yet they would install uncertainty, a strange hook that never lets go and that I'd cling onto. And then a week or a month would pass and books or clothes need to be returned and then there's a romantic reunion, tears and promises but also more fear—ever present now, a hum you cannot unhear. Eventually, the fear metastasizes into numbness.

It's nothing to do with Margot, Voytek says, I just thought it would be a nice thing. And you could see the place. You can apply to it now that you have your own book.

His eye twitches. I watch his eye twitch.

The residency is at the end of a road, a secluded piece of land surrounded by a small forest and overlooking the lake right below the cliffs the little cottage is perched on top of. There are no other dwellings around. The cliffs are steep and rocky. There are old trees, a garden and a small pond. Moss on rocks and often, thick fog from the lake. Many mornings and sometimes at dusk—according to the reviews—there's a small herd of deer that shows up to graze near the pond; sometimes they get right up to the window. I picture their curious slim faces, flicking ears, wet noses, and liquid brown eyes peering right inside. *Like being Snow White*, reads one review.

Inside there's the writer's office with walls laid out in dark wood panelling. I know because I've searched for photos online, tried to imagine my husband there alone, always failed. Any picture I'd fabricate in my mind would have a woman in it, someone just out of frame, a woman in a kimono, with delicate shoulders, watching him lovingly, a steaming cup of coffee in her hands, her breath quiet so as to not disturb her artist, her big grumpy bear, her genius man.

As for me, I have no problem seeing myself alone there, in a space that seems haunted and perfect for my gothic sensibilities; I could write a proper scary story or perhaps just a memoir, an account of real pedestrian horrors that some man critic would one day dismiss as Women's Writing.

Here's another thing I don't want to tell you but that is true. I still really miss him. I want to convince him to take it all back, tell him that I will take it all back, that maybe we can cobble some new version of ourselves where I'll just accept everything and not let it destroy me. Except that I can't because of Monster, it is too late now. But I find myself saying that yes, I would like to come to the residency and he instantly perks up and relaxes and makes a jab about me looking too pale like he's still got the right to tell me what's wrong with me. But I let it go. I catch my daughter rubbing her eyes repeatedly and she throws me a look that signals she is about to become a real four-year-old, not this unobtrusive cutout version of herself. It occurs to me that she, like me, is exhausted by pretending to be someone else, some kind of a child that she thinks would be better accepted. This makes me feel terribly guilty and selfish.

I stand up and stretch one more time to show Voytek he has made the right move by asking me to come and visit him in his lair and he asks me if he can hug me. Neither of us hugs, really, it's an American affectation but I say, Of course, and pull him close. He stiffens under my touch. I mean, his whole body stiffens.

See you in Fool's Paradise, Voytek yells as I walk away. I'm confused for a moment, then remember the residency's actual name.

# TWENTY-SIX

HERE'S HOW I would tell that story:

Once, a long time ago, something happened in Fool's Paradise. Or it didn't happen.

Afterwards, the girl this thing *didn't* happen to, complained to her student rep. She said that Professor Tak behaved inappropriately when she came to the residency to see him about her work, but also about a photo. She had just sold her first book, a collection of poems, to a small publisher. She needed an author photo and she remembered how he once said, in a workshop at school, that he had a good camera and students could come to him for headshots, free of charge.

She was asked if she would like to file an official complaint, if she would like to go to the police. The girl needed some time, she would later write on her blog. She was really conflicted, she didn't want her first book of poems—her name to be associated with any of that. She knew a thing or two about powerful men and she knew how memories get distorted, what sort of things people remember about you after time has passed: how a first book of poetry, especially a woman's first book of poetry, will be forgotten, but not a sex scandal, or at least not a woman's involvement in a sex scandal. She knew that a woman involved in such a mess might only ever be called "the crazy redhead," and never again by her actual name.

The student wanted a clean slate, she had a difficult past, stuff she wrote about in her poems, about envelopes full of cash and a specific choreography of an hour divided into five parts, the first part a greeting, the second part involving a man taking a shower, the third part her putting some music on and arranging herself on the bed.

Then there was also a story from her hometown, something about having to move schools because of a TA who got fired, a promising poet whose pupils wrote an open letter, and whose girlfriend also wrote something, a Facebook post with a picture of their newborn attached to it, a post that was hearted a few hundred times.

After two weeks, the girl officially withdrew her complaint but the stink was now in the air and it followed Professor Tak. Professor Tak who was appalled and disheartened, whose Studies in National Cinema: Polish Cinema course and Readings in Film and Television Theory had been immediately suspended. Professor Tak, who has given the Department of Humanities at the university so much, years of hard work that he could've given to another, more prestigious institution—he used to think that you couldn't find a more convivial and exciting cohort, he had always felt at home there. And to be betrayed in that way? Talks were cancelled, and so were lunches with colleagues. There were *dis*invitations and no one rallied for him, even when a malicious whisper campaign started—first, crude words from an anonymous account that were retweeted, a hashtag, #Saynototak. Eventually there was no point staying in that rotten, back-stabbing place. Quitting was not so much damage control but saving some pride, being a bigger man, his dignified lack of comment—that *was* a comment. The reputation would take a while to restore.

Around Christmas, the girl's poems were read out loud, drunkenly, in funny voices at The Demon. It was after the last call, after the bar closed to the public; the front lights were off so a small group of friends—*real* friends, not cowards—huddled in the back of the bar, around the low formica tables topped with lamps that cast a warm, reddish glow. One friend got up—almost knocking down one of the lamps—and squeaked, *It was winter and I was a soft landing/ For your desire/ My flower cold like snow.*

A Reddit thread about the incident at school had thirty-one comments, most of them anonymous. The votes were split half-and-half, into she-said-he-said. Somebody posted a broken link to an escort site. Another link to a student article about arts and depression written by the girl when she was still in high school. A screenshot of a post from her blog that was now private, for subscribers only. The screenshot also talked about depression. Her writing had clearly improved, but at the end of the article there were two lines that talked about watching a lover sleep, something about his "comforting snore." The screenshot post got three laughing-face emojis and two "lol" replies. On the same Reddit thread, somebody else posted a link to a *City Life* profile of Professor Tak where he discussed his new baby and where he referred to the baby's mother as "my roommate" and from that, there was a short side thread about how he was possibly a homosexual (which stung more than anything else that was said, even the stuff about him being a close talker and his sour-wine breath).

On the last day of 2014, the girl wrote something on Twitter. Then she deleted the Tweet. She dropped two of her courses.

In the new year, there was a new brilliant essay by Professor Tak, published in *The Atlantic*; an essay that talked about the history of Polish cinema during communism, the subversive early masterpiece of Krzysztof Kieślowski, *Camera Buff*, where the main character, an amateur filmmaker, exposes both the Party and his own duplicity.

In February, there was a film festival and a controversial talk on the subject of Pope John the II's involvement with the Solidarity movement, a strange yet plausible argument that the Pope had nothing to do with the end of communism, he was an accidental hero, perhaps was even an opportunist whose loyalties lay with the Catholic church and not with the oppressed. Although, Professor Tak argued at dinner parties, you could also say that the Catholics were the oppressed!

At the Polish embassy in Toronto, in March, there was a party celebrating fifty years of Polish diaspora in Canada and Professor Tak was invited to moderate the public talk between the former President and Solidarity movement leader, Lech Walesa, and the Minister of Canadian Heritage, Melanie Joly. Some people said Walesa was an odd choice for the public talk—having been famously and proudly working class and not particularly big on arts—but it was a momentous occasion, one that was written about in the national newspapers.

Then, in April, it was announced that a new degree would be offered at the Creative School at Ryerson that combined Film Theory and Jungian studies, specifically the idea that film can be psychoanalyzed in the way dreams can—the point is, there were going to be openings for new instructors. There was a lot of excitement over recruiting a roster of previously untapped, brilliant minds and luckily for the department, one previously tapped but now perfectly available brilliant mind. Professor Tak was courted, dined and wined; there was one special dinner that went late into the night, attended by the dean, a longtime fan of Tak's work, and the dean's wife who was ex-friends with Tak's ex-wife. This dinner happened near The Demon, where everyone had drinks afterwards, the atmosphere was electric, a promise in the air, bright eyes and talk of "subtext" and "the gaze," Professor Tak felt alive for the first time since *before* his baby was born, sad as he was to admit it. He found fatherhood tedious, he wrote in a piece commissioned for a Father's Day special in *The Toronto Star*. He was stuck in the monotony of feeding, burping, changing, napping, singing the same mind-numbing songs. On many nights—when he was particularly underslept—he would look at the infant and see something cartoonish, alien. He felt terrible about writing that but he didn't want to sugarcoat it. It was probably just stress, he was still processing the trauma of the near-cancelling at his former university.

After The Demon, after the nightcap—where he enjoyed a stimulating conversation about language, that source of life—oh, how he missed those kinds of conversations!—Professor Tak came home first thing in the morning to find his wife half-asleep in her office, still in her clothes, a pile of empty small bags of potato chips littering the floor underneath her feet. The baby was asleep in the bassinet. He didn't understand the scene, but it alarmed him, there was a sense of foreboding, which is a strange thing to think considering this was just... some mess, potato chips, how comical. It could've been her outfit, she wore a gown, her hair was piled up on the top of her head, her makeup was smeared and her face was swollen as if she'd been crying. Tears scared and bored him. He felt guilty about not waking her up, helping her to bed, but in that moment, he wrote in his notes, he had an intense urge to turn around, walk out of the house, never return, never look back. Did fathers also suffer from postpartum depression? Why wasn't *that* talked about? It was a difficult year. It was the only year where he felt truly helpless as if he himself was a baby, stuck, and with no choices but to wait till he could walk again.

The next year, there was a new book, a historical novel about the Warsaw Uprising, featuring a character named Janek, based on Professor Tak's father. The novel contained a poignant scene of Janek, unable to sleep at night from hunger, entertaining himself by thinking of preparation of all the dishes—*faworki, barszcz, mizeria, placki ziemniaczane, kaczka pieczona z jabłkami*—his mother used to make before the war. He had such a strong olfactory memory of those dishes as he'd meticulously recount the recipes, in the end he became able to genuinely taste the flavours and that's how he was able to stave away the hunger. The whole time, underneath his mattress, he collected and kept pieces of the rationed bread that he would later mold into chess figurines—he starved but he fed his soul. The novel won two awards, it was a bestseller, there were radio and television interviews, there were think pieces on hunger: physical, spiritual.

In May, the girl's first book of poetry came out. The author photo was a selfie. On her blog, she talked about selfies, claiming she had never sent a nude to a lover, to anyone for that matter—having worked as an escort made her acutely wary of indiscretions. She wrote that her livelihood used to depend on her being able to be discreet and subtle; it was against her core principles to share a photo like that; it would've been dangerous for her to do so while she worked and she retained her work ethic, her post sex-work career. She pointed out escort websites where women were photographed in sensual clothing or lingerie but almost always had their faces, tattoos, and nipples blurred. This aesthetic not only supported the ideas of seduction and mystery, but also safety.

She didn't know how the story of the nude photo came about. But there was gossip, so much gossip, even after a group of queer women came to her defense and published a poorly constructed argument in a feminist online magazine on women's self-portraits and female expression—a well-meaning take that only reinforced the rumour that there was, in fact, a nude selfie.

There were many reasons why the girl dropped out of school. She wrote about some of them on her blog. Then she shut down the blog. It was difficult to find her online, she had made all of her socials private. She changed her Facebook profile picture to one of a cat in a Christmas hat.

# TWENTY-SEVEN

LISA RUNS INTO Voytek and Margot at the corner store on my street. She describes their awkward meeting, Voytek trying to remember what it was that she did for a living—he knew it was something weird and sexy—until he finally capitulated and simply said, How is—your work?

It's a great gig, Lisa supposedly said and winked at Margot, Men pay me to abuse them.

And *she* was like a stunned horse. She has that horse vibe, right? Margaret? Marge? Mare! Whatsherface. She looks like a woman who's never worn lingerie if you know what I mean, Lisa says. She's spinning on one of the Lucite stools like a child.

I love what you've done with the joint, she says referring to me rearranging the furniture. I've moved all the boulders against the walls to open up the living room, arranged books by the colours of their spines like a girl on Instagram, and hung up white curtains instead of our usual maroon ones. I'm trying to see what the house will look like once it's truly mine, and I'm, again, trying to appease it. I haven't had the guts to get rid of some of Voytek's favourite items, his shelf with his semi-ironic collection of Polish tchotchkes, various Jesuses and folk art from the Tatra mountains. He hasn't been by in two weeks, last time was to pick up some sweaters and coats.

For once, the house is loud too, Lisa's Spotify list of electronic hits bringing the much-welcomed charge. I haven't been leaving much since Voytek's move to the nearby sublet, I've been too worried about running into him, or Margot. I have spotted her already, once in front of the house, strolling leisurely, stopping briefly and looking, zooming in on the front window, detecting me inside. Another time, I saw them from a distance while out on a run. I sprinted back home as if diving for safety. (It didn't look like they were broken up; they held hands.)

You think he's been setting you up? Very *War of the Roses*, or something. Or *Fatal Attraction*, I don't know, I haven't seen either but it's very, very toxic, Lisa says smiling and opens a second bottle of white. She has brought three bottles of Chablis and a box of stemmed glasses as a housewarming gift because I told her we were going to exorcize this place and celebrate me living in it even though there's a *For Sale* sign right by the front porch. My inbox overflows with Voytek's emails informing me about upcoming showings and his bizarre dispatches on Ruby, reminders of her routines and preferences as if I was a new babysitter and not her mother.

This morning, I woke up to a man installing the sign and immediately called Lisa. I didn't want to call, I worried you would show up and try to hit the man. So instead I'm having a party.

You hold the stem to keep the wine cold, otherwise your hand is going to warm it up, Lisa says, in a strange fake posh accent, like she's sophisticated about those things and like she won't just drink out of the bottle after the first glass. She tells me some gossip about the people we used to know, someone is getting married, a girl from our eating group who has a popular Instagram account where she flaunts her stomach and talks about loving her curves. She dances and jiggles and is often dressed in tiny bikinis or lingerie. I'm fascinated by all that flesh, and I'm fascinated by how happy she seems. Even her voice has changed, no longer monotonous and choked up like she's got a piece of cardboard stuck in her throat. Maybe it's all for a show, body positivity, curves, it's all trendy, after all. But when I remember her from group she never smiled like that, in fact, we nicknamed her "Happy" because of how depressed she always seemed.

Later, Lisa and I go upstairs to my bedroom and I open the closet. I am proud to show off how well I've parsed and organized my wardrobe. I love how the clothes hang on the rack with enough space between them to let them breathe. The one smart thing that my stupid mother has taught me was to buy well-made pieces that will last me forever. Invest in garments and expensive fabrics rather than cycle through trends like everyone else. I've inherited many of her pieces as well, a Pucci dress, a Chanel scarf and a purse, a Pierre Cardin coat and a few other items that survived the 70s and 80s. It was only after we moved here that my mother lost her resolve and started to buy cheap clothing, falling for pretty labels and incredible discounts in outlets. After years of communism, the abundance was overwhelming. My mother became a hoarder, lining up her closets with shmatas that would start to disintegrate after a few washes. The designer clothing was out of our immigrant financial range anyway, with purses that cost as much as monthly rent or a shitty car. But I stuck with her lessons regardless, working part-time jobs and setting aside money for things that would last.

There was another side to this, an incentive better than any other—I had to ensure I remained a certain size, specifically the size I was when I first got off the plane as a teenager. If I wanted to take advantage of my shopping sensibility I had to keep in mind that my classic Levis from Grade 10 would not tolerate another slice of pizza; at my age after all these years of dysfunction my body could betray me at any moment and balloon with hormones or water or stress. I had kept many of my fat clothes too, the only cheap clothing I wore after experimenting with Canadian food, and some of my more forgiving maternity pieces.

Right now I point to the box in the corner of the closet where my fat clothes live next to a bag filled with Valentine's Day bears from Voytek, and Lisa nods with recognition on reading "F.C."

Hilarious, she says. She pulls out a champagne-coloured dress from the front of the closet. She pulls the dress over her undershirt. She admires herself in the large closet door mirror, her red-dyed hair even brighter against the subdued shade.

I love these fucking doors, she says and removes the undershirt, her expression full of awe as she holds her breasts up, thumbs pinching the nipples to make them harder under the silk. She sticks her tongue out and moves her hips side to side, to the beat of the music blasting from downstairs. She doesn't look back at me, she knows I'm watching her. I whistle weakly and she laughs.

The doors are all sliding mirrors, something Voytek insisted on installing when I balked at making any more home movies. If he couldn't film it, then let him at least watch, he complained. Once he installed them, I'd often catch him staring at himself as he'd go at me from behind. He would instantly avert his eyes if he noticed me noticing and would gently push my head back into the pillow, which I used to tell myself was in the spirit of dominance, not because he couldn't handle another human being witnessing his sweaty ugliness and vulnerability. The homemade movies were like that too, a lot of body shots and a chin and hair and things going in and out but never a full face looking back.

Lisa's little performance for me is more genuine fun than this room has seen ever since I've moved here and even after we installed the mirrored doors. I've never brought you upstairs to this bedroom because I couldn't stand the idea of Voytek's ghost being here with us. I worried, also, that he would sense you here. But it's different with Lisa, we are not in love and this is just a game.

I tell her to grab a few more dresses and she does, piles them up on the bed before stepping out of her jeans and panties and trying them on. I sit in the corner on the little kneeling bench that has always reminded me of the same one I used to pray on when I went to church. I've never used it to pray here, Voytek got it at an auction and immediately employed it as sex furniture, directing me to take various positions on it as he'd try to make it more than it was, which was burdensome and put-on. In those first months I kneeled or sat with my legs spread open and moaned or stayed quiet when ordered to do so. I posed pregnant too, my belly between my legs, obscuring my pubic area, like a giant balloon with a strained belly button and massive nipples. Eventually, the kneeling bench became every other bedroom chair with robes and towels piling up on it, and, later, we desexualized it definitively with Ruby's receiving blankets and clean cloth diapers.

I sit on it and lean my head against the wooden side, sniff its deep, dark corner, try to inhale something beyond its smell, God and sex. I wonder what sort of desperate prayers it holds, if anyone's ever prayed for a life to not end or, more perversely, for a life *to* end, on it.

Lisa finally settles on a black, tight bandage dress I got from a sample sale, not a well-known designer but a beautiful size 4 that she takes great pleasure squeezing into. The whole time I'm watching her body to see how it compares to mine when I squeeze into the same dress—is there a bulge or a fold that will pop out in a spot where it doesn't pop out on me? Lisa pinches herself around the waist as if trying to please me with some flesh she will magically cajole out of her fatless body and I tell her to stop.

We go downstairs and drink wine and dance to house music. I spent part of my twenties in various warehouses and secret loft apartments with boys in black T-shirts, dancing to techno. But techno is too utilitarian, too harsh so it's soft, bouncy *house* music for the house. I imagine the house is happy. And I am drunk. Getting drunk. Sometimes when I drink, I enter a psychedelic realm, a place where it is confirmed magical things happen—things that I suspect are happening when I'm sober too but that I have no access to, limited by my sobriety. I can sense a conversation between the house and Monster, two consciousnesses that exist beyond my reality but that rule my life. Their roles are reversed; in this conversation Monster is a friendly hostess telling the neurotic shy guest, the house, to be patient and relax and the house closes its eyes and shakes its head and loosens up its shoulders and now it's a whole dance party, it, me, Monster, and Lisa like an exclamation mark in my bandage dress and the red tips of her hair and some yellow too—she has wrapped the yellow silk scarf around her neck, gifted to me from Voytek, from Paris. She shakes her head and she bounces, pulls me in for a twirly hug, she grinds her ass into me, she wraps the scarf around my shoulders and shimmies me in it, she shrieks and with ragged breath tells me bits about her clients, funny fetishes she has to indulge, a guy who asks her to dress like a sixteen-year-old boy, a guy who pays her to watch him jerk off onto his wife's sweater, a guy who pays her to stay with him overnight ($2,200) and read *Winnie the Pooh* to him while wearing a housecoat that reminds him of his mother's housecoat. There's even a guy who has asked her to feed him special caviar and the way she says *caviar* doesn't sound like she means fish roe.

I ask her to channel *me* with *you* and she unconvincingly takes my face in her hands, and I pull her in closer for a kiss while holding her by the neck. I am you. I push her back onto the daybed, giggling, I feel predatory as I climb on top of her. We make out for a couple of minutes, sloppily, and then we laugh about it and drink some more. I am not a very convincing *you*, not to myself although Lisa moans once in a way that tells me she's genuinely getting aroused. But I have no ideas as to where to take this next. (I've never been very good at girls. I have never wanted to penetrate them. I've gone down on girls, on Lisa too, but it was all performative and uninspired. The only thing I liked about the whole business was making a girl come because being a girl myself I liked to serve and please. Yet, this was not about my own ego the way it is with some men who claim they love eating pussy just for the sake of it. Many do not, their eating pussy is about being owed one; I've never been with a man who'd not try to insert his cock immediately following my orgasm. And that was perfectly fine, I wouldn't know what to do with a man who did it selflessly, I'd be suspicious of him.)

My hands stay above Lisa's waist, I am not really *you*, you'd have her-me spread and open and writhing underneath by now.

I ask if we could switch, if *she* could channel *you* now. She says breathlessly, Yes yes.

We pause our frantic rolling around and stare at each other long enough to let the energies switch between us until she nods. Ready?

Yes, I say.

She moves her face closer and grabs a handful of my hair, even yanking some of it out. I press my lips to hers and whisper, Daddy, And she bites me, her eyes never leaving mine.

I miss you, I tell her and I mean *you*.

She says, I miss you too, baby. Please don't cry.

This is perfect, I think but then she ruins it by saying, Should we call him? And when I say no, she pretends to pout, and pushes me away.

Baby, I say.

Stop it. You're the baby, She swipes her hair into a messy bun. She's red in the face and her eyes sparkle. She shakes her head. And then in a split moment her eyes seem to darken and she falls back onto the pillows and says, You've always been so bad at sharing. So bad. Your real thoughts, sharing your food, sharing your pills…

She sounds exasperated and I don't know what she's on about but I sit still and wait—I know I'm waiting for *something*, I can feel the secret percolating right under her surface, waiting to burst out. It's not me who's bad at sharing my real thoughts, it's her. Or we're both bad at it but she's worse than me. Lisa is full of shit, with her inconsistent stories, secrets, unfinished business and mysterious men that accompany her to parties who might or might not be clients. Some are introduced as boyfriends, some are not. I've chalked up Lisa's secrecy partly to her affinity for substances—her trying to piece together various blackouts—but there's also her natural shade of untrustworthiness and the side where she plays a character in her life, a mysterious siren with a dark, albeit fabricated past, her fake rough upbringing. In group she once shared a story of parental neglect, of staying under her grandparents' care and eating out of cans. Later, she told me she was bored in the session and felt like she had to entertain her audience. She has admitted to being jealous of my immigrant lore. I've often wondered if she was forgetting what was real and what wasn't, the way some of us do when we get ourselves so deep into the mire of lies that it's easier to just keep drowning. Yet, I love her the way I've always loved imperfect people. Perhaps she could tell I would love her less if I knew she was empty and without a good story.

My father once told me there were three tests for real, deep friendship: One, taking a three-day-long road trip together.

Two, having a celebratory final drink in the town square while the Nazis invade and bomb the town. Three, calling up a friend in the middle of the night to help you get rid of a body, no questions asked. Lisa might go on the road trip if I was the one driving and there were enough pills, and she would probably drink during the Nazi bombing, but most likely inside a panzer.

Before she spills her big secret, I already know. I don't know if I've always known but I must've sensed some of it or Monster has because it is quiet inside me, lulled by my friend's little-girl voice.

As she talks, I lie down opposite of her, sink into the pile of pillows, and close my eyes, trying to remember the event she's describing. We were at some gala where she was my plus-one and I was my husband's wife. My husband had a new book about the Warsaw Uprising out that was in the running for one of those national contests only the elderly care about. He was already a rock star professor, an uncancelled one, whose publicist told me drunkenly she had a crush on me; she giggled that she Googled pictures of me. She said she was more into girls anyway. I nodded, she touched my cheek, sloshed away.

Later on, at the same party, the publicist said to my husband, Hold my phone and he did and there on the screen was her naked selfie. The mythical set-up I've heard versions of was happening right there and then. I didn't see but Lisa took me aside and said, I thought you'd like to know. She had been standing next to my husband and she glimpsed the screen. She looked out for me like that. She said Voytek handed the phone back to the young woman without saying anything but Lisa noticed his eye twitching uncontrollably.

I felt nothing. It was nothing, I didn't get upset, I was tired from the baby at home and from my husband being famous and I wanted to go lie down and take off my scratchy dress and the heels that hurt my feet. I ordered an Uber and stood outside smoking, Lisa unusually quiet with a dark cloud hanging over her. It was obvious she didn't want to leave the party. It was all new to her, the glamour of academia and publishing, the sweaty cheese and grapes and wine in plastic glasses and men in rumpled suits and women with kooky necklaces, the young, pretty publicists who—Voytek joked—were not pretty enough to be publicists of real celebrities. I had brought her to keep me company and she had enjoyed herself; I watched her all night stumbling around happily in a gown, laughing with her head thrown back, the men's eyes on her. Later, I spotted her in a dark corner flirting with a young author whose book described his childhood in a Balkan country.

When the car arrived, I told her in the most upbeat voice I could muster that she must stay, and she said, You sure, you sure? And I said I'm sure, I'm sure, and we hugged desperately, dramatically, and Lisa pretend-cried, Please ring me when you get home sweetheart, or I'll be worried sick, she sniffled in a mock-proper-lady tone, and then we laughed and I felt generous about letting her stay.

It was only that one time, it was nothing, just being drunk, Lisa says now after telling me about the rest of the night, Voytek confessing he had always wanted to be paraded on a leash—might as well be paraded on a leash, he allegedly told her, referring to me.

And you know how I feel about sharing. Or owning people. I mean outside of my job, you shouldn't have those kinds of... claims on real human beings, you know that. I was drunk. And I felt terrible for him. I mean, I know he's full of it. And I even thought of asking you first, like maybe even getting your permission, but how? I knew he was a piece of shit to you but I also thought I was doing a good deed. It just happened, Lisa says about sleeping with Voytek and I stop myself from asking if a leash was involved.

So a good deed?

It wasn't about him.

Was it about me?

It wasn't about you or him. It was just a mistake. He reminded me of my clients, he sounded so pathetic. I was like turned off but I don't know, also turned on. But not for him, just for having that power over him? I think? He's pathetic, Yoveeta. He's a pathetic, old man, Lisa says, doing a similar thing to what the couples therapist was doing which is making me want to defend Voytek—or maybe my choices of men, or I don't know what because I don't know what I should want here. I am angry so I look around for something to throw and smash but there's nothing tangible nearby except for the too-large pillows but also the yellow silk scarf, hanging over the daybed's railing like a tongue. I grab the scarf and I throw it with great force but it pauses mid-air once I throw it; it unfolds and flows, slowly to finally land gently and majestically on the ground. And this is the opposite effect I wanted, it is so ridiculous that all I can do is burst out laughing at this display and Lisa starts laughing too and then we're folding over our non-bellies, our messy hair, over the pile of pillows and thighs and we're hugging each other and it's fine.

In the spirit of our outburst, I pull her up with me and we launch off the bed. We run outside to the front porch. The *For Sale* sign is jammed into the small patch of dirt where my gardening efforts have never flourished because of too much shade. It's a perfect place for the sign, obnoxiously right in front of the house, the thick wooden column with the threatening announcement and the name of the agent printed on the board that starts swinging lightly, back and forth as soon as I kick it for the first time. I catch a glimpse, a shape, a shadow moving within shadows, the bent arrow of a coyote's body. I shake my head, look again and it's gone. I'm wearing ballet flats and my foot and ankle hurt from the impact but it doesn't matter, I am fueled by all my angry energy that courses through me from the tip of my head, all the way down to my toes. Lisa runs back inside and runs back out with her sneakers on, and we start kicking the thing back and forth and as it loosens more, we throw ourselves against it and push it with our starved bodies, swing hard till it finally falls over. There's a big ugly hole in the ground, the longer, flat pieces of stone around it remind me of a picked fresh scab and it's an apt analogy since this feels like a minor but violent medical procedure, the kind you can get to extract a big splinter—or a *For Sale* sign from your house's tongue.

I wrap my arm around Lisa's shoulder and we both rest against each other briefly, breathing heavily, winded from all the excitement. I'm suddenly in a really good mood, not just drunk but genuinely content. Adrenaline. Lisa elbows me gently.

I look over and it's my Italian neighbour staring at us, her mouth open in an exaggerated, dramatic fashion, bushy eyebrow knotted in disgust, hands wrapped around a broomstick she seems prepared to swing at us. I can hear her son whining from behind the door, unintelligible begging sounds and banging like a big wild animal trying to get out.

Hey Sofia, how's it going? I say cheerfully and give her a big wink. I've never addressed her other than "Mrs. Stacielli" having grown up with the Euro trappings of having to respect your elders.

She closes her eyes and mutters something to herself, probably an ancient curse that will turn me and Lisa into foxes.

Gimme a hand will you? Lisa says and tries to lift the sign to no avail.

Why? Just leave it there, I say and she shrugs sure and I watch her kick it hard in frustration and shriek, *Motherfucker, my toe!*

Lisa.

Is everything okay? A woman's indignant voice from the sidewalk interrupts our special moment and I lift my hand and wave at her, a woman with a stroller, whose features I can't quite make out in the dim streetlight, Yes, all good, everything is great!

The woman waves back, unsurely. I wave again. She dislodges, pushes the stroller, looking back once, twice.

To my right, the neighbour is now whisper-shouting at the son-animal behind the door but the banging and the whining only gets louder so she too must cut short her entertainment for the night. She drops the broom. There's some wrestling with the doorknob and once she twists it open she pushes at it with her large body overpowering the small man on the other side. The door bangs against the wall, there's real shouting now, and more whining and then the door slams shut and he wails.

They're usually very sweet, I say and Lisa giggles, wincing a bit as she examines her foot out of the sneaker now.

Mission accomplished, I guess, I say. Sorry about your foot.

It's fine. I just thought that we should maybe, like hide it, you know, so it doesn't exist? But that's obviously as crazy as kicking it in the first place. It's all crazy, she sighs softly nodding at the defeated sign on the ground. You need a better plan, like an actual plan, She's looking at me sheepishly now, her voice wavering. She probably figured out that she's lucky, she can't believe her luck, I'm such an instantly forgiving friend. But it's not that I am. And it's not even that it's easier to forgive—her, Voytek—now that I have you. It was just a pity fuck, which irritates me more than any of it, that someone pities the man I don't want. Anyway, it's not that I'm a forgiving person or I am blinded by love. It's not that. I just suddenly don't care. And this realization makes me happier than kicking the sign.

# TWENTY-EIGHT

THE SIGN IS back in its old spot the next evening. Earlier, I left to get Ruby and we spent a whole afternoon in a park and ate at Wendy's instead of coming home for dinner. Ruby had a Kid's meal with a frosty. I bought a salad, GREEN-coded, of course, without a dressing. I took a sip of her frosty, fifty calories of cold liquid sugar, faintly flavoured with chocolate. I sloshed it in my mouth and then I spat it out into my cup of water. I let her watch a show on her iPad about talking dogs, to kill more time. I wedged myself into the corner of our plastic booth and texted with you about a new trend on TikTok of people ranting about their worst exes. When a sufficient amount of time had passed, and Ruby's eyelids became too heavy to keep blinking her sleep away, we left and walked back a different route, trying to avoid my husband and Margot, a large loop that took us through tight, graffitied alleys, "a nice ventuwe," as Ruby called it.

I kick the sign, back in its place, but it doesn't budge. Ruby stirs in her stroller. As soon as I'm inside, my phone rings.

I see you're home, Voytek says. His voice is soft and gentle, the same cajoling voice he'd use when he'd tell me I was delusional and needed to get help, the same voice he used when we first started sleeping together and he would ask me to let him do things to my body, *put this on, give me your wrists, turn around, show me how wet you are.* This is a voice that makes me forget that this man wants to destroy me. It's a trap, but I'm so tired. Tired of walking, tired of hiding, tired of being in-between. My body reacts to the voice the way it reacts to the voice—my muscles relaxing despite themselves, my pussy throbbing—and something inside me whines, *You can tell him anything so tell him everything, beg him, talk to him.*

How do you know I'm home? I say, stupidly. I don't know if he can see the house from his sublet but probably because how else? Or maybe he installed cameras while he put the sign back in the ground. I wouldn't put it past him.

I was in an Uber. I saw you walking by with the stroller. It's late. I don't think this is good for Ruby. Children need routine.

Ruby is fine. This is our routine.

(She's fine. We're fine.)

I can always take her more if you need a break, he says, as if I was falling drunk in the streets with the toddler in tow, like his old alcoholic memoirist friend.

It was disturbing to see the sign, he says. Violent. Are you feeling violent?

I am feeling fucking violent and you have no idea just how violent, I think. Instead, I say, We're not selling the house. I didn't see the reason for the sign.

He sighs, You can't do that. That's not going to change anything. I don't want to have to be firm. I want *you* to be well. I want *me* to be well. I want *all of us*—I still have love for you.

This is good to hear. I know he does—he's not someone who lets go easily of his things and I am his biggest, most broken thing of all—but him saying it is a reassurance. It means I still have him, or a part of him. And I really need whatever I have of him, for now. I am not done yet.

Please just don't sell the house, just let me live, I try weakly. (I mean let me live in the house but I also just mean let me live.

Just let me.) I say it only to say it *one last time*, feeling I must stamp this moment.

He sighs again, Misiaczku, we have to stop this nonsense. This isn't good for you. Or for me, or for Ruby. It's not going to end well.

It's not going to end well, I think but say nothing. Too late now.

Or you could just let go. We could find you a nice apartment, a condo. Two bedrooms—

Who's "we?" You and Margot? She's gonna find me a place now too?

More sighing, Please, please, please stop with this jealousy.

This is another one of Voytek's little tactics, calling me jealous as if I indeed were one of those women who is unhinged, who installs spyware on phones, who follows her man in a car for no reason, who screams if the man says something about a celebrity's perfect ass, who is suspicious even of his elderly receptionist. The kind of woman who wants him so badly that she is pathological about her claimed territory, who is so possessive she cannot help herself but bring up all of her delusions about other women every chance she gets.

I've often wondered what I would be like After Voytek, if I'd still make comments that showcase my insecurity—or if this so-called jealousy is only a consequence of my husband's indiscretions, not my inherent flaw. I have never had a chance to test it because until you, I haven't loved anyone as much as I once loved him. I am excited to find out what I would—*will* be like.

Well whoever "we" are, I'm not interested, I say.

Kochanie. I don't want to fight with you. How's Ruby? Voytek says. He manages to soften his voice again, even more now, on a brink of a lisp. Like he needs to placate me because I'm not only unpredictable but also maybe I shouldn't be trusted with my daughter.

Asleep in her stroller. We had a long walk. *Kochanie*?

Where did you girls go?

Are you trying to soften me up?

Not everything is a conspiracy, Yoveetka. Might I send you some listings? I know you're running out of money, how much longer—Please. I only want to help. You should take her out of the stroller, she needs to be in her bed.

I know he knows I'm running out of money because I had to submit all of my financial records to his lawyer. He is also running out of money according to his financial records, except he isn't. Or at least his sister isn't. Or his parents who have sent him to a private school. His parents who have bought this house. He's always been filing his taxes as if he's on the brink of poverty, an academic and an author who has never experienced luxury other than that offered by his generous friends with places and yachts and for a longer time, his first wife who was the daughter of an English judge.

You don't want to hel—I lower my voice, backtrack, suddenly aware of Monster fully awake inside me. (*I forgot*, I tell it and it pings back that it knows I forgot but it is here to remind me that I need to slow down—*slow down and lure, lure this man* like the Slavic rusalkas, the water lake nymphs drowning unsuspecting men who fall under their spell, die for a promise of beauty.)

I finish off softly: I don't want to fight with you either.

Then let's not. Do you want me to call you back so you can finish the bedtime?

Just leave it alone, please, I say. The bedtime is finished. Anything else?

No. Yes. Please put our daughter to bed.

I notice that I'm sweating. I don't know how much longer I can manage to not hang up on him. Or scream. So I think of you, nothing specific, just the way you look at me when we fuck, intently, with love. Then I think about how you kiss me, your hands palming my face.

Voytek says something about his sister finding a condo building with new units in an affordable range. Gotta get a jump on that, they won't last long. The market is shit. We're only getting older. Even Ruby is getting older. No one cares about the arts anymore. I am talking. Maybe we can all live in the mountains one day like we've always planned. I am still talking. Or who knows? Even go back to Poland!

I don't retain everything that he says, I stop interrupting and mostly lose him for good once he starts going on about having to organize a memorial for an old classmate who wrote an important book on intelligentsia mass shootings during World War II, a man I recall only by the peculiar black and white photographs he had in his one-room apartment where we had a dinner party at a foldout table. They were photographs of teenage boys posing awkwardly in frilly nighties, sheer robes or boa feathers, silly and forced fetish stuff. I'd bring up the photographs to stop this boring tangent but he is full on monologuing now and I think how I wish they'd call him again to do those TV spots from back when there was much better arts coverage, when it was par for the course to always wheel out one pasty, grey-haired European male to opine about things in some dusty TV studio with a fake bookshelf in the back. But they don't have those shows any more, no one debates, unless you consider twenty-somethings in bikinis debating things like the *vibes, connections* and *energies* of their fellow contestants on one of those simpletons-fucking reality TV shows. TV is dead. *Intellectual discourse is dead*—I don't know who says this, maybe Voytek, it sounds like a sentence he'd say, he keeps talking and I keep not interrupting. Maybe Voytek could get a Twitter account or a YouTube channel where he could be a controversially outdated thinker, but technology baffles him and besides, they already have much more controversially outdated thinkers with huge incel followings occupying that space. I should blame television being dead, and the media and society for his straying. It is clear all this man wants is to be listened to, and now only a woman can give him that and one woman is not enough for a man of his intellect, I certainly wasn't enough.

After he's done talking he says, I have to go, as if I was the one keeping him. I am so exhausted that I have no energy to wake Ruby up and give her a bath and put her in bed. She looks content in her stroller, her rosebud mouth half-open, her breath milky and sweet. I remove her jacket and cover her with it. I wheel the stroller into my office where I lie down on the daybed where you and I first made love and I dream about the house turning into a boat and saving us from a storm.

# TWENTY-NINE

SEX IS A life force, a physical act that is spiritual with its power of creation and destruction.

The geisha Saba Abe killed her lover by strangling him with her obi. She kept his severed penis in the folds of her kimono for days, a gruesome lover's memento. But before that, they spent a sweaty weekend barely separating for food or sleep, their genitals almost permanently reattached. Not attached because they were two parts of one in another universe and their earthly union made them whole. Just like you and me. The other geishas who brought food complained about the smell of fucking, but some were happy to watch the lovers together.

When you open the door bleary from lack of sleep or something else I feel it instantly, that draw, a pull that I feel whenever I'm near you but that I forget when we're apart, that electric field specific only to us.

*Hey baby*, I think and I smile at you and you close your eyes and take a deep breath and open the door wider to let me in. It's like you don't have a choice. I sympathize but I also don't have a choice.

I'm not claiming to understand anything beyond rudimentary physics but the definition of the force of attraction is any type of force that brings objects together even if those objects are not near each other. The first force is the gravitational one,

"What goes up must come down." The second is an electric force and this is the one I believe is at work with us, where one of us has lost too many electrons (you) after becoming positively charged and the other has gained too many electrons (me, Monster) and becomes negatively charged. The pull is instant when two objects of opposite charge are in close proximity, and the electrical force causes these objects to come together. The third force that may cause attraction is the magnetic force—a north magnetic pole is brought into close proximity to a south magnetic force, we stick.

What? you say as I blather on about physics, and you sit down on the only clear surface, an office chair pushed against the wall.

I look around. What happened to your place? There's a rust-stained blanket half-thrown up on the loveseat littered with fast-food wrappers. The big chair has a mass of cables wedged in its crevices. There's a pile of clothes on the ground—laundry, clean or dirty, who knows? The glass coffee table bears dusty white traces of whatever has been going up your nose. I count three empty baggies but there's a little shiny white rock in a glass ashtray and there's a tiny folded square that looks untouched. There are glasses with various brown liquids, and one wine glass stained purple with residue. Empty cigarette packs and another glass ashtray full. Two empty plastic pop cups.

What is this?

You look momentarily puzzled—as if you have no idea—and run your hand through your hair. Then you look at me, I've missed you. I didn't think you were coming today.

Okay, I say. Okay. What happened?

I've been thinking. Then I fell apart.

I take in all this information, what is spoken and what isn't. I don't need words but I ask for words, I ask for more because I should. I set down my bag. I don't know what I was expecting, coming this early to surprise you but not this. I suppose I wanted to catch you. Now that I've caught you, I understand that you don't know how strong you are and I still have to show you. I *need* you.

We stare at each other without talking. Even Monster is still. Then I watch you open the little folded square, tap some of the powder onto the glass surface of the coffee table. You've found one clean spot. You take out a credit card, break the powder in uninspired taps, make two thin lines. You take a straw and put it against your nostril. I watch you.

So is this like a nervous breakdown?

You look up sniffing loudly, No. I don't know.

Are you okay?

I'm not. I'm fine.

I'm sorry.

It's fine. I just need for something to happen.

I'm going to lose the house. Something *is* happening. Isn't that enough for you?

I don't want you to lose your house. I want you to be happy.

I'm not happy. But I'll be okay. In Polish, we don't say, "I like it," or "this is good." We say, "*może być,*" which means "this can be." As in, I give my permission for the continued existence of this here thing.

Jesus, you sigh, and bend over the glass coffee table and chop the lines one more time, make them into two more even rows. This is not good for good girls, it's bad stuff. You gesture at the powder with the straw, press your finger against your nostril as you inhale.

Oh get fucked. What is it?

Daddy's medicine, you say and inhale the second line. It's 8 a.m. It's too early or too late to fall apart.

I have no idea what to do, how to show you. I walk up to you and then kneel down and lay my head on your knees, the way

I used to in those first, starry-eyed days we spent together. You would scratch my scalp, run your fingers through my hair. And you do it now but your hand shakes, it's a performance you're putting on for me. I'm uncomfortable on the floor but I don't move, I have to rescue you because I *need* you.

I get off my knees, and Monster rises within me. Your eyes are unfocused, dead inside. I need to shake you up. I gesture for you to get up and you do, you stand motionless witnessing this, dead inside or not, I need you to *see*. I need you to see that I am hungry or Monster is. I've been starving it, I wanted to know what will happen, and now, finally, I know, feel something shedding from within, a witch, a dragon, an egg, a phoenix, or none of these but yet some alien creature that's never been seen before, wet, silver-lavender. The seven screws in my broken clavicle have melded with my bones or melted into them. I am all light and titanium. A dragon! And an afterbirth of scales and sinew, and thighs bathed in blood and juice, hair in the trees and howling wind and early morning mountain fog and the ocean and all the fish. I am delirious, so many smells, flowers in the middle of a June or July kind of night, jasmine, every hair on my body electrified.

You blink, your amber eyes, two rocks to create a spark, start a fire. Then it's here. Your lips on mine feel charged and yet soft, a current being passed back and forth as your tongue explores the inside of my mouth, our mouths together again, sucking into each other.

You move closer and I press myself against you and Monster opens its dragon wings, unfurls and wraps them around my arms that I wrap around your shoulders, and we're carried all the way to the ceiling, or at least it feels that way when you pick me up and I coil around your waist, still kissing you, drinking you and letting you drink me back. I am a life-giver, I am giving you my life. You are giving me yours, I feel it pulsing in your tongue, sneaking down my throat, my empty stomach.

You carry me to your bedroom and you lie me on the bed and undress me. You are shaking all over. I don't know how long you've been up; I can feel the fragile junky energy emanating from you. I caress your arms as you remove my dress. I massage your head as you pull my panties down. I keep touching you, never stopping, never not connecting with you, my hunger full-blown, my insides pulsating and waiting for everything you're about to give me.

There's a large, yellow envelope on the bedside table and as you lower your head to shakily lick me between my legs, I reach for it and reach inside it and pull out the soft leather belt I knew would be there.

I am not nervous.

I feel you suck gently on my clit, little powerful pulls, the pressure is almost too much, almost too distracting but I will not be distracted; now that I am here, it seems as if I'm just following steps I'd learned long ago, the steps I've been reciting in my sleep and while awake, unaware of having been reciting them but in this moment I follow one, two, three, the belt is around your neck. You look up briefly and in the semi-darkness our eyes meet, yours no longer dead but full of fire; to cool off, you dive back into my sea, and you keep on sucking and I slowly move my hands away from each other, I unbend my elbows, I stretch—you lose your rhythm, your tongue touching, your mouth trying to find the source again—and I stretch my arms wider and wider, I open my legs wider too, pull on the ends of the belt to mash your face into me, your fuel is whatever powder is helping to make this happen, baby. I love you, and you agree that I love you and you love me too, you show me. I rise higher and higher, my mountain, my sea, and this is the one way we can be together without a home, this is the only way I can satiate Monster and myself; the three of us are one, no more misunderstandings, no more filling my holes with the wrong dicks and carbs, no more plugging your holes with drugs or finding more holes in empty, inhospitable pussies. As I pull and pull—and you let me, you are complicit, you understand; none of this would be possible without you letting me—you start to cough and shake and twitch, you move your mouth away just in time for me to finally fall over the edge, explode all into myself, it's a flutter and violent bucking and my thighs clamp around your head as I orgasm right into you.

But maybe it was more grotesque than that, uglier than I'm remembering. It takes almost five minutes for an adult to choke to death—I let you go with a minute to spare. What did you imagine before step one, when the soft leather touched the skin of your neck? Did you picture your future, back at your dirty glass table, or dying in your cubicle stuck on some meaningless deadline, maybe eating the office birthday cake forever with co-workers you don't even like, some blurry woman at home, a dental hygienist, someone who does teeth, or maybe real estate, someone who is not me who fights with you over taking the recycling out or who was going to call the landlord about the broken toilet, who is sarcastic about the toilet seat, it must've been you who left it up since you're the only one with the trained peepee, or not trained enough, etcetera? Or did you picture me and my ultimatum? Or was it none of that?

I fall asleep next to you and I drape your heavy arm around my concave belly. I dream of nothing. When I wake up, the day is fighting its way into the bedroom, the strong afternoon sun filtering through the blinds, slicing our bodies into light and dark.

I feel full. I truly love you.

I never understood what people meant when they said it was all that we needed, what was I not getting, why couldn't I get it, why was I tired, I was tired of hearing love love love.

I know I've experienced it. With friends, with family, with men, with my daughter; I fell in love with paintings and authors, and drugs and yes, definitely food. But the cult of love? How could love just on its own make everything better? Didn't you need the object of it to be there to fulfil you? How could love itself give you joy? Didn't it have to be reciprocal?

I've been in pain over loving men, I've debased myself, destroyed my days and my solar system, removed my sleep, focused solely on getting love back, on trying to stir desire, on being wanted, admired, and I made myself tragically unhappy.

But now that we're here, and now that I'm thinking about it, I know that my mistake was believing that it was transactional, that it needed to be returned. It doesn't. The gift is in me loving you, in being capable of loving this deeply and ultimately, this gift is freedom. For the first time in my life, my contentment is not conditional; my contentment is that I am able to feel. And your sacrifice last night is the ultimate gift, you would do anything for me indeed and I will never doubt you.

Yoveeta? Your sleepy voice breaks through.

You're alive! I giggle and you giggle back but right away you start to cough and cough and you cannot stop. Your forehead is clammy when you're done.

I get up to get you some water. Back in the living room I have to look at your nervous breakdown again so instead of getting you water right away, I grab a garbage bag from underneath the sink and start filling it with all the trash, empty bottles and containers. I get some paper towels and a cleaning spray and scrub the table, the white powder sticking to the wet towel.

What are you doing? you rasp from the bedroom, Where's that water?

I'm cleaning up your mess.

Okay, you say and that's it. You can hear me spray and wipe, so for a moment I worry you'll come running and start losing your shit over "Daddy's medicine" which is no longer possible to consume, but you don't. I've given you a lot of tests over the past few days and you're passing every single one. It's almost your turn and you can ask anything of me, I promise you. We will start with this book, you can ask me to destroy it, of course, or to publish it—however you want to celebrate our love, privately or for all to see. I'm fine with either.

Once I'm done cleaning, I attend to you, first with the water, later with my mouth; our day is long, warm inside, under blankets, stretched, unrushed, the softest day we've had so far. There's an angry, red ring around your neck and I gently massage some vaseline into it, as you hang your head, waiting patiently, until I'm done. My fingers remember the diaper rashes and delicate hurts of my daughter's first months, how I had to relearn to touch skin that could only be touched with devotion and nothing else. That's how I touch you.

You stare at me, your wolfish eyes: amber and black and something of the water, like its depth if that was a colour, you hold me by my hips after I climb on top of you, and look down at you; you look like a boy, wide sensual lips, your curated six-o'clock-shadow that I know you trim every three days. I grind my pelvis into yours, deep enough it hurts a little, but I want, need you that deeply. I get out of my head, send myself all the way down my throat, my chest, my stomach, till I reach the tender walls wrapping around you, all movement and charge. You bounce me up and down, fast, you're lost in fucking, too fast for me to catch up, ride this wave out with you, your hips pistoning into me with that same desperation you contained in your words. You grip me harder. I urge you to let go, to come for me, I bear down and feel you expand even more, I am so attuned to you that I swear that as you climax I can feel you ejaculate, and as you do my uterus contracts once, twice, a fist opening and closing, trembling, and suddenly I'm tumbling over into my own surprise orgasm. I collapse on top of you and you wrap your big arms around me, head on your chest, listen to your fast thumps, I close my eyes and see red rapids rushing, so much blood, so sweet and rich.

And I grab back at you, grab the back of your head, dive my tongue right in, clean out your insides, your darkness, your sadness, the diamond that's turned back into coal, your pineal gland, your soul. A praying mantis bites the head off the male and he still copulates with her, headless. Once he's done, she eats him. I am that, an insect eating you from the inside, a predator, a parasite, all those things men have called me, jokingly and not.

Afterwards, we talk again, keep bridging all that time we've missed. You tell me about your father's violence, your first fear. You tell me about that girl who used to cut herself, how she carved your name on the inside of her thigh and how that scared you and turned you off. You keep touching your neck as you talk and I wonder if you can feel the beginning of the scales multiplying underneath your skin. I don't want to bring it up yet, I wait for you to discover it on your own.

You say about your sad girl, But now I don't know why that scared me so much. I wish I had stayed. I could tell she could tell that she was scaring me when she started talking about it. She told me about one Christmas when she had a big fight with her old boyfriend and how she just sliced into her hand when she was preparing a salad, on purpose...and she felt calm. She said she didn't have those urges often and she had it under control but it made her excited and she felt like I was the only person who would understand. I didn't understand at all. I didn't know what she wanted me to do. Tell her it was fine? Yell at her? Help her? We were driving in this terrible snow storm, it was already so tense. I remember I could barely see the road. There were no exits for some ridiculous amount of time. And I wanted to warn her about me, that I *was* scared and not as open-minded as she thought but she had already started talking and I could tell that she could sense that right away and thought she said too much already and then she was like, fuck it now, might as well tell him everything. I wanted to shout at her. Just to tell her to shut up. But I was so worried that if I started shouting, I would lose my focus, it was really truly fucked outside, these large trucks swishing by. And she kept talking and talking and then it was too late. I wanted to just get away from her, that's all I could think about.

I picture this girl in the passenger seat saying things faster and faster and more hysterically, trying to make it sound normal and then sensing your tension and then her voice quivering, her gesturing with her small hands. Maybe she's crying. And you can't comfort her, because with each second that passes you're growing more repulsed with her.

I don't know why I thought of that, you say once you're finished. You say it was worse than a car crash, what happened that night. You could've prevented it, but only by telling her to hide that monstrous part of herself from you.

I know why you thought of that story, of course. You're letting me show you *my* monstrous side and you're still here—even better, you want to see even more. And you will.

We stay in our den for the rest of the night, nursing each other and fucking each other till we are all better or at least well enough to part again.

# THIRTY

I WALK AROUND the house and touch the walls, mindful, slow strokes as if it was you, your skin. I kneel and press my forehead against the wooden floors and listen to the house's heartbeat. I smile in every mirror and when I do, there's a glow that pushes from the inside and it illuminates my teeth. Lisa has given me some sage and told me to smudge window frames, but she lost me at *setting an intention*, yet now that I'm doing my own made-up ritual I feel that I'm doing something similar, setting an intention. I don't smudge the windows, I am wary of using other people's spirituality to help my own causes. If I were to do this the Polish way, I'd invite a priest, have him bless the door with a sign of a cross and some holy water. I don't believe in God, so I do whatever feels most authentic to me. I go into every room and touch every wall. I spend the most time in the master bedroom where I get up on the bed and pray. What sort of prayer, I don't know. I let words run through me and enter the house via my touch, I listen for words back and I hear: *white, light, truth, light, light.* I wait for bigger, more profound words to form and to echo back but later when I think about it, those are the perfect words because they contain all that needs to be said and echoed back.

I haven't eaten in twenty-four hours, my body feels like the words, light, and truth. I am light. After I am done with the house, I wash and condition my hair, take a long bath and shave all of my body hair, massage coconut butter into my warm skin, rub magnolia essential oil in my wrists and behind my ears. Earlier this week, I bought a long, wool winter dress whose colour is described as "birch," and a pair of white Wolford stockings. I dress myself slowly, as if I were being dressed by others, smooth out every unevenness and wrinkle, I lace my new Coach booties with care and choreography worthy of going viral on TikTok, had I filmed it. I'm wearing very little makeup, channeling ease and cleanliness or, more accurately, purity; I execute each pampering gesture with the same mindfulness I gave to the house.

I leave and I walk. This is probably the second craziest thing that I do that day: I walk. It's a long walk. I don't walk all the way—I take the Go train to Guildwood and then walk from Guildwood to Fool's Paradise. The residency was once a home of Doris McCarthy, a Canadian landscape painter who donated her home on the Scarborough bluffs to the Ontario Heritage Trust that later designated it an artists' centre. The photographs I've seen suggest this place is not even in Ontario, but somewhere much more untamed, like the Atlantic coast. If you squint, you can convince yourself that the still lake waters are the rough black and white edges of the ocean, that the tall cliffs are shipwrecking rocks, dramatic and dangerous. It's impossible to imagine the city that surrounds this place is only a few kilometers away. I've always loved those kinds of places, pockets of completely different worlds in unexpected locations: a drawbridge deep in the woods of a ravine dividing two neighbourhoods, a wild forest on the edge of an industrial park, a cove with white pristine sand metres away from a public city beach, height-dizzying cliffs at the end of an inner-city road, and so on. Voytek claims to suffer in nature unless it's his beloved Tatra mountains, the only place he has ever had a spiritual experience, outside of a cunt. He used to tell that particular joke at dinner parties. It would always make me laugh extra hard, so hard that people would direct their attention to my laughing and not to the joke. I wanted to protect him from embarrassment more than I wanted to protect myself from embarrassment. In any case, what I'm sure most appeals to Voytek about it is not Fool's Paradise's remote location but that there is a mentorship component, meaning he is contractually obligated to host workshops or one-on-ones, meaning there is nothing wrong with him inviting those who are a *real talent*.

The sun is warm, and the day feels like it belongs to early September; only the bare trees give away the fact that we're later in the year, November already. I've memorized the directions and they're fairly easy, south and then east, the location of the lake like a pin in my internal map of Toronto's edges. I pass bungalows on the left and on the right more bungalows but these with tall trees in the yard, part of the woods that grow on the escarpment. I think how nice it would be to have a backyard with trees like that, the front facing the city, the back in the country, two worlds in one. I'm rarely jealous of people's wealth, cottages and sports cars and plastic surgery. Vacations I'm jealous of, like everyone else; vacations exist to make the people who are not on them jealous. No one is truly resting on vacations, not with social media, where you have to report those things with proper hashtags that say things like #chilling. And I'm truly jealous of houses; I've only ever wanted to have one thing in life, a home. I never specified what kind, if it was a feeling or an actual structure, but with Voytek I got both. It worked. Lisa says it's my fault I am not wealthy since I've never asked for it; you have to *manifest* what you want otherwise the universe has no idea. As ridiculous as it is, this concept of manifestation serves me on a day like today because if you think about it, what will end up happening is me helping fate from getting derailed, and what will happen will be me fulfilling a manifestation. I could argue I have no choice. A glitch in the system and I am here to fix it. (I wish I actually felt as nonchalant about it as I tell it here but I don't, I'm not nonchalant at all and I'm trying to make sense out of something that makes little sense. I'm not even trying to make sense, I'm trying to survive, fate has nothing to do with it; I'm not sure I believe in it, but maybe I believe in helping it.)

I packed lightly for my trip; in my backpack, a birthday gift for Lisa, and my See by Chloé dress—my favourite, I wore to my book launch, where I met you—wrapped around a bottle of Manousakis Nostos Crete that I ordered especially from the restaurant you took me to when we were first falling in love. Everything about today needs to be deliberate and meaningful, a series of spells or part of a ritual, a plan I am following, however abstractly, intuitively.

The end of the paved road turns into a country road that is flanked by the woods on both sides. The journey is now blanketed in almost silence, save for the sound of rustling and the wind and little animals scuttling around preparing for their winter sleep. I imagine I can hear the lake too, its non-existent crashing waves, but what I'm really sensing is the deep, ancient hum of a still body.

The cottage is a one-storey-tall building, white siding and slanted roof and wide windows and a chimney. It's not a city house pretending to be a cottage, it's the real thing. Voytek's Mercedes is parked outside. There's a small pond and a garden and old, stooped trees without leaves, and beyond the edge, the lake, vast and deep, steel blue. It's just like in the pictures, except everything seems a shade darker.

I knock on the door and wait. I'm suddenly nervous, jumpy. I am Voytek's student all over again, an aspiring writer who is unsure of the words she wants to tell her story in, words that don't exist in the Polish language and also words that only exist in Polish, words that are closest to my heart, what's underneath my scales. He will reassure me that it's okay to try, that I have the right and the permission to use this borrowed second tongue and not only that—that I can use it flamboyantly, that I can even showboat in it, prove to the native speakers that I am better at it, or that I at least have a more direct line to my soul, and understand how to express it. He has never said those kinds of things but he did tell me that if he could do it then so could I, and that I should never apologize, in the same way he never apologized, just took the whole new alphabet like it was a chunk of clay and finessed stories out of it that he knew were beyond language; language wasn't important, it was only a vehicle and as with anything it took practice to learn how to drive it, master it. He is the man who could extract the right words from me—he's responsible for the bridge that I walk on that moves me between languages, between my heart and my head. He's responsible for this story too. He is my maker in our mythology, and I do what mythological characters do, I return to my maker, now more powerful than him.

Yoveetka! You made it! He opens the door wide, all excited as if I were indeed new and a student, somebody he'd been pining for all semester—discreetly, never overtly—a woman he has never touched and wouldn't dream of touching if I, his wife, were to confront him about it.

Please come on in, I just put some potatoes in the oven and I'm going to get started on the fish. I'm afraid I didn't think this through well enough so no Polish dishes tonight.

It's okay, I brought this Greek wine. It'll go well with the fish. I had it before.

Leave the shoes on, leave them on, He says and closes the door firmly behind me. I fumble with my backpack, unveil the bottle. The house is warm like the inside of a glove.

Oh? What is it? Where did you have this? he says as I hand him the bottle and he inspects the label, the line drawing of the old man on it. Hmmm, I don't know this wine. Who recommended it to you?

Oh, I recommended it to myself.

No, really. Did Lisa tell you about it?

Why Lisa? I say and remember Lisa's confession about him, and I have to look away from Voytek's unshaved jowls that, angrily now, I think look like a ball sack.

Your boyfriend?

No, not my boyfriend. I read about it, I say. In one of my girly magazines.

He seems satisfied with the answer.

I follow him to the small, dark galley kitchen, past the living room with the wood-panelled walls I've seen in pictures. The window looks out right onto the yard and the lake beyond it. It's still early but the sun has disappeared, perhaps never to be seen again.

There's deer every morning. A whole herd. They come up to the window and peer inside. It's quite enchanting, Voytek says behind me. He's too close, I can feel his breath on my neck. I'm standing in the awning, looking into the quickly darkening backyard, trying to make out deer that aren't there.

Help me set the table, he says and we walk back into the kitchen, where he points to a drawer containing utensils and napkins. He moves around the room like it's his own. Voytek is one of those people who feels confident in kitchens, who is instantly familiar with their layouts; at friends' dinner parties he would always try to make himself useful—or, depending on the host, a nuisance—asking if he could help and without waiting for an answer, grabbing a bottle to uncork or a salad to toss.

How is Ruby? I say suddenly remembering that something very important is missing, feeling guilty that I forgot all about her until now. He's left her with his mother and I didn't argue, didn't point out that I should be his first choice for childcare if he couldn't do it; I needed to be alone.

She's fine. She's happy to be with Granny.

He pours me a glass of wine and asks me why I'm suddenly distracted.

I was thinking about your mother. I was thinking about your family, how perfect you all are. Were. Are, I say, somewhat truthfully, guessing this pleases him; we both know that he has the better family, one that passed the immigration experiment with flying colours. He has better everything, brain and manners and experience, and it is good of me to acknowledge that sometimes. The only thing I have better is maybe my looks but that also has something to do with him—it is a confirmation of *his* better taste, his ability to land a thing like me.

Thank you for saying that about my family, Voytek says in a tone of voice that tells me I should've been praising the family more frequently. Maybe if I had we wouldn't be here now, he wouldn't have to turn to others to be recognized for his greatness—imagine? Of course, I don't really think that, this is just my Female Rage flaring up, all my resentments, things I want to say out loud but don't.

We sit down to eat at an oval table in the little alcove that's a part of the kitchen, another wide window looking out onto the yard, the dark row of trees in the distance bringing to mind a horror movie, a madman on the loose with an ax.

I've been thinking about this whole book-writing business, Voytek says. How your self-help—

It wasn't self-help—

How your memoir—

It wasn't that either—

The point is, how it did so well, all those interviews and media, much better treatment than I've experienced with any of my writing, my academic work or even documentaries. It's frustrating but let's face it, confessionals sell, people are voyeurs, everyone posts their dinners online.

I mean, it's not new. Your observations, I say and try to quarter the potato in the way that would look like I've eaten most of it even though I'd only had a bite. Over the years, Voytek has never acknowledged my eating habits directly, the most he'd say was at dinner parties, warning hosts about me *doing weird stuff with food.* Sometimes when he would prepare something that was in the RED category, I'd imagine he was watching me closely as I struggled with it but I was probably just paranoid. He has never made any comments about my post-dinner disappearances to the bathroom, the frequent showers I used to take after lunches...I was always grateful for that, grateful for him being so tactful as to not expose me, embarrass me. I'm sure most of it had to do with the fact that he would have to picture me vomiting, being disgusting, his beautiful thing that *was* truly a monster underneath—and maybe that would be something he'd have to feel responsible for; not my eating disorder but the fact that he let himself be fooled.

He says, I know. I think of this new book that I'm writing—I'm excited and scared to go there, to tell *my truth*, His laughter is short, sheepish. He waves his fork in the air as if to dismiss those words, The point is I want to write something more commercial. You know, it's not the writing or ideas or even the plot that people gravitate towards with books. The writing can be shit. The plot can be shit. The ideas can be half-baked. He takes a big gulp of his wine.

I get excited that we're having this conversation. It's exactly like when we were still dating, those frantic alcohol-soaked hours in dark bars where we'd discuss ideas and *the industry*, and sometimes people, but especially assholes who didn't *get it*, who were not real artists, who were fakes.

I am excited and then I am not because it occurs to me that it's not that he thinks I am the only one who would understand—no, we're in his own special play and I am just a student visiting my old professor. I am a *real talent* who shows up to be mentored and have ideas bestowed on to her and it doesn't matter what I think of those ideas, I just have to listen and agree. And if I'm to be honest, even on those first dates, where I felt more alive in Voytek's presence, when I was falling in love with him, building a life with him, I always just agreed. It is depressing, in part because it isn't so unusual; it's a common dynamic in relationships where there is an imbalance because of age, prestige, money, or something else. And it's depressing because maybe we both were always just doomed having to act out those parts, the Student and the Professor; Voytek is as much of a casualty of this arrangement as I am.

Maybe none of it can be really simplified in those terms. But I feel regret, like a fist clenching, wrapping around Monster's pulsing need, this need to straighten everything out, make it even. I could never make it even, this is nonsense math although something has to be subtracted. Sacrificed.

Voytek says, So all I'm saying is that talent or even brawn, none of that makes a difference. You know what makes a difference?

No, I say even though I know.

What genre and *who* is writing it! A pretty girl who is sad. A pretty girl who is sad and who's brown? Even better, ideal, actually, he says, visibly pleased with himself as though he'd won a hand in cards. And the genre is Myself, Me, and I, my Sad Thoughts! Visibility and whining. Visibility and whining sell. Sales make a difference. I don't want to be deluded anymore, believe in this artist craft or vocation even, I want to be cynical and an asshole, books are just a product, like anything else people attach their face to, I'm going to start an Instagram account—who's gonna stop me? I'll be the Old Expat Man on

TikTok, talk about my "trauma" immigrating, the communist oppression, why not?

I recall how just the other day, I imagined a Twitter account or a YouTube channel where he could post his thinky thoughts and now I debate telling him but I don't know if he'll take me seriously or if he'll get paranoid about being mocked so I stay quiet. He keeps taking sips of his wine, he's finished his fish, attacked his salad, usually a slow and mindful eater, he's fired up with his audience of one: I'll go viral, I'm going to become a brand and it won't matter how good my product is—the quality is not important—all that will matter is how much someone is willing to pay for it, He wipes his mouth and stares at the purple smudge on the napkin a beat too long, and then he laughs and I laugh too. He pours himself another glass.

I don't even buy that he's only just arrived at such tired, offensive, cliché conclusions this late in his life. But, then again, he's always been a little behind, reluctant with progress, for example technology: he's lamented the loss of our landline, boycotted Apple products until his ancient PC desktop gave out—which he considered a conspiracy—and he's been mostly happy to be buried in print books and handwritten notes. He turns off all of his electronics when writing, refuses to use Slack or Google Meet with his students, not even Zoom—he hates Zoom—and he keeps office hours religiously and you cannot get a hold of him on weekends. I love this about him. I even love this rant because although it is so naive, it is this naivety and bitterness that endears me to him, that makes me think I need to protect him, help him find his way in the world again. Except that now it's too late, I think, and realize I already miss him even though he's still right here, in front of me.

Well, *you* were certainly onto something with your clever little book, he says. Ideas don't matter anymore, not really. Only how sad you are. So I'm going to write about how sad

I've been, how this thing here—he gestures around, he means the residency—showed me something about people and how you can't trust anyone, not even with your best intentions. How even your best intentions can destroy you if you're not careful, if you don't play the game. Well, I'm traumatized too! I've been oppressed just like everyone else! And I've overcome those things. And now I have a book about it and it's gonna be—

Who are you angry with exactly? No one has cancelled you, I say, because this is true. The incident at the residency happened before the #MeToo movement, he has never closed his office doors when talking to a student, unless he had already prepared and delivered her grades, or it was them who would close the door, and he would open the door again, like they were stubborn toddlers. But I understand what he's saying, he has felt the sharp tip of the public shaming scythe against the back of his neck, has seen some of his colleagues disappear, get in trouble for the "most innocuous things"—writing a romantic poem, lending a book by Henry Miller or Neruda with highlighted passages, stealing a kiss, or having a consensual fuck—and that was wrong, all wrong, it was all a big misunderstanding and he could explain it all.

There is more—more rants, pontifications, observations: *But how do you even measure talent?... Of course there have been exceptions to the rule, like Houllebecq... I don't believe that you have to be in pain to create art, that's nonsense... Everyone hates each other in the arts because there's so little money going around, what, two, three grants?*—he is really working himself up, he gets another bottle of wine, opens it, tops my glass and his.

I don't touch my wine. I need to be clear-headed. I'm telling you all of this so you understand the gravity here, what is at stake—my love or whatever is left of it, my thoughts about the future, the betrayal of my younger self, who was happy to be this man's only listener, who, in fact, lamented not being the only one.

I've eaten most of the fish, and I've successfully destroyed the potato arrangement so that it looks as if I had more than one bite. I feel satiated and calm.

The plan is to go for a short walk, to look over the cliffs, walk back here and watch a show perhaps—there's a documentary about Andrzej Żuławski  and the making of his cult movie, *Possession*, a movie that—Voytek complains—is impossible to get a hold of online, you have to order a Blu-ray disc from the UK and it's a lot of money. We should see it, it would be better to see it before the documentary but we'll have to do with what we have, won't we? A walk will be nice. Cold, brisk walk! For our mental health. We have to be careful not to walk *too* close to the edge, but it's really spectacular once you get closer and see all that infinite dark surface; it's a full moon tonight, and the sky is clear, it will reflect in the water.

I think about the bluffs, the day of our non-wedding wedding, how we drove out near here and had that picnic on the edge, eggs, smoked salmon and cold wine, and how Voytek wanted to make love out in the open but in the end changed his mind. Tonight is the eighth anniversary of us becoming a couple, that afternoon in his office. I will not bring it up, it is too hard to talk about, that perfect fragile beginning, while we're here at the end, right by the place we promised each other there will be no end.

After dinner, we sit in the living room and he lights a little fire in the old-fashioned fireplace, not one of those electric ones; you need real wood and matches—and lighting fluid, *if you're a baby*, which Voytek reminds me he isn't as he struggles with the matchbox and the little tower of sticks. Once the fire is lit, we sit on the opposite ends of an ancient couch, with loud, flowery upholstery and arms adorned by wooden curlicued rests. It's pitch black outside. Voytek has moved onto whisky, and has poured me a glass as well, which

I don't touch. When he isn't looking, I empty it into a potted plant, hoping the soil will absorb and break the alcohol so that the plant goes unharmed.

Votek tells a story about Ruby, how she decoded letters in a sign, *Wal-Mart*, he makes a joke about Ruby growing up to be on welfare. I laugh and think about how I learned to slip makeup inside my sleeves like I was doing a magic trick, when I first discovered department stores on moving here as a teen, how I couldn't believe you could just walk around with all that stuff around and nobody watching you pick through it.

There's a charge in the air and I know it stems from Voytek's drunkenness, he frequently pauses to stare at me with those hungry eyes I remember from years ago, the same eyes that said he was at my mercy and all I needed to do was to give him a sign, any sign. And every time I catch him doing it, I give him the sort of smile I would give to Ruby for performing a simple task, a quick stretch of lips that acknowledges I see it and appreciate it and we don't need to do anything else about it. I don't want to ignore it because I need him pliant, I need him to be needy and ignoring it could make him angry, abrupt; he could stand up and announce he's calling me an Uber and this has been a mistake, a throwback to one of our early breakups when he would ship me off back to my apartment in a taxi.

As he talks, I discreetly look around: pictures of landscapes on the wall, an easel with a half-finished painting of some kind of bird of prey, and frail, dusty curtains on the smaller window. There's a sense of many people having gone through here. It feels strangely familiar although maybe it's from years of imagining Voytek here. I thought I'd feel hostile towards it but I don't feel hostile in the least, I feel safe and welcomed, like I could write a book here, maybe my next one. Maybe, like Voytek, I could get cynical about it, pen something about being sad, again, something that could make me rich. Or maybe I could write something else, an experimental novella about murder in paradise that will sell 234 copies and never pay out its advance.

He tells me about an opera he saw, a new rendition of *Carmen*, done in a contemporary style, the characters wearing jeans and bondage clothing, how he cried at the end even though he hates when people mess with perfection, he hates this insistence on making everything *cool*, edgy, it's already edgy, it's a universal story, a story of love, sex and humiliation, and social class... He talks and he talks but as he goes on, something starts to happen—the words become muffled, distant, strange, as if they were in another language that I used to know but I'm no longer fluent in. It's not that he's losing my attention but it's as if he's exhausted *all* my attention, as if he got to the end of our communication, as if I had only enough Voytek bandwidth and now it's spent. I've experienced something similar with my mother, one day everything she said stopped making sense because it was all nonsense for so long my brain could no longer parse her words, could no longer compensate to comprehend. It's as if I'm listening to him underwater but I don't want to interrupt him, this evening, this warm glow of the fireplace, this perfect evening with us safe inside, and the darkness outside, and the treacherous cliffs, so I try to look like I'm listening. I watch him, watch his mouth move, remember this fierceness, the insistence on dazzling whoever would listen with opinion and interesting facts, his cultured upbringing—it was this difference that I fell for, he was so different from all the men, boys, really, who couldn't make me stay. He was a grownup, fully formed; he didn't talk, drink, or fuck like a student, he was a teacher, my most important teacher, like my Best Friend's Dad but better, he had places to go, on television, in the newspaper, on stage.

Now he talks about this place, the cottage, the story he wants to tell. Something about regrets. I can't untangle the words and they clamour and climb on top of one another and then fall apart, fall down.

# THIRTY-ONE

AFTERWARDS, WHEN I get to the bottom of the road, you're right where you said you'd be, a true friend, now that you've been tested. I'm shaking all over, my teeth are chattering, quiet porcelain clink noises that fill the heavy silence in the car.

Can you—can you help? Help me, I say. I say that because I can't stop thinking of the rainy afternoon in Voytek's office. It's a film playing on a loop, zooming in on the details, goosebumps as he kissed my stomach, his breath so hot on me, I can feel it still. The door rattled. We paused, he pressed his finger to my lips. The door rattled again. And he bent his head—that fluffy grey hair I loved touching—and kissed me again, softer, silent kisses, the tip of his tongue teasing the sensitive skin, where one day there will be a C-section scar—the *only* visible scar of his doing—his finger still pressed against my lips, my giggles bubbling inside my mouth and dying then starting again as the door rattled and rattled.

You hold my wrist, squeeze, Hey, hey, you say softly.

What did I do?

Nothing, you did nothing, Yoveeta. I'm here. I'm here, you say and reach across to try to pull me towards you, an awkward move, the stick shift between us like a comma.

I wiggle out of your grasp, push (*push*) you away a little too violently, Just leave me, leave me be, I snap, my voice high-pitched, unrecognizable, like there's another much smaller woman inside me.

What do we need to do? you say calmly.

I don't fucking know. I'm sorry. You should probably go, I say, although I'm convinced I will die if you go. I will run towards the cliffs.

I'm not going anywhere. Tell me everything.

So I tell you. I take a deep shaky breath and I tell you. I tell you about this morning, praying at the house, how later I took the train, how I walked to the residency, how the fish was too salty and how Voytek wouldn't stop talking, how the more he drank, the more he talked. How he kept looking at me, giving me those come-hither eyes, how I ignored it. I tell you about him coming back from the kitchen with another glass, how he stood there in the door and then just stared, openly, and what he said, something about me being cruel, how I tried to laugh it off. I tell you how he suddenly lunged, more like stumbled actually, towards me—the glass shattered, the sugary brown whisky splashed my white tights—how he pulled me up to stand, hugged me and then wept into my shoulder, how he grabbed my head and tried to kiss me and how I didn't know how to move my head away from him exactly, I had never refused him before and my Voytek-programmed body reacted and we kissed. I have to tell you everything, even this part. I have to tell you how I thought then of Ted Bundy's line, "Sometimes I feel like a vampire."

After the kiss it was as if he came to—even though the opposite was happening; he kept drinking towards a blackout, but for a moment he sounded sober—he said he made a mistake, maybe it was all a mistake, no, it was probably a good thing, but isn't it the most vicious design just because you separate, it doesn't mean your feelings do? Do I ever think about the past, do I have fond memories, or is it all just the bad stuff? Do I remember our non-wedding picnic? Not far from here?

I tell you how then we put on our jackets and boots and went into the yard, went into the dark night, passed the pond, the trees surrounding the property and seemingly taller than they were just a couple of hours ago, more ominous, a setting for a horror flick still, and us walking till we reached the edge, not quite the edge but right up to the sign with a stick figure falling off of a triangle. It was very quiet. There was a full moon. I felt calm. I thought of the 1940s Moonlight Murders in Texas, an unsolved serial-killer case where in a space of one month three couples were brutally attacked in lovers' lane.

But to Voytek I said it was perhaps because of the moon that I felt this calm, its feminine force soothing me somehow.

Voytek said, The moon. Feminine force.

The way he said it, I felt embarrassed.

Yoveeta, you say, your voice gentle, your hand on mine, squeezing. Don't cry, please. It's gonna be okay.

It's not gonna be okay, I look at you. Please don't—

I won't, you say, and I'm grateful. (There was a thud, a short yelp, a crunch, and then silence, an otherworldly pause that felt like the lake, the sky, the whole world holding its breath.)

Alone, I walked back to the cottage. I felt calm again, slow, like a minute would split into two minutes, two minutes into four and so on. I was an automaton, methodical, deliberate, I watched my boots, their rubber half-moon tips; I watched my gloved hand turn the knob on the front door, I watched myself walk through the narrow hallway and into the kitchen and then the alcove where we ate, and then back to the kitchen where I washed the dishes and wiped the counters, wiped the sticky whisky stain on the floor, everything I touched. It didn't matter, dozens, hundreds of people went through this house, DNA all over, just last week, Voytek gave a workshop that I'm sure was attended by all of his protégées.

I watched myself go into his bedroom and this is the only time I shut off watching, I didn't want to see—his things, his sleep, his book on the bedside table, his intimacy, his vulnerability, his old-man slump, his threadbare boxer shorts on the floor—but I was there for a reason so I reached for it, and entered the password, pleased, I guess, and a little surprised that the password was one of the many I'd memorized. I got it on the second try, Ruby's birthday, 12032014. I erased the last four texts between me and him. I sent a text to Margot, *I really need to see you. Please come see me.*

I had no idea if it would work. I didn't know what their communication was like and I didn't want to risk trying to be too *him* about it, maybe how Voytek communicated with me was specific to the two of us, although I didn't think so. Simple was best here, no need to get too creative, cocky. But I did remember that he called her *baby* in that first email I read and that was something he'd never called me. I sent another text: *Baby?*

An expectation, a demand. Baby? Please. Come.

And then I watched myself walk out of the bedroom, and through the living room—the half-done bird of prey painting catching my eye with its one finished eye, watchful—and past the alcove with the dinner table with no dinner on it now, and past the kitchen, and the narrow hallway and out the door, down the gravelly path, down to the unpaved country road, back to you.

I want you to ask how it *felt*. But you don't, so I volunteer: It felt as if it were me. Jumping. I felt that same drive, every moment I've ever had on every subway platform or a balcony of a highrise and once, on the top floor of a huge dance club, Circa. That lemming instinct mixed up with all my self-destructive urges. Ultimate freedom beckoning, only a few small steps—but freedom tinted with fear, of pain, of landing badly, of survival. The memory of my first, only jump when I shattered my clavicle, proof that I would not succeed. It was almost exactly that, except the difference was I wasn't the one to die. It hits me again.

We should go and check. This is insane.

It is insane, you say, But no.

I open my mouth and close it. This is what I've asked of you. You are doing as told. You love me. And I need you.

My chest is rising and falling, I'm shivering, the realization dawning on both of us, your face pale in the dim streetlights, our panic—is this the end? But then you blink slowly, one steady click, much like the shutter in your camera, capturing something no one but me has seen, unfurling, becoming, my trembling, shimmering, insides exposed and beautiful. In that moment all I hope for is not a peaceful resolution; my one wish is for you to see Monster truly, its beauty, the shy unveiling of it—and my wish is granted as I catch the awe in your eyes.

You place your hand around my wrist and you say calmly, so quietly, your words are cold and still like the water of that night, I'm not going to leave. No matter what happens. And please consider that nothing might happen—that's the most likely outcome, actually.

This is a promise. And with that you prove to me that I can be grounded again, and that you understand.

You start the car and we drive to Lisa's birthday party. On the way, I change into my silver dress, the colour of the moon's shadow, the lake.

You park a block away from Sotto Voce and I fix my lipstick in the mirror. We don't talk. We haven't talked because there's nothing else to say. In the mirror, my eyes are black, my pupils shot, obscuring the green almost entirely. Voytek used to look into my eyes and call me *chwast*, a weed, the green reminding him of his childhood summers in the Polish countryside, thistle specifically. That was the weed he had in mind, its spiky hands and purple hair, the beauty and softness with the impermeable armour around it. That's what you are, he once said, incredibly proud of the image, the writerly metaphor, naming the weed so specifically. I think he was sensing Monster, felt it and experienced it but never recognized it. He had only weeds to draw wrongness from, the inappropriate flowers, the lesser flowers. But still, flowers.

The bar is packed, bodies in black—in Toronto everyone always wears black, every party like a funeral—clustered around the tables in the too-small space. There is a DJ shoved into a corner, men and women recognize each other, hook arms and elbows around each other and kiss, and say things like, *Oh my god, I haven't seen you in so long*. You squeeze my shoulder as we wiggle through the bodies, their cold cheeks and perfume, the bartender asking what will we have—double shot of tequila twice, you say—through blue and red blinking lights, we move forward till we reach the table where the queen of the night is sitting and I say—as if I were there the whole time, waiting and waiting—Why don't you want to open your gift? Open it before someone steals it, And I hand her a shiny black box containing a champagne-coloured silk dress, size 4, a copy of the dress she pulled from my closet just a couple of weeks ago.

Oh my god, guys, where were youuu? Says Lisa getting up, her spiderly arms looping me and you into a sloppy drunken hug, her kisses juicy and smelling of vodka. Where weerrre youhooo?

We were right here, I tell her. She looks at me, head tilted, eyebrow tilted re-*eally*, but I don't flinch, don't falter, I have only two choices: commit or confess. So I commit, say, Really. What's the matter with you? Is it because you hate your gift?

She looks confused and then mortified, hand to mouth, big eyes, Oh my god, I'm so sorry, no, I love it, I'm sorry. I'm soo trashed, girl. You know how I get, oh my god, is this the famous?—

You are quick, sharp, you pull her towards you and kiss her on both cheeks, envelop her in a hug, Lisa, it is so nice to meet you. Finally, you say, your *finally* is so earnest I do a double-take, wonder for a split-second if you and Lisa have met, and then I remind myself that it isn't *you* I'm thinking of, you are pure, and mine.

You smile at me, your eyes are calm. Lisa looks at her bare wrist, an invisible watch, and smacks her forehead. Man, she says, I should slow down, I gotta last until midnight. I was born at eleven-fifty-five if you believe my mother, I feel like she just made that up, you know, she was a very absent mother—

I exhale.

Lisa opens the shiny black box and takes out the dress and I swear, she tears up. She says, I just *love* it. I was seriously thinking of stealing it from you, did you know? And because it's funny and cheeky—or perhaps honest and desperate—I say, I know you were, girl, I know you.

Later, I feel your breath on my neck as I open the door to my house. You know, there's a coyote infestation in the bluffs? You whisper, your hand on my hip, pushing me inside.

I know, I say. I know because I looked it up, I'm not stupid. (Google: *It appears that in fact coyotes could eat the remains of a human.*) The chances are exactly 50-50, it might work out or it might not, just like everything else. I push you gently away, look at you, you are mine, my hybristophiliac, my true love.

And we are here and here is home, this is my home, my walls that I will paint white, my daughter's room that I will turn into my office, the attic that I will open up to make a room for my daughter, all the renovations, all the possibilities, the future, finally, with you in it.

I take your hand and hold it between my legs and you press firmly, press and release, press and release. Now that we're here and I know what I am and what this is, I feel unrushed, safe. I lean against you, my face against your shoulder, breathing you in, your minty cologne, my heart thumping wildly in my chest, a whole constellation before it erupts, cascades, swallowing me briefly, releasing. A shiver passes through my iridescent body as I unfurl the scales, the feathers. I'm so beautiful. I know you can see it too. You've witnessed a miracle: a woman whose monstrosity turns outward, against something other than herself.

My legs give out from underneath me but you catch me before I fall, and you kiss my tear-stained face all over, It's okay, it's okay, you say. But I'm not sad, I'm the opposite. No more longing, no more hunger, I no longer feel it. I'm satiated.

# AFTERWORD & ACKNOWLEDGMENTS

My *Monster* is an intimate, special book to me. As we all grapple with the Alice Munro revelation and her daughter Andrea Skinner's story, it seems more timely than ever to address the issue of women writing fiction. Everywhere on social media and outside of it, people are talking about wanting to examine Munro's fiction all over again to explain the atrocity in her personal life; lots of people are saying they understand the detachment and moral dilemmas in her short stories much better now because she was obviously writing about herself. We will never know, but why do we think that about women's writing? And why women? Is it because we are incapable of coming up with stories with our little girl brains? Jokes aside, I believe that real life does inform fiction but more often than not fiction is not real life, nor a thinly veiled account of it.

I called *Monster* "autofiction" and gave the protagonist my own name to poke fun at the fact that people see women's writing as autobiographical. This is something that I've heard all of my female writer friends complain about. Even with my first novel, *Guy*, written from the title guy's first-person point of view, I was asked if it was based on my ex, presumably my son's father who is a public person and who's known for dressing well and appreciating women.

Then in 2022 I got a letter from a lawyer written on behalf of an ex-lover who threatened to sue me for my book *Possessed*, which he believed was about him. He had never read the book, not even the first draft. I once said he might've inspired a character and that was that. I was writing *Monster* at the time and what that ex-lover did inspire indeed was my decision to give the book some elements which might seem autobiographical. Maybe because of that, the book seems special to me, and intimate, and I feel it was something that needed extra care and protection.

I was over-the-top-happy when Anvil Press made an offer to acquire *Monster* as they are my favourite indie publisher and I knew they would know exactly how to care for it. They have published the work of Nelly Arcan, one of my favourite authors, who was famous for her semi-autobiographical novels, and who I believe possessed an incredible imagination that inspired mine. I identify with Arcan in as much as when she used to be interviewed, people tended to focus on her personal life—I feel like she would get my insider joke. So this is to say, first of all, thank you to Nelly Arcan and thank you to Anvil Press's Brian Kaufman for being a stellar editor and publisher who was very patient with me both with the book (and some of my short fiction); Karen Green who is the most hard-working publicist in indie presses and a brilliant copy editor. Loved meeting you in Toronto!; Jessica Key: can't wait to see what we organize together! And Clint Hutzulak at Rayola.com for the cover design.

And further thanks to:

Emily Keeler for her sensitive, thoughtful and respectful edit. I was incredibly lucky to get you as my editor and not once did your intelligent suggestions make me cry.

Jules McCusker for the stunning cover image of a woman in distress that used to exist only in my head and that you've executed perfectly.

Sam Haywood for taking the best care of our *Monster*. This book is for you.

Eva Oakes for your exceptional feedback and brilliance.

Beta readers extraordinaires: Jeff Dupois, Sean M. Turrell, Brian MacDonald and Lisa Hannam, Tim Rostron, N.S. (who this book is not about either) for reading, for all your support, always.

And, besides Nelly Arcan, these four women who are also my favourite writers and who read and (based on their blurbs) understood *Monster* sometimes better than I did: Laura Albert, Alicia Elliot, Tamara Faith-Berger, Heather O'Neill.

Thank you to Hugo who is the reason I write.

Thank you to Canada Council for the Arts without whose support I wouldn't have been able to create.

Jowita Bydlowska is the author of *Possessed,* the best-selling memoir *Drunk Mom,* and the best-selling novel *GUY*. She's also a prolific short-story writer, journalist and a professor. She was born in Warsaw, Poland and came to Canada as a teenager. She lives in Toronto with her son and their chihuahua.